Execution of Justice

Execution of Justice

Patrick Dent

Chapter One

Safi, Morocco

The young American did his best to look casual as he approached the Moroccan bar. His eyes constantly scanned for incongruities – anything more interesting than an infinite expanse of sand and about a dozen rugged four-wheel-drive vehicles. He saw none.

The bar itself looked ancient, having a wooden frame plastered with a tan adobe, making its color indistinguishable from the surrounding desert. The slate roof appeared on the verge of collapse. The windows were arched and glassless, about twenty feet from the ground, with heavy wooden shutters latched open with hasp locks.

Elan had selected attire generic to the region. His tan robes concealed his slightly trembling hands, as well as the Colt .45 automatic in his shoulder holster. Luckily, the desiccating atmosphere evaporated sweat, helping mask his anxiety.

The locals called the bar Shaqra, although it bore no markings either outside or in. Elan grabbed the huge iron ring serving as a doorknob and pulled. The thick wooden door eventually surrendered to his will and swung open with a creak, attracting the attention of some of the locals inside. Rheumy, bloodshot eyes turned toward the offending desert sunlight cutting through the dimly lit room, but quickly lost interest when they saw Elan.

Elan blinked as his eyes adjusted to the darkness. The main room was large, with about a thirty-foot ceiling. The only light had to fight its way from the open windows through thick clouds of hashish, opium and tobacco smoke. The air hung motionless. In the center sat a square bar. A solitary bartender cleaned his fingernails with a US Army issue bayonet. No wait staff was visible.

This is it, Elan thought, *the next fifteen minutes will decide the course of my career.* Elan knew his Arabic heritage was the main reason Major Briggs had selected him for Operation Sierra. Nonetheless, he prided himself on the progress he had made. For the past six months he had worked his way up through the Moroccan black market, establishing contacts and credibility through a series of increasingly larger business deals.

With a little help from Uncle Sam, Elan had been able to produce enormous quantities of valuable merchandise ranging from toilet paper to Soviet AK-47's. Now, he waited to meet the man who ran the most powerful and despicable enterprise in the region. Tartus ran an ancient business, one whose tentacles had only recently infiltrated Western civilization. President Nixon declared Tartus' operation a threat to national security and sanctioned the creation of the Sierra task force. Elan felt honored to be selected as the principle Sierra operative - Sierra One. Men such as Tartus stained the reputation of good Arabs all over the world. Elan would take enormous pleasure in bringing this heinous operation to its knees.

When Elan reached the bar he ordered whiskey in Arabic, with the hint of French accent so common among Moroccans. He had lost his university grammar and enunciation months prior. The bartender gave him a menacing look, but reached below the bar and placed an unopened bottle of Jack Daniels on the counter. When Elan did not reach for the bottle, the bartender begrudgingly produced a glass of questionable cleanliness, giving Elan a look saying *now what; you want me to drink it for you too?*

Elan paid the exorbitant price of fifty Dirham - equivalent to about twelve US dollars. Such robbery, commonplace in countries who forbade alcohol, did not surprise Elan. Still standing at the bar, he poured himself two fingers, neat. *Just one drink,* he vowed, *I need my wits about me today more than ever.* He took his bottle in hand and began working his way through the crowd; scanning for the red neckerchief Falon told him would identify Tartus.

Falon, perhaps the nastiest man Elan had ever met, frightened Elan despite his training. A calm sadism in the man's eyes distinguished him from Elan's other business contacts. Elan knew Falon would relish killing him at a leisurely pace if he suspected he were an American agent. He repeated the mantra to himself - *Remember your training. This is your job.* While others wanted American and European creature comforts, Falon shopped for dangerous merchandise – rocket-propelled grenades, anti-tank weapons, heroin, and much, much worse.

In a city where black and brown were the predominant wardrobe choices, Elan had little difficulty spotting the red neckerchief. His pulse quickened. He smelled the fear on his upper lip as he considered the man he prepared to meet. It had taken months of courting Falon to gain an audience with Tartus. Men that cautious were not to be underestimated. He downed his drink in one motion and approached the man who would become the instrument of his destiny.

Elan estimated Tartus was about forty years old. Tartus' face - lean, taught, and weather-beaten from years spent in the desert – carried no expression. Elan felt Tartus' coldness even from a distance. The tables surrounding Tartus were all empty. All Elan's training and months undercover had led to this moment. He braced himself to initiate a conversation with one of the world's most venomous and clever men. Although Falon's treachery made him a local icon, he lacked the fear and respect Tartus enjoyed.

"Hello," Elan said in Arabic, meeting Tartus' level gaze, "I notice the weather here is much harsher than in the South."

"But the opportunities are so much better," Tartus replied, completing the code phrase. "Please, have a seat and let us discuss such matters."

The cordiality in Tartus' voice belied the brutality and heartlessness Elan knew were the staples of his trade. He forced himself to maintain contact with Tartus' soulless, obsidian eyes. Those eyes evoked primal fears from Elan's genetic memory. Images of alligators and sharks flashed through Elan's mind – ancient predators, machines designed exclusively for killing. Elan, a seasoned combat veteran, felt the first familiar tingling of fear. As always, he tried to let the adrenaline work in his favor.

Elan hoped his training had prepared him for this encounter. Although Elan did not subscribe to the Christian concept of the Devil, Tartus gave him reason to reconsider. Tartus had the presence of some supremely evil denizen of the underworld, visiting Earth in search of souls to steal.

When Elan sat, Tartus immediately began his business. "So, you have gone to a great deal of trouble to talk with me. What makes you think I have any interest in what you have to say?"

Elan calculated that Tartus would respect nothing less than complete candor, and replied, "Well, that you're here, for one thing. And that I have access to merchandise that would bring a much greater price than your normal wares."

"So Falon told me. And what, exactly, is the source of this wonderful merchandise?"

"America, of course. West coast. California." Elan paused to let the statement sink in. Tartus' eyes probed Elan, searching for any sign of weakness. "Surely there will be abundant profit for all parties involved."

"You propose something with great risk." Tartus' hard eyes bored into Elan's face.

"High risk, high return," Elan quipped. "Besides, you don't impress me as a man afraid of a little risk." This statement skirted dangerously close to arrogance, but Elan had to pass himself off as a calloused murderer, a man who knew fear merely as something he saw in the faces of his victims. He behaved as Tartus' equal.

"You should not confuse wisdom with fear, my friend." Tartus' voice took on an icy, challenging edge. "However, I am still listening."

"I have a friend who is a travel agent. His operation is a perfect front for moving merchandise of this sensitive nature through American customs."

Tartus' eyes narrowed to slits. He leaned forward on his elbows until his face nearly touched Elan's. "Just like that? You appear out of nowhere and want to cut me in on your foolproof enterprise?"

Elan forced himself not to back away from Tartus. At this distance, he smelled curry mixed with alcohol on the man's breath. "Tartus, like you, I'm a businessman. I don't have the network you have, and I don't have access to the end users. That's where you come in. We're both familiar with the Brazilian and Philippine crap flooding the marketplace. I propose moving a top-end product into the market, the business opportunity of a lifetime. I can deliver in quantity. How does one unit per month sound?"

Tartus mulled this over for a few seconds that seemed an eternity to Elan before he responded, "You do make a good case. I'll discuss this with some of my high dollar clientele and meet you here tomorrow at the same time with an answer."

As Elan stared into those reptilian eyes, he kept the most important poker face of his life. Inside, he surged with triumph. He looked at Tartus differently – meaner.

"This conversation is over," Tartus said. He stood abruptly and walked toward the exit. When he opened the door, an intensely bright light flooded Shaqra, temporarily blinding anyone whose eyes followed him. After exiting the bar, Tartus turned left into the parking lot.

Elan's mind struggled to process what had just transpired. Did he just cut a deal with Tartus after his first meeting? If so, this mission would exceed his wildest imaginings. He couldn't wait to call Major Briggs to arrange the sting. Once they had Tartus in custody, they could begin to dismantle his entire operation, beginning with that beast - Falon.

After waiting an excruciating five minutes, Elan recapped the bottle of Jack Daniels on the table and left. Outside, he squinted against the desert glare and turned left toward the parking lot. As he walked toward his jeep, he began to plan Phase Two. He would need at least two squads from special ops, maybe more. From what he had observed, Tartus would have several layers of security, ranging from well-paid locals in the crowd to short range snipers armed with AK-47s. Tomorrow, he would earn his captain's bars.

Elan's pensive trance twisted into an anguished mask when the garrote unexpectedly snapped his head back. The piano wire cut through his esophagus, trachea, and both carotid arteries before his mind registered that he had grossly miscalculated Tartus' business ethics. As he lay on the ground with his life force rhythmically gushing into the Safi sand, Elan thought of the daughter he would never see again.

* * *

Langley, Virginia

Special Agent Robert Fulton sat at his desk, drumming his fingers as his mind raced. His new assignment exhilarated him. The Director of Central Intelligence had sanctioned him to solve the single biggest economic threat to America's future - the OPEC oil embargo. If successful, Project Crossfire would be the crown jewel of his career with The Agency. This project, right on the heels of his promotion to Director of Middle Eastern Operations, would make him top contender to become the next DCI.

He reflected with pride upon a life of hard work and the commensurate rewards. After his Cum Laude graduation from MIT with a degree in mechanical engineering, he had entered Officer Candidacy School in the Marines. He made Captain by the age of twenty-five, resigned his commission for a detour through the FBI Academy. His six-year career with the Bureau had been stellar in every respect, peaking when his two-year deep cover operation had culminated in the capture and conviction of one of the biggest cocaine dealers in Miami.

Shortly thereafter, his supervisor told him the CIA wanted to talk to him. The DCI commanded an audience. At that point, he knew he would be a player. Robert Fulton would make a difference in this world. Of course, intelligence work was not conducive to glory, at least not the public variety. Fulton's sole glorification would be in his own mind and within a tight group of coworkers. Such was the nature of covert ops. People who required validation from others were speedily identified and expunged from the program for security purposes. Fulton derived his satisfaction from knowing he served the cause of freedom. Project Crossfire, for instance, would shift the balance of power in the civilized world, and no more than a handful of people would ever even know it took place.

The enormous question in his mind was how to bring this multi-billion dollar juggernaut to a grinding halt in the space of a few months. American citizens were waiting in line for hours to purchase their paltry allocations of gasoline. President Nixon had declared the embargo to be a national crisis, urging Americans to conserve power wherever possible. By presidential order, air conditioning units were to be set at seventy-eight degrees during the summer and sixty-eight degrees during winter. While the most powerful nation on the planet shivered and sweltered in their homes, the OPEC nations grew richer by the day.

Fulton ran through recent events, searching for leverage to use. Since the Fourth Arab-Israeli War had begun, tensions were high among the Arab nations. Syria, with support from the Soviet Union, had launched an offensive against Israel during Yom Kippur in 1973, ostensibly over a territorial dispute. The sneak attack on the Jews' holy day was an insult of the highest magnitude to Israel.

The Arab extremists saw the fight with Israel as a Jihad, a holy war bringing religious purity to the Middle East. They referred to the conflict as the Ramadan War, named after the Muslim holy month. The moderate Arabs wanted to avoid conflict with Israel to remain in the good graces of the United Nations. The UN and especially the US were strong supporters of Israel, and the moderates saw no profit in making an enemy of the US. Some of the more liberal Arab factions even entertained the idea of recognizing Israel's status as an independent nation, thereby qualifying the Arab nations for membership in the UN.

Although the Arab nations constantly bickered among themselves on political and religious issues, they presented a united economic front. Every time the Oil Council met, they further reduced production, driving oil prices through the ceiling. They had an economic stranglehold on the West.

The US had begun to drive a wedge between the Arab nations when Anwar Sadat rose to power in Egypt. Sadat appeared all too happy to accept strong economic support from America. However, Egypt carried merely one voice among seven in the Oil Council, and none of the Arab nations would publicly make a stand against the all-powerful Saudis. The President deemed Diplomacy too sticky and slow to resolve this issue in a reasonable timeframe.

The king and prime minister of Saudi Arabia, Fahr al-Azon Al Saud, kept his hand on the lever the Arabs used against the West. Fahr led the Oil Council and was perhaps the only man who could bring an end to the embargo. Fulton had to find a way to get to Fahr.

As he ruminated at his desk, Fulton's face lit up. The answer wasn't to influence Fahr. The answer was to *become* Fahr. What if the US led the Oil Council? With control over the world's power supply, the US would be politically and economically omnipotent. But, how could such a thing come to pass? Once Fulton knew the right question to ask, the answer became obvious.

Fulton jumped from his seat and began to pace the office, wringing his hands in nervous energy. Would it work? Yes, he believed it would. Could it be covered up? Yes, although doing so would require a certain level of ruthlessness. But, as his father liked to say, if you want to make an omelet, you have to break a few eggs.

The details were already beginning to crystallize in his mind. He sat at his desk and began to make notes. He had much to do in an extremely compressed time frame. Special Agent Fulton had a war to start.

Chapter Two

Beaumont, South Carolina

John Drake Jr. secured his place in history during the third game of the District Seven playoffs. At eighteen, John found himself standing at the doorway to adulthood, staring into the vast, undiscovered country lying ahead. At his back he felt the gradually increasing pressure of his parents, pushing him through that porthole into a threatening and unknowable world. As he peered, he saw murky shadows – unfocused images formed not simply by his own desires, but also by those of the people who shaped his life. In those shadows, he saw John the baseball player, John the Game Warden, John the foot soldier in Vietnam, John the employee at Drake Enterprises.

John comforted himself by believing life had a defined set of rules. If I do *A*, then *B* will happen. He envisioned the future as a multiple-choice question - a finite set of possibilities that he may select from based on his actions. Today, John would learn the answer to all his questions was 'none of the above'.

History shows that gigantic forces are often balanced on the minuscule events of a single person's life. Such people are the instruments of fate. If John had fully understood the consequences of his actions, he probably would have been paralyzed by indecision. If he had known that millions of lives would be saved or lost based on a split-second decision, he might have acted differently. But, of course, his crystal ball worked no better than anyone else's.

In a typical early summer day in Beaumont, the South Carolina sky cast a white-hot shade of blue, without a cloud in sight to protect the players and fans from the Sun's brutality. A faint, intermittent breeze taunted Beaumont's citizens with the insincere promise of relief from the sweltering heat. The gnats and mosquitoes focused their assaults on every available ear, eye and nose, inexorably drawn to the moisture there. The weather-beaten bleachers were crammed with people fanning themselves, licking ice cream cones, slurping soft drinks, and sweating.

Slick arms rubbed against each other as people squirmed in wasted effort to find comfort. The sole leniency came from the ancient oak and pecan trees, providing afternoon shade to the home side stands. The visitor's bleachers, in the Southern tradition of selective hospitality, were in direct sunlight.

John noticed that his girlfriend Tammy had lucked into a shaded seat. Nonetheless, she periodically used a napkin to blot the sweat from her forehead. She smiled and waved as John caught her eye from his position in front of the dugout. He warmed up by gently swinging a bat weighted at the tip with two batting rings.

Tammy and John had been going steady since tenth grade, and were due to begin the ramp-up toward matrimony. Although he knew Tammy would support him if he attended Clemson University in the Fall, he also knew she feared their bond would wane during the four-year separation. That was why John had proposed that she move to Clemson with him.

In the background, John heard the chants of a few restless children who had mustered enough energy to play their own baseball game behind the stands. Although school had been out just two weeks, it wasn't even a distant memory to them. John admired their ability to live in the moment. As far as they were concerned, this summer day would last forever.

John noted that his father sat as far away from Tammy as possible. John Sr. divided his attention between his son and the talent scout from Clemson. He had made significant contributions to Clemson over the years; so, when he requested they send a scout to this particular game, they could hardly refuse. Although he could easily afford the tuition, he had told John he wanted him to learn to care for himself. John knew his father fully expected him to play for the Atlanta Braves after graduation, but he didn't want to follow his father's dream. He would use baseball if it earned him the degree he would need to become a Game Warden. After that, John planned to resign his bat.

By the dugout, John swung his bat lazily, loosening the powerful muscles in his torso. Not a notable team player, John did enjoy competition for its own sake. The winner of this game didn't matter to him and would be forgotten in time. Unlike his teammates, John did not consider his senior year the pinnacle of his life. While the others would be content to take jobs in the local mills and spend the next forty years reminiscing about the glory days, sucking on Bud long-necks; John considered his life to be just beginning.

In John's mind, sports were the bread and circuses of twentieth century society. The ancient Romans knew how to entertain the masses – give them young warriors to admire and vilify. Varsity sports? Not much different in John's book.

Most people would rather watch than do. Why else would entertainers and athletes attract such crowds? John realized mediocrity offered a cozy bed, and coziness was the cornerstone of Beaumont society.

The crowd stood for the national anthem. The citizens of Beaumont placed their hands on their hearts and gazed with awe at the baseball diamond symbolizing everything they lacked - fame, heroism, and the chance to be noticed.

John sneaked a peek at the coach, who kept him in stitches most of the time with his exaggerated gestures and statements. Coach Stanch sweat profusely. Having run out of dry clothing and appendages for his face, he was merely moving sweat around with his timid-but-macho gestures. His gut protruded comically over his pants, and he spat tobacco juice at regular intervals. The kids got a kick out of his bumper sticker saying, 'Use care passing, driver chews tobacco'. True to the sticker, an indelible brown stain decorated the driver's side of his Datsun 240Z. He waddled over toward John.

"John, I hear there's a recruiter in the stands from Clemson," Coach said, pushing the brim of his hat up to improve his eye contact with John.

"Hey, Coach, maybe this is your big chance to get into college," John jibed.

"Look, you wipe that shit eatin' grin off your face. This could mean a scholarship if you pitch good this afternoon." Coach's gin blossoms grew bright red. The enlarged capillaries in his bulbous nose resembled a poorly done tattoo. "Besides, we ain't won the title in seven years. Your team needs you. Look at 'em." Coach pointed at the visiting team. "Don't you want to teach these guys a lesson?"

"Last time I checked, I was a student, not a teacher."

"Well, for your information, you ain't a student no more. You remember that little shindig we had two weeks ago? Well, that was your graduation, in case you didn't notice. As of now, you're no different from the rest of us."

"Coach, I think I can safely say I'm *nothing* like the rest of you." John smiled widely.

"You still think everything's some kind of joke, don't you?" Coach said. "I'm telling you that dog won't hunt in the real world." The coach's face softened somewhat. "Look, all I'm saying is keep your focus. Think about that scholarship."

"Focus? What would a pot-bellied loser know about that?"

"You listen to me, you little tick turd." Coach emphasized each syllable by poking his finger into John's chest. "That attitude is the only thing standing between you and a pro career. I know the training you do, and you got the talent. You're probably the smartest kid to come through this school ever. But out there in the real world, people won't put up with your crap." Coach spit a well-marinated strand of Beechnut between John's feet to punctuate his sentence. He stomped away to toward the dugout.

John did train heavily, but not for the reasons Coach Stanch thought. John had boundless physical energy that he constantly discharged. Before school each day, he logged in three miles, three hundred push-ups and five hundred sit-ups. After practice, he ran another five miles. He followed this regimen regardless of the sporting season. To John, exercise equaled life. It took him to a place where the world and all its troubles ceased to exist.

John interspersed ample reading with his exercise. As his eyes scanned the page, his mind left his body and traveled to exotic lands of the past, where bad guys acted like bad guys and good guys usually won. In the world of literature, right and wrong were clearly defined for all to see. No one's father vacillated between hero and villain. No one's mother both enabled and welcomed her husband's cruelty. In books, the greatest minds in history had recorded their wisdom for the benefit of future generations. There were only three times John felt completely free – reading, exercising or communing with nature.

By the time the game started, even the most acclimated people were sweating profusely. John, however, stood completely dry in the direct sunlight dowsing the pitcher's mound. He seemed to have a natural immunity to the plagues of the Southern summer. Heat, mosquitoes, even poison ivy did not affect him.

Five foot nine athletes were rare, but his 230 pounds of muscle and unparalleled explosive strength more than compensated for his height. He tucked his shoulder length black hair under his cap as he waited for his mother to throw out the first pitch.

For eight innings, John hurled the white orb across home plate time and time again. His power and accuracy were unwavering as the innings wore on.

No sweat corrupted his brow. No fine motor quivering affected his form. A well-oiled and finely tuned machine couldn't have been more consistent. John knew the Clemson scout would want to chat after the game. He had no way of knowing just how irrelevant that thought would become.

At the top of the ninth, John continued working on a shutout. He had talent, no doubt, but he knew his father manipulated him, reliving his youth through John. The John, as his children called him, had been selling him on a pro baseball career for twelve years now.

If John wanted to realize his dream of becoming a Game Warden, he would have to play his father's game - baseball.

As so often happens, John worried about the problems he would be unlikely to face. John's visions of the futures he envisioned had a life expectancy of just over two minutes.

John's best - and really only - pitch was his fastball. As early as tenth grade he had been clocked in the low nineties. Number 12 stepped to the plate in the top of the ninth. John had already struck him out in the fourth, and that had simmered beneath Number 12's skin for the past hour. The boy's face stiffened with concentration. He clenched his teeth and stared directly into John's eyes as he raised his bat. From the pitcher's mound, John saw the muscles in Number 12's jaw flexing. The batter took two violent practice swings, then nodded at John.

John's first pitch flew high and inside. Number 12 fell over backwards, narrowly avoiding a shattered jaw.

"Ball!" called the umpire.

Number 12 regained his stance with anger in his eyes. The muscles in his jaw flexed rhythmically. He spat before saying, "Oh, you wanna play? Come on, punk. Let's get it on!" He raised his bat again, this time crowding the plate.

John had no intention of letting Number 12 get inside his head. He lifted his left leg seemingly to the sky and put his entire weight behind the second pitch. Number 12 nearly ripped himself in half trying to get a piece of it.

"Strike one!"

John adjusted his cap, picking up a bit of pine resin from the brim. With all his strength, he released the pitch that ultimately would impact the balance of power in the Western Hemisphere into the next century. The ball struck Number 12 in the hip. He went down, screaming in anger and pain.

Number 12 rose awkwardly and limped hurriedly towards the mound. The bat still hung in his hand. His gait teetered as he attempted to spare his left hip from the rigors of quick movement. His eyes burned with fury. His teeth bared in a feral snarl.

John became instantly calm. He let his glove drop to the ground. Whether Number 12 kept or dropped the bat did not matter. John could neutralize either scenario quite easily. A heavy implement such as a bat had a fight span of one attack move only. After the first swing, the bat's momentum would throw its user off balance and leave him vulnerable for precious seconds.

Time slowed to a crawl as John's senses were heightened by adrenaline. Two hundred spectators were shouting out their opinions as to what each of the boys should do. John's mind drew into focus, filtering out the din of the crowd. He heard Number 12's cleats digging for purchase as he sprinted. He heard his opponent's lungs wheezing for air with each stride. Coach Stanch already waddled awkwardly toward the plate. Brown spittle ran down the left side of his chin as he gasped in the moist heat. John waited.

Number 12 hurled the bat away fifteen feet before he squared off against John. He had no way of knowing this act would have profound implications.

"You did that on purpose, asshole!" Number 12 spat.

John waited.

"By the time I'm through with you, you'll be crying for your mamma!" Number 12 thrust his chest out, clenching both his hands into fists.

John waited.

Number 12 decided to take the conversation to the next level. John saw the telltale dip in Number 12's right shoulder, indicating the opening roundhouse right. The natural human reaction would have been to back away from the punch, but John ducked forward, letting Number 12's arm pass harmlessly over his head.

The attempted roundhouse told John Number 12 had little fighting experience. He was a showman. A lighter punch, such as a jab or uppercut, would not have been telegraphed and would likely have connected, paving the way for a more powerful follow up. John knew the next punch would be another roundhouse right. He had fought Number 12's type many times. They always overextended themselves and lost balance within the first couple of punches. He straightened and waited for the right moment. By this time, there were dozens of people rushing toward the mound. One way or the other, the fight would be over in seconds.

"Scared to fight?" Number 12 said as he threw a haymaker at John's face. *This is it*, John thought to himself, taking note of Number 12's posture. He saw Number 12 would lose his balance with this swing. John ducked inside and to the right, assuming a crouching position. When Number 12's arm extended completely, John saw his right foot come off the ground. Number 12 could not stop his spiral momentum. In a split second, he would fall forward and to his left. Instantly, John extended his legs and pumped his right fist directly into Number 12's heart.

Number 12 froze, bent over at a forty-five degree angle, his momentum having been neutralized by John's blow. He quickly found himself in a universe without air. A few seconds later, he fell to the dusty ground beside the pitcher's mound. His muscles were so tight he seemed like a statue that had been toppled by juvenile delinquents. As he lay on the ground, Number 12 felt a tightness in his chest like he had never imagined. His left arm went numb. His jaw tightened. His heart stopped beating. And since no one present had any emergency medical training, it never started back.

Chapter Three

Langley, Virginia

Special Agent Fulton fumed with tension, though it was barely ten a.m. He had already removed his jacket and loosened his tie. He had no time for formalities. These days he arrived anywhere from six to six thirty in the morning and worked until seven or eight at night. Fulton didn't fear hard work. He had just one fear – failure. A successful execution of Project Crossfire would be a career milestone for him. And time worked against him constantly. He had much to do. His secretary buzzed in, "Sir, Mr. Carlton is here."

"Thanks, Joyce. Please send him in."

Carlton entered the room with obvious trepidation. As he approached Fulton's desk, he removed a handkerchief from his back pocket and mopped sweat from his shining pate. He wore his typical work clothes – a starched, blue Oxford shirt, pressed khaki pants, and penny loafers. Fulton suspected the penny loafers would be replaced with well-worn boots as soon as Carlton returned to his car.

The two men exchanged greetings, Fulton poured them each a cup of coffee, and after a few minutes of small talk, they got down to business. "Mr. Carlton, first I want to thank you for coming in," Fulton began. "Second, I'd like to dispel some common misconceptions people have regarding the CIA, if you'll permit me." Fulton walked around to Carlton's side of the desk and sat on it with one leg, creating a more intimate connection with Carlton. "Most people form their perceptions of the CIA based on Hollywood. They assume the CIA abounds with duplicitous spies, secret agents, assassins, and other nefarious characters.

"The truth is we're predominantly bureaucrats, but bureaucrats who pay well when we put work out for contract. Our specifications are quite demanding, as you will soon see. Few can adhere to them." Fulton paused before continuing. "I understand you are an excellent metal worker, with a top-notch crew."

"Well, I've been in the business for twenty-two years, and have over two hundred years experience in my team. I'd say we're pretty much up for any challenge," Carlton responded. Fulton pleasantly noted Carlton's even voice and his relaxed posture. He took Carlton at his word.

"Mr. Carlton, the job I have in mind will require an extraordinary understanding of metal stresses and strains, as well as heat stability. The tolerances are what I consider 'world class'. You're not likely to encounter limits tighter than ours."

"What is the project, by the way?" Carlton ventured.

Fulton handed Carlton a schematic representing a small part of a picture that, in its entirety, was known only to Fulton and a handful of technicians. Carlton located a small piece of paper with a large dollar figure stapled to the last page. He only took a quick glance, enough to count the zeros. "I need three sets of cylinders, one hundred forty six each, built to these specifications," Fulton said.

Carlton studied the schematics for some time. Carlton's expression of shock when he reached the last page made Fulton smile. Carlton finally responded, "Wow, these babies are tough! May I ask what they are to be used for?"

"Mr. Carlton, this is the CIA. We pay well because we require the highest quality in the world. And, as you may have surmised, we strongly dissuade curiosity. Am I making myself clear?" Fulton stared directly into Carlton's eyes for several seconds.

"Yes sir, I understand."

"Excellent, then. Will you take the job?"

"Mr. Fulton, for what you're offering, I'd be a fool not to."

"I'm just looking for the word 'yes', Mr. Carlton."

"Yes," Carlton replied.

"One other thing, Mr. Carlton," Fulton said, leaning forward on his elbows, "This project has an extremely aggressive timeline. I'll need the first hundred and forty six units delivered within the next ninety days, with each subsequent set delivered every sixty days."

Carlton couldn't quite conceal his shock. "Mr. Fulton, I'd have to drop every other project I have, and work my men double time to meet those requirements."

"Welcome to the CIA, Mr. Carlton. I don't think the math should be difficult. This is not a difficult business decision for you. I suspect you know other contractors who can take over your existing projects."

After staring at his lap for about a minute, Carlton looked up into Fulton's eyes and said, "It'll take me a week to clear my schedule. Can we agree that the clock starts ticking next Monday?"

"Mr. Carlton, I do believe we have a deal."

After the contractor left, Fulton felt the knot in his stomach relax, having solidified this critical aspect of Project Crossfire. *You'll never know what you've done for your country*, he thought. But then, no one would ever know what Fulton had done for America either. At least he knew. That would have to be enough. In his line of work, that would always have to be enough.

* * *

Beaumont, South Carolina

Incarceration differed from John's imagination of it. All his life, he had felt imprisoned by his father's roughshod rule. But his father's prison imposed an intellectual loss of freedom, the knowledge that certain actions carried certain consequences. He still had choices in the Drake household, no matter how unpalatable those choices were. When Sheriff Woodson had slammed that high tensile steel door shut and bolted it, an unnatural claustrophobia enveloped John.

He realized a few things quickly. He would not leave the six by nine room until someone else decided he could leave. He would eat only when someone else decided to feed him. He couldn't take a walk, read a book or magazine or even take an aspirin unless someone else allowed it. *How would it feel to spend twenty years like that?* He thought about all the animals in zoos around the world and wondered if they lived with this feeling. Even the most comfortable prison was still a prison.

The room sported a stainless-steel toilet with no lid, a sink with cold water only and a cot bolted to the concrete wall with an inch thick gymnastic pad as a mattress. They took his watch, so he had no sense of time. This was his universe until someone else decided to change it.

He lay on the cot and tried to clear his mind. He wondered how the boy he hit felt right then. John's father had taught him to abhor violence by doling it out on a regular basis. Although The John brought out the rebel in him, John remained peaceful at heart. He regretted hitting that boy so hard. He could have held back, but he didn't. Why? Nausea chewed at the lining of his stomach.

At some point, the walls no longer felt as if they were closing in on him. Eventually, he drifted off to sleep, but his slumber granted no solace. He dreamed of his father, the man who had taught him the unique skills that would soon make him among the most influential men of the late twentieth century. In his dream, in tenth grade, first session report cards had just come out.

* * *

The John chose a ten-foot bullwhip, truncated to five feet, for behavioral modification. This shortening minimized collateral damage to lamps and other fragile household items. The John was remarkably considerate in such matters.

The smell of whiskey permeated the room, and although John knew the scent well, his kid brother did not register it as he huddled in the corner, crying as silently as possible. John grinned at Perry, giving him a wink to ease the kid's discomfort. More than anything else, John wanted to shield Perry from the scene to follow.

"Get on the bed!" The John bellowed to his son, who, knowing the drill, was already stripping off his shirt.

The first strike from a bullwhip immediately raises a welt roughly the diameter of a small cigar. Whenever a subsequent blow lands across one of these welts, the skin splits and blood spurts out.

The John swung the whip with the fury and passion of a Golden Gloves champion, searching for just one more victory in his life. When he had no adversary to defeat, a poison began to build in The John, slowly at first, but always reaching a crescendo. Every blow, every time his whip permanently reshaped his son's flesh and mind, a little of that poison would drain out of him.

The white scar tissue on John's back helped to ease the pain, but his deepest scars, and the source of all his strength, existed solely in his mind.

The sound of leather skillfully used against human flesh continued. Each lick sounded like something between a firecracker and a rat-tail from a wet towel. The John utilized all the techniques he had learned as a champion boxer and a scratch golfer. Every swing originated from the soles of his feet, initiating a progressive torque throughout his body, culminating in a super-sonic whip velocity.

The John swung as hard as he could, as many times as he could. For a man of 50 years, his effort carried considerable enthusiasm. John did not register the passage of time. He floated outside his body.

The John, bathed in sweat, stood above his son, covered in blood. They looked like gladiators exhausted from battle, but not ready to quit.

When The John's right arm completely gave out, he switched to the left. Though not a southpaw, long years of perfecting his jab and left hook had given him substantial control and power in his left arm. The revolting sound of leather upon flesh resumed.

Finally, The John reached a point where he had his hands on his knees. Doused in sweat and gasping for breath, he glared at John with an unbearable rage. He still had fight left in him. He always had fight left in him.

John turned, staring evenly into The John's hardened eyes. As The John wheezed for oxygen, his eyes stinging with sweat, John smiled and said,

"You can start whenever you're ready."

* * *

"Breakfast, John."

John jerked upright, rubbing the back of his neck with one hand. He shook his head and squinted at the Sheriff, raising his other hand to block the glare.

Sheriff Woodson resembled a well-fed bear that ate mostly from dumpsters. He weighed in at almost three hundred pounds. His salt and pepper moustache completely concealed his mouth. The hair on his arms formed a thicket. But, when he opened his mouth, the macho illusion evaporated.

A big man, Woodson was cursed with the voice of a Boys Choir soprano. That tiny, high-pitched voice coming out of Woodson's mouth resembled some weird ventriloquist's act. Physically, he could take any of the roughnecks around Beaumont. But instead of respect, he usually got ridicule. They thought he didn't hear them making fun of him, but he heard more than they thought. Over time, this had made him mean.

Woodson slid the traditional Southern breakfast of eggs, grits, toast and sausage through the slot in the bottom of John's cell door. He spoke without looking at John.

"There was this kid I sent to Juvi a few years back. I thought he was basically a good kid, so I kept an eye on him. His name was Mario. He was a tough guy, just like you. In Juvi, he was tough shit - let me tell you. He was in the gang that ran the place. But, two weeks after his eighteenth birthday, he got pinched for grand theft auto. That little stunt landed him in Wallbash.

"Now, here's this kid who's used to being the toughest thing around and suddenly he's just another punk. That's their favorite kind of new guy, by the way. They love the ones who fight back. They love to bring them down a few notches.

"Mario was raped so brutally and so often that his anal sphincter was damaged beyond repair. They had to sew it shut and give him a colostomy bag. Can you imagine wearing one of those for the rest of your life?" Woodson looked at John as if he expected him to answer. When he didn't, Woodson continued. "Well, about a month later, Mario comes into the infirmary again and his colostomy hole is infected. You know what it turned out to be? Gonorrhea. *That's* the kind of place you're gonna spend the next twenty years in."

"Twenty years?" John said, "Just for a fist fight?"

"Fist fight?" Woodson said, his face growing purple, "Son, that boy is dead."

John couldn't respond. This couldn't be true. This couldn't be happening. He had killed only one living thing in his entire life, and that damned dove still haunted him. Now, they were saying he'd killed an innocent man. He wondered if they were right. His hands began to tremble. He felt light headed. There had to be a mistake – mixed up medical records or something. He just punched the guy.

"You're going to be charged with murder, son," Woodson said.

"Sheriff, I, I mean, I didn't... you know it was an accident. You know I'm not a killer."

"I don't know any such thing. What I do know is you have a history with this boy. I also know you hit him with that ball on purpose. I've been watching you pitch since seventh grade, and I know the control you have."

When the Sheriff spoke, John saw his moustache move, but his mouth remained hidden. This unsettling him quietly, John felt his neck and face getting hot. Anger suddenly consumed him for no apparent reason. He responded to Woodson with volcanic rage.

"You don't know shit," John spat. "You think you're something, don't you, riding around in a squad car, busting kids for drinking beer and smoking pot.

'To protect and serve', huh? Well, who exactly do you protect and serve? That is, besides yourself."

"You think this is a game? Huh?" Woodson said, "You think this is funny? This ain't high school, where you can shoot your smart mouth off and just get detention. You're an adult, son, and that's the way you're going to be tried. You can play games if you want, but all Parker needs do is convince twelve people you're guilty, and snap - it's slammer-time.

"Let's see how that mouth serves you when you're in prison for the next 25 years to life. I bet those boys in Wallbash will just *love* your mouth." The Sheriff made a kissing noise from behind his unkempt moustache.

"I always knew you'd amount to no good. You're in so deep this time, even your daddy won't be able to get you off." Woodson's gin blossoms were further reddened by his anger. John couldn't guess whose side Woodson would choose. Although The John was officially his friend and political ally, Woodson clearly resented the man's influence and power. "I've just got one question, John. I've seen Clay, Marciano, Louis, all the great heavyweights fight, and I've never seen a person killed with a single punch. How'd you do it?"

"I don't know," John replied, his tone calmer now. John knew if he got worked up, his cage would feel all the smaller for it, so he tuned Woodson out and closed his eyes. At times like this, when he wanted to speedily shut out the world, John focused his entire mind on a single word, phrase or thought, to the exclusion of all else.

When the Sheriff realized John had tuned him out, he left in a huff. "Yea, they're just gonna love your mouth," he repeated as he loped away.

After a few minutes, John silently picked up his tray and began his breakfast. He finished everything but the sausage. Having nothing else to occupy him until lunchtime, John stood on the toilet to improve his view to the outside world. Behind the county lockup opened a massive cotton field, an ocean of white swabs extending for over a mile. The field reminded John of the tops of the clouds as seen from above. The John wanted all his children to experience flight at least once, so he arranged for John, at fifteen, to be taken up in a C-130 from the local Air National Guard unit. John remembered every detail of the trip. Possibly his most pleasant father-son memory.

Beyond the cotton field was the edge of an enormous pine forest. John knew that forest well. He had been exploring it since he was six. Over the years he had found several rich veins of petrified wood, two openings to underground streams, the occasional deer or dog skeleton, and his most prized find - a rusted WWII bayonet. The bayonet's handle had been rotten with age, but John had remedied this condition with a thick layer of duct tape.

Doves swarmed overhead, devouring every insect in their paths. Above the cotton field, doves glided and swooped as they gorged themselves on the ample supply of mosquitoes in the Southern air. John had read somewhere that Doves each consumed over two thousand mosquitoes per day. That did involve a lot of eating, but about a million too few by John's reckoning. The doves reminded him of the painful incident that made him a vegetarian.

As the day progressed, he saw the heat waves rising from the cotton. By mid morning, a glimmering mirage overtook the center of the field. It resembled an enormous black pond.

When the Sheriff brought John's lunch, he saw the boy hadn't moved. Woodson noticed that John had not touched his sausage. "Not hungry, Big Boy?"

"I don't like sausage," John said blandly.

"What's the matter? Stomach getting' a little queasy thinking about those Wallbash boys? Well, don't worry, I'm sure you'll get your fill of sausage once you're in the slammer." Woodson giggled as he slid John's lunch tray into the cell - barbecued pork. John grimaced, knowing he would have to get by on mashed potatoes and string beans. If this represented prison food, he didn't have to worry about the next twenty years. He'd starve to death in a few weeks. Somehow, he doubted that Wallbash would accommodate a request for a vegetarian diet.

* * *

Judge Phillips' receptionist stood the instant she saw The John enter. Without a word, she immediately escorted him into the Judge's office. The John made it clear he was not one who liked to wait. He stormed across the generous length of the office and put his fists on Phillips' desk, leaning forward, encroaching on the man's personal space. "Don, you and I go way back," The John began.

"Yes, we do, John, but we're talking about a murder charge here." Phillips did not back away. They both knew the reason for Drake's visit. Phillips maintained John Drake's penetrating gaze.

The John knew there had to be the illusion of compromise - the face saving out for one's opponent. He already knew that Phillips would capitulate, but he still had to go through the motions. Diplomacy required The John to give

Judge Phillips the impression he possessed some semblance of power. The John and Phillips participated in the strut and dance, fulfilling the ancient ritual of negotiation. The John always won the psychological victory. He knew this. Ultimately, the quickest route into a man's brain passes through his wallet. And victory doesn't come cheap.

Phillips betrayed his discomfort by drumming his fingers on the desk.

"That's horse shit, and you know it. This is an open and shut case of self defense." The John's face reddened with anger as he slammed his fist on Phillips' desk. The vibration knocked over the judge's pen box, but Phillips did not set it back up.

"That," said Judge Phillips, lifting his arms with the palms facing the ceiling, "is for the Solicitor to decide."

"Well, until he does, my son should be at home with me. What do you think he's going to do? Run away?"

"It wouldn't be the first time, John. Besides this is an election year. How would it look if I released John and he ran off?"

"Don, you want to talk about elections? Over half the people in this town owe me money. I've been poor and rich so many times I can't remember. What if I developed a little Christmas spirit in July this year? You know how they say people vote their pocketbooks? Well, I have a lien on damn near every pocketbook in town!"

"John, calm down. You're acting as if we haven't been friends for twenty years. Of course, I'll help your boy. I just want you to understand the consequences of this favor. The arraignment is just a formality. I'll release him into your custody, but you'd better keep him out of trouble until the trial or even I won't be able to help him."

Chapter Four

Fort Benning, Georgia

Major General Jeremiah Dalton reclined at his desk with his eyes closed. He slowly leaned forward and glanced about his familiar surroundings. Dalton, an emotionally austere and mentally disciplined man, set up his office to mirror his self image. Though the space was large, the furniture was sparse - just two large metal desks forming a right angle. No family pictures on the desks. He had selected gunmetal gray for the walls and ceiling, with over two dozen colors to choose from, and he sported a grand total of about ten framed photographs, each from a different area of the world.

The General's uniform was custom tailored to accommodate the upper body capable of one hundred push ups per set. From his physicality, one would place him in his early thirties. But, his eyes emanated a cold knowingness that one could not acquire in less than fifty-five years. Dalton's response to his thinning hair was to cut it all to the 1/8 inch standard for incoming recruits. His cheeks were hollow. His face had the look of granite just beginning to set in. Dalton's eyes were a brilliant blue, and when he looked you in the eye, he appeared to be looking down the barrel of a rifle.

Hundreds of details swirled through his head, none finding a comfortable place to land. This made Dalton uncomfortable. He normally organized and filed his thoughts neatly away as if they were paperwork. But today, his mind seemed fuzzy. He couldn't focus on any one thing for fear of neglecting another. This had been happening more often lately, ever since he had launched Operation Sierra.

And Operation Sierra wasn't exactly a success story so far. The first deep cover operative had been publicly beheaded when his confidant, a man named Falon, turned him over to the Moroccan authorities as a drug smuggler. It had taken months of small transactions to even gain an audience with Falon. It took months from that point to win his ear, to see if he could arrange a meeting with Tartus. Obviously, the question would have benefited from better timing. It cost Dalton a highly trained soldier and set the operation back damn near twelve months.

The second operative, Lieutenant Elan, used much more aggressive tactics. He tried to pass himself off as a kingpin in the Moroccan black market. Within three months, he had set up a personal meeting with Tartus. But, Dalton thought, there's the slight problem that Elan had failed to report on the meeting for several days now. Elan, if alive, was in Tartus' custody. Dalton hoped Elan remembered his training on torture tactics.

"General Dalton, Major Briggs is here to see you," the intercom barked. This jolted Dalton out of his detachment. His hand hovered over the intercom button. *What was Briggs doing dropping in without an appointment?* Dalton knew one thing – it wasn't to deliver good news. He rubbed the bridge of his nose as he pressed the speaker button. "Send him in."

"Yes Sir."

Major Briggs entered the antiseptic office, closing the door behind him. Dalton knew Briggs always arrived a little nervous and he liked to keep it that way. He had been toughening Briggs' skin for years now, but the kid had a long way to go before he could handle the heat of full-bird. Dalton had a mouth like a scalpel. Other men could *tell* Briggs he'd screwed up, but only Dalton could *convince* him.

Briggs removed his headgear, came to attention and saluted Dalton, who reciprocated.

"Sir! Major Briggs reporting."

"At ease, Major. Have a seat," Dalton said, knowing already he wouldn't like what Briggs had to say.

Briggs was third generation army and looked it. His square jaw, athletic build and thinning flat top blond hair made him look like a Rock 'em Sock 'em Robot. His headgear tucked into the precise ninety-degree angle formed by his left arm. When he sat, his spine remained rigid, never touching the back of the chair. "Sir, we have a problem. Elan is dead."

"Details," Dalton snapped, leaning forward on his elbows. He strained to keep a poker face. He couldn't let Briggs see his anxiety. In reality, Operation Sierra would earn him a third star if successful. The flip side meant it could also cost him his command.

"We lost contact with Lieutenant Elan four days ago. We know he was operating near Safi, in northern Morocco. He had a meeting set up with Tartus, but we didn't get the exact time or location before we lost contact. At first we assumed he had gone under deep cover, but yesterday the Safi medical examiner contacted the US Embassy in Rabat about a body found in a Safi landfill. The passport on the body matched Elan's cover ID. He was essentially decapitated, Sir.

"The local authorities wrote it off as the mugging of a tourist. I've arranged for the remains to be incinerated. Officially, he died a hero, saving six injured soldiers' lives before the Viet Cong got him. We gave him the Silver Star posthumously. I thought that was a nice touch. Basically, we are back to square one, Sir."

"Damn it!" Dalton slammed his fist on his knee. Though Dalton knew the familiar sting of sending men to their deaths, this business of doing it one at a time was particularly unnerving.

Major Briggs judiciously gave the General time to collect his thoughts. The office sat silent for at least five minutes.

General Dalton spoke at last, "Next steps?"

"Well, Sir..."

"Speak up, Soldier!" Dalton demanded.

"We're running out of Arabs."

Dalton glowered at Briggs. The message in his eyes said it all – this had better not be a joke. "You want to run that by me one more time, Major?"

"As operatives, Sir. The combined Special Forces units have only one remaining Arabic speaking soldier – Lieutenant Amin. It would seem we've nearly depleted our supply."

Dalton stretched back and put his hands behind his head. "Where is Amin stationed?"

"Fort Bragg, Sir. He's a weapons specialist."

"Has he been approached?"

"Yes Sir. He is preparing as we speak."

"Good. I want you at Bragg tomorrow morning to brief him."

"Yes Sir. Anything else, Sir?"

"No. Dismissed."

Major Briggs stood at attention and saluted. When Dalton returned the salute, Briggs performed a surgically precise about-face and exited.

* * *

Beaumont, South Carolina

John's arraignment was quick and perfunctory, as promised. Judge Phillips remanded John into The John's custody. The judge gave him a trial date expedited to six weeks. John had to sign a few papers, and then he walked out into the afternoon sunlight as a free man.

So many things he had taken for granted, like the ability to go outside, see the sun, to walk more than nine feet in a row. His brief stint in the county lockup gave him a preview of what the next twenty-five years might hold - deprivation of nature's every form in a place where souls stagnate and rot.

His mother walked beside him, holding his upper arm with both hands, as if the slightest breeze might whisk him away. The John walked ahead to his Mercedes. He stopped in front of the car and leaned back on the grille, facing John. He crossed his arms high on his chest. He had a scowl on his face, making John cringe inside. The two of them had not been alone together since the incident. Gloria kissed her son on the cheek and walked to her car. She and The John always drove separately.

The John didn't mince words. "Son, let's get one thing straight from the start. I don't give a damn whether you did it on purpose or not. I don't want to hear your side, understand? The point is, accident or not, no one will railroad my son. You just let me take care of everything."

"So you're telling me killing isn't wrong." John said.

"Exactly," The John said, "There is no right. There is no wrong. There's simply whose side you're on. The sooner you accept this simple fact, the better off you'll be. That's what all these hippies don't understand about Vietnam. The war isn't about good vs. evil. It's about allegiances."

Even after eighteen years, John's father still had the capability to surprise him. He appeared to be angrier with the Solicitor, Dave Parker, than he was with John. It slowly dawned on John that this was a turf war - and *he* was the turf. "Dad," he ventured, "Would you please drop me off at Mud Dog Road? I'll walk home from there."

"I don't see the harm," The John replied, "But don't you even *think* about running away. My word is on the line and I'll break you before I break it. I would be *unrestrained* in my disappointment. Do I make myself clear?"

"Don't worry, I'll be home for supper," John said, taking a sudden interest in the ground between his feet.

"Well, get in."

John sat in the passenger seat, staring wordlessly out the window. The events of the past twenty-four hours just wouldn't add up for him. Not until later would the full impact of those events sink into his mind. The John did not talk at all, knowing silence can be the most effective form of speech. It worked. By the time he dropped his son off at the head of Mud Dog Road, The John shook fiercely.

John walked over two miles before he reached his favorite spot. He sat on a large rock formation overlooking Sugarcane Lake. The details of his surroundings soothed him as he unfocused his attention. Ants performed their small but organized tasks. Birds were moving deeper into the forest, sensing the upcoming storm that meteorologists would not detect for some hours to come. The surface of Sugarcane Lake lay as smooth as glass, responding to a recent drop in barometric pressure. The abandoned shack near the dam periodically creaked, though no one detected a wind. The rope swing formed a right angle with its own reflection.

After about an hour, a rustling in the woods interrupted his trance. Tammy emerged from the bushes and sat next to him, leaving a couple of feet between them, sensing his need for personal space. John and Tammy had a habit of never saying hello or goodbye. They sat; completely comfortable in the silence so many people feel the irresistible urge to fill.

When Tammy spoke, she began in the middle of a thought, as they liked to do with each other. "It's that asshole Solicitor, Dave Parker. What's the deal with him and your dad, anyway?"

"He and Parker were business partners in the sixties. They owned a gas station together. Anyway, something happened between them, so my dad sold out his half interest in the station, and opened his own station across the street. He worked nights selling insurance door to door, plus pulling in whatever money he could by taking small loans to subsidize the gas station. He sank every penny he had into the station, always selling below Parker's price. In the end, he sold gas at less than cost for almost a year before Parker declared bankruptcy.

"Then, he bitch-slapped Parker at a party years later, but Parker felt too embarrassed to file charges. So, yea, I guess you could say Solicitor Parker and The John aren't the best of friends." John spoke robotically. Emotionally, he felt completely inert, like the rock where he sat. He wanted to feel something, but the feelings wouldn't come. He reached out and hugged her tightly. When the tears came, they came in a torrent. Neither spoke again until dusk.

John broke the silence. "Tammy, I don't know who I am. Everything I thought about myself just got tossed out the window." He had his head in his hands. He saw tears dripping on the rock between his legs. "I've always thought I was the opposite of my dad, but I'm beginning to wonder if I'm exactly the same. Maybe deliberately being the opposite is exactly what makes me the same. Now, I'm a murderer on top of everything else."

"No, you're not," Tammy began, but John raised his palm toward her face.

"When I was twelve," John said, "my dad took me on my first hunting trip. He's an expert dove hunter, and wanted to teach me the basics. I had this little 4-10 shotgun, but I was still afraid of it. He taught me to hold it tight against my shoulder to minimize the kick and to squeeze the trigger with the gun still moving along with the target. Your natural instinct will tell you to stop, then shoot, and you have to overcome that instinct to hit moving targets.

"Well, by blind luck, I actually shot a dove out of the sky. But, when I walked up to the bird, it was still alive. I still remember it looking at me with those tiny black eyes as if to say, 'Why have you done this to me?' I was horrified at what I'd done. Then Dad walked up and casually grabbed the dove by the head and rung its neck to kill it.

"I threw up from revulsion, then ran and hid in the woods until Dad left. I knew he was disappointed in me, thought I was weak, and I couldn't face him. I walked home late that night and climbed in my bedroom window.

"Since that day, I haven't killed anything other than insects and haven't eaten one bite of meat. I keep trying to go back to that point in time, when I was innocent. I keep telling myself *that's* the real me, not the angry rebel I've become. I haven't been particularly successful so far, and now I've killed a human being. That's a mortal sin, Tammy. I killed that boy and all the children he would have had, and their children, and so on. Essentially, I've killed thousands of people. I'm a *mass* murderer. I've become the thing I hate and fear the most – a monster like my dad."

"John, I know it was an accident and so do you. You're nothing like your father. You're gentle and kind and have a heart the size of Texas," Tammy said, giving him a light kiss on the cheek.

"I've got his genes, Tammy."

"Yes, but you also have something else, something more powerful than genes – free will. Nobody, not even your father, can turn you into something you don't want to be. He tried to make you a killer on that hunting trip and he failed. Don't you see? You decide who you are – only you."

Extreme circumstances have a slimming effect on the mind. A billion worries coalesced into one thought. "Tammy, will you marry me?"

Tammy didn't move a muscle for three seconds. Then, her face burst into sunshine. "Yes!" She screamed as she threw her arms around his neck.

Neither of them thought about prison as they walked back to Mud Dog Road. As always, they took the path bypassing the lake. Tammy laid that law down. John never understood Tammy's fear of water. They took swimming lessons together as children, but she wouldn't even look at a body of water now.

John and Tammy walked directly to his parents' house to share the good news. The plantation-style home – white, two-story, with columns, sat on several acres. Eartha, the maid, answered the door. John had always loved Eartha. She was a second mother to him. After a brief chat, John and Tammy walked back into the living area.

The John sat in his wing-backed chair, reading the Beaumont Times. Al Capone's fishing rod hung above his head. The John claimed Capone gave it to his father to make good on a bet.

An uncomfortable silence filled the room. As John inhaled to speak, The John dropped the paper by two inches and barked, "I don't want to hear one syllable of complaint. Do I make myself clear?"

"Yes Sir," John responded, "Mom, Dad, we've got some news."

Gloria leaned forward, put her arms on her knees and intertwined her fingers. "What is it, John?"

"Tammy & I have decided to get married."

The room grew silent as this proposal sank into their minds. Gloria looked shocked, but this didn't surprise John, as she was prone to melodrama. For almost a minute, The John did not look up from his paper. John realized too late that he should not have done this in front of Tammy.

The John finally spoke, "Son, this is a bad idea."

"I don't know why it matters to you. This is one decision you will *not* make for me." John said.

"This girl…" The John began.

"Her name is Tammy," John interjected.

"This girl is not cut from the same cloth as the Drakes."

"John, you're much too traumatized to make such a decision," Gloria added.

"We've made our decision. You two can choose to attend the wedding or not. I don't care which. But, you can't stop us. We're both legal age."

"You think it's as simple as that, huh? You're of legal age, and can do whatever you want, just to spite me?"

John saw the cauldron begin to boil behind his father's eyes. His parents thought of Tammy as 'trailer trash'. He had hoped her presence would be advantageous. He assumed their middle-class manners would work in his favor. It was uncouth to insult Tammy to her face. Civilized people would do that later, over a mint julep.

The John put his paper down and stood slowly. He walked until his nose reached the spot one inch from John's. He stared into John's eyes, but John held his ground. He maintained eye contact. It was no longer him against his father, something bigger than both of them was on the table – the formation of John's own family. At this range, John smelled a hint of his father's Old Spice.

"You do what you want. I don't give a damn!" The John looked John up and down as if sizing him up for a fight. When John did not respond, The John stormed out of the den toward the front door. A moment later, John heard tires squeal.

"John, you can't go through with this," Gloria sobbed, "Please don't do something you may regret the rest of your life just to hurt your father and me."

"You're talking about Tammy like she isn't even here!" John screamed. He clenched his fists at his sides, shaking with rage. "What gives you the right to judge her, or me for that matter?" He shoved his finger in Gloria's face as he spoke.

Tears were now streaming down Gloria's cheeks, "John, I know it hurts you to hear this, but you're not making a good decision."

"What the hell does that mean?" John spread his arms in the fashion of a scarecrow.

"This is something you'll just have to trust your mother on, Honey."

"Trust?" John spat, "What do you know about trust? A mother who allows her children to be beaten."

"John, don't you know I blame myself for every one of those beatings every day of my life? Please, listen to me. I was just a teenager when your father married me. I never knew any different. Every day I pray to God for the courage to stand up to him, and every day I fail. How do you think that makes me feel? I'm afraid to stay and I'm afraid to leave.

"Honey, please trust me about this. She's not right for you."

"Mom, I'd rather follow my own heart and be wrong than follow someone else's and be right. Tammy and I are getting married. This is our decision, and it's final." Before Gloria could respond, John calmly grabbed Tammy's arm and led her out the front door.

Chapter Five

Beaumont, South Carolina

John nervously adjusted his tie as The John parked his black Mercedes sedan in the handicapped spot and squeezed his massive shoulders through the driver's side door. Gloria approached them across the lawn.

The Beaumont courthouse presented an awe-inspiring work of nineteenth century architecture to the practiced observer. The interior was 100% mahogany, worn to a smooth finish over a period of 156 years. There were huge cannonball cracks in the exterior red bricks. These cracks had never been mended, to remind the locals of Sherman's march through the South during 'The War of Northern Aggression'. Stout granite columns braced either side of the front entrance.

John saw his mother take note of the ever-present group of hippies waving banners protesting the war. They seemed to have unlimited time on their hands, and used it to demonstrate at any event providing an audience.

"Look at that, John. It's so tasteless," she said.

"Mom, they're just fighting for what they believe in," John chimed in.

"Fighting?" The John snarled. Gloria quickly cut her husband off by saying, "Well, Republicans don't demonstrate. We just write checks."

The John chuckled at his wife's little quip and put his hand on the small of her back, ushering her toward the courthouse. The John walked briskly, wearing his usual calm demeanor. His strides were long and confident, causing John to lag slightly behind. Only John noticed The John's occasional nervous twist of his West Point ring. For him, that tiny gesture was a full-blown conniption fit.

John did not have to presence of his father. In the six-week period since his arraignment, he had lost almost twenty pounds. His face stretched gaunt. He had black semicircles under his pink-rimmed eyes. He looked malnourished. Even with a fresh haircut and suit, something about him looked wrong. It would have been easier for him if the trial had occurred immediately after the incident. The waiting unnerved him. He had never been more frightened. When he saw the Solicitor crossing the well-manicured grass of the front lawn, he avoided the man's steely gaze. *So, this what I've become*, he thought, *a coward?*

John's head felt encased in molasses forced himself to face Parker. Time slowed to a crawl. John had weathered The John's abuses for the better part of two decades, but that had hardly prepared him for lifetime imprisonment. He had always been able to focus on the freedom he would enjoy when he turned eighteen. Now, this one ray of hope was in question. By force he managed to look Parker directly in the eye. Parker had the gaze of a junkyard dog. An icy calm washed over John. It was the calm of utter hopelessness.

* * *

Parker stood before the jury, pompously straightening his silk jacket by the lapels. He had chosen his navy-blue Brooks Brothers suit – conservative, respectable, and a nice complement to his sapphire blue eyes. Before beginning his opening arguments, he made brief eye contact with each juror.

"Ladies and gentlemen of the jury, I want to tell you a story – a story of a boy on the wrong path in life, a boy who is not beyond salvation, but a boy who has committed a heinous crime nonetheless. I will demonstrate that the defendant, John Drake Jr., has a violent history. I will further demonstrate that John Drake Jr. has unleashed this violence on the beloved deceased, Clarence Buchanon, in the past. Ultimately, I will demonstrate that this was not an act of self-defense, but one intentionally instigated by Mr. Drake when he first attempted, and then succeeded in striking Clarence with a speeding baseball. Clarence merely defended himself.

"Clarence's fatal mistake was dropping the bat, wanting to give a fair fight to a man who'd just attacked him with a deadly weapon. Clarence clearly demonstrated that he had no deadly intent when he threw his bat away. Mr. Drake, however, did use deadly force, a force he was well aware he possessed. His initial attack was with a hundred mile an hour fastball. He followed that with a blow to young Clarence's most vital organ, his heart. That, Ladies and Gentlemen, is murder, plain and simple. Thank you."

His Honor, Judge Philips, spoke, "Mr. Felts, you may proceed with your opening statement."

"Thank you, Your Honor." Felts' heavy-set frame and gleaming pate stood in stark contrast to Parker's trim appearance – by design. His navy sport jacket, a cotton blend, and his khaki pants were both wrinkled. He had a blue-collar charm especially effective with rural juries.

Parker, in his shiny silk suit, didn't realize he might as well be wearing a spacesuit as far as these people were concerned. Before Felts began his statement, he mopped the sweat off his brow with a handkerchief. Parker thought it a sloppy gesture, but acknowledged it might appeal to the working class. Despite his ruffled appearance, Felts charged the highest fee of any defense attorney in South Carolina. Felts turned to address the jury.

"Ladies and Gentlemen, we all know baseball is an American tradition. We also know that occasionally, pitches accidentally hit batters. This unfortunate occurrence is not limited to high school ball, but is not uncommon in professional baseball. Men who dedicate their lives to the sport, men who are paid handsomely for their unique talents, still sometimes make mistakes. They are only human, are they not?

"That's what young John is – a human being. He has hopes and dreams just like we do. He also has regrets. He regrets the terrible accident that claimed Clarence's life. He regrets being born into a society divided by race, where a boy – either white or black - might be judged by the color of his skin, rather than the facts. My opponent, Mr. Parker, will no doubt play the race card during this trial. He'll tell you John hit Clarence with that pitch because Clarence is a Negro. I know John Drake Jr. and I know he is no racist. I have merely one thing to ask of you. Cast your votes based on the facts, and nothing else. Thank you." He slowly returned to John's side at the defendant's table and elegantly squeezed his paunch into the wooden chair.

"Mr. Parker," the judge spoke, "Please call your first witness."

"The prosecution calls Mr. Thomas Stanch, coach of the Hornets."

The coach waddled up to the witness stand, carrying a Coke bottle into which he periodically expectorated his Beechnut juice. The bailiff swore him in before he sat.

"Do you mind if I call you Coach?"

"No sir, near everyone does."

"OK, Coach, how long has Mr. Drake played for the Hornets?" Parker asked.

"Since seventh grade. I guess this was his sixth season."

"And how would you characterize his performance during those six seasons?"

"Damn talented player. I've never seen such power and control in a boy his age. I just wish he would adjust that attitude of his."

"Power, control, and attitude." Parker paused between each word for dramatic effect, looking again at each juror. "In those six seasons during which Mr. Drake nurtured this power and control, how many times have you seen him strike a batter with a pitch?"

Coach scratched his head and looked at the ceiling, as if he were taking a math test, and had secretly written the answers up there. "I don't recall any, come to think of it."

"Objection, Your Honor!" Felts exclaimed, "Hearsay."

"Sustained," the judge said.

Over the next thirty minutes, Parker extracted incriminating information from the coach, focusing his inquiries on John's attitude and propensity for violence. By the time he finished, he had painted John as a fist-ready reprobate. When certain there was no more water in the well, Parker informed His Honor that he had no further questions.

"Mr. Felts, your witness," the judge said.

Felts approached the stand and stood with his hands in his pants pockets. When he spoke, he faced the jurors rather than the witness. "Coach, do you believe John hit that boy on purpose?"

"Objection! Calls for speculation!"

"Sustained."

"Your Honor, the coach has trained this boy for six years. I merely want his professional opinion on the likelihood that the pitch was deliberately malicious."

"Mr. Felts, you may continue this line of questioning, but you will rephrase the question."

"Thank you, Your Honor. Coach, are you aware of any animosity between John and Clarence?"

"You mean did they hate each other?"

"Yes, sir."

"Well, I don't claim to know the mind of any man, but John and Clarence have duked it out a couple times before."

"Were any of these alleged fights potentially lethal? Any weapons involved?"

"No, not that I'm aware. You know, boys will be boys."

Parker had to give him credit. Felts did his best to present John as a pacifist at heart. He pitched an unfortunate accident. Clarence instigated the fight. John threw a solitary punch. Hell, he didn't even eat meat, so how could he be a threat to anyone? His questioning lasted a little over forty-five minutes.

"No further questions, Your Honor," Felts said.

"Mr. Parker, next witness, please."

"The prosecution calls Mrs. Josephine Buchanon."

Mrs. Buchanon, at Parker's suggestion, wore the same black dress and veil she wore to Clarence's funeral. An enormous woman, she lost her wind by the time she reached the stand. Before she sat, she leaned heavily on the railing encircling the stand. When she finally dropped into the chair, Parker winced, hoping it wouldn't collapse. Although the mahogany chair squeaked in protest, it bore the load.

"Mrs. Buchanon, is there anything I can do to make you more comfortable? Some water, perhaps?" Parker asked.

"Mr. Parker," Judge Philips interjected, "this isn't Howard Johnson's, please get to your point."

A ripple of laughter moved throughout the courtroom. Parker appeared unfazed.

"Sorry, Your Honor, I was merely attempting to offer whatever small comfort I can to this lady who has just lost her baby." After allowing thirty seconds for his statement sink in, he began his line of questioning. "Mrs. Buchanon, can you describe for the court the relationship between Clarence and Mr. Drake?"

"That boy hated my son! He beat him close to death twice, both times at baseball games." Mrs. Buchanon slammed her fist on the railing.

"Why do you think Mr. Drake hated your son, Mrs. Buchanon?"

"Objection! Calls for specu…"

"Overruled. Mrs. Buchanon, please answer the question."

"That boy is just like his daddy, he hates black folk!"

"Objection!"

"Sustained, the jury will disregard that answer."

"Your Honor, I don't want to further upset this lady who has been through so much grief recently. No further questions."

"Mr. Felts, your witness," said Judge Philips.

Felts stood, mopping his forehead again. "Mrs. Buchanon, do you recall the dates of these alleged altercations between Clarence and John?"

"Yes Sir, June 6, 1971, and June 14, 1972."

"My, you have an excellent memory," Felts said, giving an accusatory glare to Parker. Parker's great strength was witness coaching. To him, a trial resembled a Broadway production and required just as much rehearsal. "Do you also remember the causes of these fights?"

"Yes Sir, both fights started as arguments over baseball."

"Then why, Mrs. Buchanon, do you accuse John of having racial motives?"

"Because I know his daddy, and the acorn don't fall far from the tree."

A murmur spread throughout the courtroom. Felt's face flushed with frustration and embarrassment. Parker noticed it was difficult for him to meet his gaze. He flashed his most arrogant smile at Felts.

"Your Honor, I'd like that answer to be stricken from the record."

"Agreed, the jury will disregard the answer."

Felts kept his cross-examination brief. "No further questions, Your Honor."

"Very well, court is recessed until 2:00 p.m." Judge Philips banged his gavel once to signify the beginning of lunchtime.

* * *

The John stormed into Judge Phillips' office, slamming the door open against the wall. Besides Philips' wife, no other human would dare such an irreverent entrance. The John quickly focused on the occasional nervous tics of Phillips' neck.

Placing both his fists on Phillips' desk, knuckles down, The John leaned into the judge's face and shouted, "Don, this is a fiasco. My boy is being railroaded!"

"John, it is highly inappropriate for us to be talking."

"It is highly inappropriate for my son to be prosecuted for murder!" Veins stood out on Drake's forehead. Philips noticed for the first time that the two central veins formed a giant purple Y. Drake began to pace, pumping his hands into and out of fists. "My boy is in there facing nine black jurors. You know he doesn't have a chance! Christ, I do these people a favor by loaning them money whenever they ask, and they make me out to be a villain!"

"John, calm down."

"Don't you tell me to calm down! Who the hell do you think you are?"

"John," Philips said in a soothing tone, "You have to calm down before I can help you."

"I'm listening," Drake said, facing the judge with the stance of a prizefighter.

"John, you know I can't determine the verdict, but I do control one thing – the sentence."

"That's what I'm here to talk about. We have a phone call to make."

"To whom?"

"An old friend."

* * *

In the conference room, Parker looked around the table, individually studying Felts, Drake Jr. and especially Drake Sr.

"Well," said Parker, "I'm waiting."

"We'll plead guilty to simple assault," Felts responded.

"Gentlemen, if you will excuse me, I have a case to win." Parker had reason to display arrogance, knowing demographics were in his favor.

"Don't play games, Parker," Felts said, "We all know that any jury, no matter how well stacked, is a wild card. The three whites could lock this up and we'd have a mistrial. How lucky do you feel on the next draw?"

"The county is 88 percent black."

"Less than half of whom are registered to vote. That makes them ineligible for jury duty. So, let's talk."

"Manslaughter."

"Now I'm the one who should be laughing. We'll plead out to involuntary."

Parker studied John Drake. He wondered if Drake had the judge in his pocket. If so, the kid could get off with as little as six years. Still, weighed against a full jury trial, this was not a bad proposition. He had gotten off to a strong start, but the defense could bring in every one of the two hundred eyewitnesses, stringing this out for weeks, and making the jury forget why they showed up in the first place. He slowly took out a Camel, no filter, and lit it. As he exhaled, he stared not at Felts, but at John Drake Sr. He looked closely for Drake to betray his hand, but the man was carved from stone. *I guess you don't make it to General by being weak in the eyes,* he thought. He decided he would agree to the plea bargain.

"I accept, involuntary manslaughter."

* * *

John sat in his defendant's seat, already knowing the outcome of the trial. It reassured him, knowing his fate in advance. But even so, the level of corruption he had just witnessed shocked him.

"Hear Ye, Hear Ye. The court is now in session, the Honorable Donald Philips presiding," the Bailiff proclaimed.

"Mr. Drake," Phillips began, "I understand you have decided to change your plea to guilty of the lesser charge of involuntary manslaughter. Is this correct?"

"Yes, Your Honor."

"Mr. Parker, do you agree to this?"

"Yes, Your Honor."

"Very well. The defendant will rise." John stood.

"John Drake Jr., you have pled guilty to involuntary manslaughter, a crime carrying a maximum penalty of ten years in prison. There are mitigating circumstances surrounding this case, such as your lack of criminal record of any type, as well as the ambiguity of your intentions. The enormously influential Mr. Parker has also inspired me with his statement that you are 'not beyond salvation'. Therefore, it is the sentence of this court that you be inducted into the United States Army, where you will serve your country for a period of no less than six years. If you are disqualified from military service for any reason, you will serve the remainder of your sentence in prison."

Judge Philips banged his gavel, thinking of the new boat he would be able to buy before the best of fishing season passed, complements of John Drake Sr.

Chapter Six

The Desert South of Safi, Morocco

Lieutenant Amin nervously wiped his palms on his robes. When he had accepted the assignment for Operation Sierra, he had known there would be risks, but he had always known the Army would be there for him. Now, here he stood in a Third World country under a false identity even Uncle Sam would disavow. He had never felt more alone in his life.

The desert showcased all its grandeur just before dawn. The eastern sky's orange hue shone undisturbed by clouds, smog or city lights. Amin stood alone in an infinite sea of iridescent white sand. A lone dust cloud grew on the northern horizon. After a few minutes, Amin made out the shape of a deuce and a quarter truck, approaching rapidly. No other vehicles accompanied the truck. Good. So far, Falon had kept his word.

The truck stopped beside Amin's car at precisely six a.m. He recognized Falon in the passenger's seat. They had agreed that Falon would bring just one man, but Amin couldn't help wondering whether the truck contained a full platoon of armed militia. In reality, it didn't matter. Falon wouldn't need a platoon of men to take Amin out. The rendezvous, by its typical nature, placed Amin in a compromising position. Black marketers tended to be somewhat cautious.

The knowledge that he had a sniper behind a nearby dune calmed Amin. From a hundred yards, the shooter would have little problem dispatching Falon and his driver should the need arise. Of course, killing Falon would destroy his entire mission. Falon was the gateway to Tartus.

The driver remained behind the wheel as Falon walked toward Amin, his robes flapping in the stiff desert wind. Falon stood lean and tall, perhaps six feet. The Moroccan desert had sand blasted pock marks into his face. His irises were large and jet-black, and his perpetual squint concealed the whites of his eyes, giving him a demonic look. He had an insincere smile, like the grin of a cat about to pounce upon its prey. He spread his arms in an open gesture of greeting.

"My friend. How are you?" Falon asked in a friendly tone, as if the two men were old fraternity brothers. He spoke formal Arabic, virtually devoid of the French accent so common in Morocco.

"I'm well, Falon. It's good to see you. You're a punctual man, I must say," Amin responded in Arabic, consciously regulating his breathing.

"In this trade, the only contract a man has is his word," Falon said, "I trust you had no problems acquiring the cash?"

Amin opened the trunk of his car and produced a medium sized brown leather suitcase. He opened it, showing Falon the two hundred fifty thousand American dollars. Were the money not strapped down, the desert wind would have scattered it within seconds. Amin grinned to himself for anticipating this detail. To Amin, both the victory and the devil hide in the details, so he kept them under constant watch.

Falon again flashed his synthetic smile. "Follow me," he said, walking toward the back of the truck. When he pulled back the tarpaulin, Amin braced himself. If this were a trap, he'd have a second at the most to hit the sand and let the sniper go to work. Even then, his odds of survival would be somewhere between thin and call-a-priest.

But the tarp came back to reveal merely crates – dozens of them in varying sizes. Falon stepped into the back of the truck and emerged in seconds with a four foot by two foot wooden box. The box bore the insignia of the US Army. Falon lifted the lid and Amin saw that he just might survive this transaction. Inside were a dozen LAWs – Light Antitank Weapons.

"Would you prefer a demonstration?" Falon asked.

Amin swallowed before he answered. "No. That won't be necessary."

"Well then, I believe our task is complete for the day," Falon said.

"Yes, it is. May I contact you soon to make other arrangements?"

"You know where to find me. Just go to Shaqra and wait."

Amin stood by the crate until the truck disappeared over the horizon. Then, he packed the crate in his truck. The LAWs had served their purpose of getting him one step closer to Tartus. Selling them would further establish him as a player. Arms trade was not one of Tartus' mainstream businesses. Today's transaction would establish Amin as a high-level business associate, but not enough to gain him direct access to Tartus. Baby steps. Amin would be taking things up a notch on his next transaction. To get the big game, you use the big bait. Amin hoped he had established enough credibility today to take things to the next level.

After a few minutes, Amin's sniper gently lifted the meshing he had been under and scanned three hundred sixty degrees before he stood. Only then did he gasp for fresh air. Even at dawn, the sun had already begun its merciless beating of the sand. The temperature was easily one hundred. He waved to Amin, who returned the gesture. Amin knew the sniper was a happy man because he didn't flex his index finger today. One-shot, one-kill, universally regarded as the most intimate form of combat, sometimes disquieted even seasoned snipers. Amin did not envy the man's job.

All the while, multiple AK-47s held crosshairs on their heads. The Arabs were inventing desert tactics thousands of years before the US Army existed. The key to finding someone in the desert is glare. American snipers concealed themselves well, but always left the tips of their scopes bare, making them easily seen by the trained eye. All four of Falon's men radioed in the clear shot signal, but he ordered them to stand down. Business was business and one did not shoot one's associates until it became profitable to do so.

* * *

Beaumont, South Carolina

John's circle of friends held an intimate going-away party at Fat Jack's trailer the Saturday before basic training. The initial shock and anger began to wear off, and John adjusted to the change of course his life had taken. A military life wouldn't be so bad. Besides, you *do* get to play with fun toys. Plus, they would provide a decent housing allowance for a married soldier. Aside from the likelihood of being shot, overall this seemed a workable situation.

"Hey man, you really think you're going to 'Nam?" Fat Jack asked John as he passed a joint to Skeet, who waved it away. Fat Jack, close to 400 pounds, acquired his nickname honestly. His shaggy and frizzled blonde hair hung so coarse it appeared weightless. He had forearms like Popeye, disproportionately large even for a man his size. He had to hold his arms at a funny angle when he walked, always appearing on the brink of teetering forward. Like a sea lion, Fat Jack consumed his body weight in carbohydrates each day – mostly in the form of hops, barley and oats. He had the look and attitude of a Viking king with the vocabulary of a well-trained mountain gorilla.

"Probably. Who knows?" John responded, "They say it might be over soon. I might get lucky."

"Come on, Skeet, take a hit," Fat Jack insisted.

"You know I don't touch that stuff anymore," Skeet said.

"How long has it been?" John asked Skeet.

"Two years, three months, and sixteen days," Skeet replied with pride. For Skeet, the decision to clean up his act had been precipitated by ninety days in juvenile lockup at the age of sixteen. The judge suspended the balance of his thirty-three month sentence, pending good behavior.

Skeet and the state of South Carolina did not see eye-to-eye on the topic of marijuana as a cash crop. Skeet had the honor of being the first person in the county ever to get busted with over a pound of marijuana. DMV revoked his driver's license for the entire thirty months of his probation. In just over two months, Skeet would rejoin the world of drivers.

"How about you?" Fat Jack said as he nudged Tammy.

"I'm fine," Tammy responded coldly.

"*EAT SHIT!*" Fat Jack burped out loudly. Tammy cut him a sharp look, and he didn't quite meet her eyes. "I'm sorry, Tammy. You see; I have this condition. My doctor says there's a little man living inside my head, and he can only speak while I'm burping. *BITCH!* You see what I mean? I can't control that." All the men present were howling with laughter.

"Well, you're right about one thing. There is a very little man living inside your head. And his name is Fat Jack," Tammy said, refusing to look directly at him.

"Hey man, pass that thing over here!" Patch jumped in. Patch had lost his left eye in a DUI related car crash at the age of fifteen. He blamed his addiction to narcotics on his extended convalescence period, when he was inundated with prescription painkillers. Once, John, Skeet and Fat Jack had compared notes and discovered no one had ever actually seen Patch eat. They concluded that the delicate balance of the various drugs in Patch's system must have mummi- fied him. He was a living, breathing chemical robot. He even had that mummy lethargy thing perfected.

John watched his friends with detachment. He wanted to rise above this place, these people. He wanted to be middle class, and these guys had already topped out on the social ladder. Once he and Tammy were in Georgia, the game of life would be reset. They would live in a middle class neighborhood. They would make middle class friends. John knew he could do much better than this. If the military took him out of Beaumont, so much the better.

John looked forward to crafting a new life with Tammy. Watching the erosion of his parents' relationship over the better part of two decades taught him that marriage becomes a lifelong project. You must not only weather the storms; you have to constantly repair the damage they cause. John reeled in his thoughts and tuned into Fat Jack, who had been gesturing at him for several minutes.

"John, I need to ask you something," Fat Jack said, leaning forward onto his elbows. "You remember that fight we got in with those Peachtown guys back in football season?"

"I remember," Patch said, clearing his throat, "That's the day John let me get my ass kicked."

"Well, you see, John," Fat Jack continued, "That's what I wanted to ask you about. It was three guys against three and you took your guy down in one punch. Then, you just stood there and watched Patch get his ass beat. Why?"

"It was a fair fight - one on one," John answered.

"Fair fight?" Patch jumped in, "There's no such thing as a 'fair fight'! There are won fights and lost fights, but there are no fair fights." Patch fancied himself a philosopher, and loved to pontificate on topics ranging from the meaning of life to the rules of engagement for schoolyard fights.

"That's real deep, Patch," Fat Jack said in a sarcastic tone. Patch ignored him.

"Patch," John said, "This may surprise you, but you and my father agree on something. He says there's no right and no wrong, there's simply whose side you're on."

"The man's a genius!" Patch exclaimed.

They spent the next several hours rehashing stories of cars wrecked while drinking, cars wrecked while racing - wrecked cars in general. Patch grew progressively higher until he reached the pinnacle of conscious thought. Then, he had an epiphany. "Wait, wait, wait, I've got an idea!" Patch said, "Instead of letting Uncle Sam shave your head, let me do it."

"Right," John said.

"Wait! An even better idea - let me give you a mohawk. That way, they'll think you're crazy from day one. *Nobody* will mess with you." Patch brimmed with bright ideas when he reached what he called "the zone".

"There is no way you're giving me a mohawk!" John said.

"All right, I'll make you a bet!"

"I'll tell you what," John said, "You polish off that pint of Jack Daniels in one swig and you can give me the mohawk."

"Man, you're crazy!" Patch said, "I've been drinking all afternoon." Then, upon further consideration, he added, "What if I don't finish the bottle?"

"Then you owe me fifty bucks."

Patch went blank for a few seconds as he did the math. "You're on," he said, as he broke the seal on the pint and lifted it to his lips. The first couple of chugs went down reasonably well, but about halfway through the bottle, Patch's body began to jerk as his stomach bucked, and he regurgitated Jack Daniels and stomach acid into his mouth. Then, in one swift motion, he emptied the contents of his mouth and the bottle into his stomach. Although extremely unhappy, his stomach eventually surrendered and retained the Jack Daniels. Ironically, Patch slept while Fat Jack gave John the mohawk.

* * *

The next morning, John walked into the breakfast room wearing a baseball cap. As usual, neither he nor his father acknowledged the other's presence. They had long ago fallen into a mutual disinterest. He smelled his mother's traditional breakfast of bacon, eggs and grits coming from the kitchen. Although Gloria didn't understand John's decision to abstain from eating meat, she supported it by making him an extra serving of eggs and grits. As he took his usual seat to the left of his father, The John reminded him of proper table manners.

"Hats off at the table. You know that." Somehow not saying 'good morning' was perfectly acceptable, but wearing a hat at the table was gauche. John knew this would not end well.

When John removed the hat, he thought his mother would pass out from shock. She dropped the platter of breakfast, the coffee cups shattering on the tile floor. John saw in her eyes that she was witnessing an abomination. She shrieked and ran out of the room, crying.

The John had a different method of expressing his discontent. His left jab caught John by surprise, and cost him his lower right canine. John spit blood and tooth into his hand and looked at his father with contempt. His mind scrolled through hundreds of memories of belittlement, beatings, vacations, gifts, wages, and promises of inheritance.

The John's seemingly complex pattern of brutality and reward were quite simply explained by one word - control. Control over others. Control over objects. Most importantly, control over himself.

In all fairness, The John did mete out occasional expressions of love. John easily spotted his father's love, as it took only one form - material gifts. These gifts were usually proportionate to the severity of the physical and mental tribulations he visited upon his family. John took eighteen years to decipher the incomprehensibly simple economy of the Drake family. The gifts were not apologies or acts of atonement. They were a fair wage paid for his family's obedience.

John finally decided that, if he could change The John, violence would certainly not be the method. It also didn't make sense to stage a rebellion the day before he left home for good.

"I'll go shave," John said calmly as he walked back toward his bedroom. Another trait he and The John shared: they were both men of few words.

* * *

John faced Fat Jack as they stood in Fat Jack's yard. They were both wearing jeans and both had their hands in their pockets. John hated to ask such a favor, but had nowhere else to go. John called this event 'the changing of the guard'. Late Sunday afternoon, T minus one evening. John was exhibiting some signs of nervousness – rubbing the back of his neck, pacing constantly. Inside, he trembled with fear. His entire life would change in just about twelve hours.

All week long there had been reminders of the approaching deadline, as John set his affairs in order. He had managed to find homes for almost all his worldly possessions, taking to basic training a simple bag containing two civilian outfits. Uncle Sam didn't even permit wristwatches. John didn't mind, though. He wanted to forget everything about this place and start fresh. Of all the tasks John had to perform, he dreaded this one the worst. Aside from Tammy, John would miss his dog Vonnegut most of all.

"I've always been afraid of that dog. Why don't you find someone else to take care of it?" Fat Jack said.

"Him."

"What?"

"Vonnegut is a he, not an it," John replied.

"Well, pit bulls make me nervous. Haven't you heard the stories of them killing people?"

John sighed with exasperation. "Pit bulls are much less dangerous than people. The only reason you're afraid of him is you can't speak his language."

Fat Jack responded by barking repeatedly. John couldn't help but giggle.

"Look," John said. He produced a wad of foil and unraveled it, revealing a piece of steak. He handed the steak to Fat Jack.

"Here, you feed this to him, and Vonnegut will understand you are his friend. Be sure you hold it below his mouth."

Fat Jack did as instructed. As he crouched down on one knee and extended his arm, Vonnegut approached at first with trepidation, but finally could not overcome his primal desire for meat. He delicately clamped his teeth into the steak as Fat Jack released it. Vonnegut then lifted his eyes to the sky and practically swallowed the morsel whole.

"Keep your hand down," John advised.

A few seconds later, Vonnegut licked Fat Jack's hand, relishing the new friendship he had made.

"What does Vonnegut mean, anyway?" Fat Jack asked.

"He's a writer."

"What does he write?"

"Books," John replied with a smile.

"Aw, come on, Man."

"Well, basically he does not believe in free will. He thinks God has already created the past, present, and future. Therefore, we appear to have free will simply because we can't see the future, which is fixed anyway, at least from God's perspective. Get it?"

"John, I love you, man, but sometimes I have no idea what the hell you are talking about. Nobody controls my future but me."

"Don't be so sure." John winked. "What if I decide to kick your ass five minutes from now? Would you be in control of that future?" They both enjoyed a good laugh.

Chapter Seven

Langley, Virginia

Special Agent Fulton ducked into the Blue Hose Diner at precisely eleven forty-five. The place bustled for a Tuesday. Grey suits and USAF uniforms were packed into every table and booth. He scanned the front section, peering over the bobbing sea of heads. The diner had a Scottish tavern motif, the blue hose being a reference to the battle stockings worn by bravest Scottish warriors. All the wait staff wore kilts and blue hose, a look that Fulton thought diminished the image of the blue hose and the real soldiers who wore them. He heard bagpipe music coming from the rear section.

"Robert! Over here," Peter called. "I've got us a table in the back." Perky Peter. Peter's constant cheeriness annoyed Fulton, whose mind never strayed far from his work. Fulton's coworkers kindly referred to him as 'focused'. In truth, he tended to obsess a bit - perhaps more than a bit.

The two shook hands and navigated the crowd to their table in the bar section. In the rear section, the lights were considerably dimmer, creating an atmosphere of conspiracies and secret plots. Two men were playing darts in the rear – cricket, judging from their conversation. Men with beer guts pushed against the bar, staking out their little pieces of territory on the bar top as they guzzled Scottish ale from half-yard glasses.

The bar area overflowed with humanity, but tables were open for dining. Crowds seemed thinner to Fulton in dim light, and the background noise maintained a level that would interfere with recording devices. As they sat in the most private booth they could find, Fulton tucked his tie into his shirt.

"What's good today?" Fulton asked.

"The Bannocks." Peter paused. "It's a barley and oat biscuit baked on a griddle, then served smothered in melted cheese. You've got to try the Bannocks. It's a new addition to the menu." Peter's father owned a restaurant, so he unofficially assumed the task of choreographing all matters of cuisine. They each ordered Bannocks with 'wee heavy' ale. 'Wee heavy' meant the strongest brew on hand.

They made small talk until the food came out. Then, they ate like hyenas, attacking their food. Neither was a breakfast person, and both were famished. As their blood sugar stabilized, they became more man and less animal. They began to ease into their own semi private world.

"How's work?" Peter asked.

"Can't complain. Got a lot going on, though."

"Hey, that's job security. Can't argue with that," Peter grinned. "What I mean is, how's 'Fulton's Folly' coming?"

Fulton's crew nicknamed his leviathan ship, Prometheus, 'Fulton's Folly'. The Prometheus, a monstrosity of Fulton's own design, was the crux of Project Crossfire. Fulton's inner circle had doubts they could overcome the engineering challenges of the Prometheus in the given time frame. Although the nickname was partly in jest, it got under Fulton's skin.

Fulton's grimace lasted no longer than a millisecond. He assured himself Peter didn't catch it. There were a few Gremlins in the project, but if Peter asked him if the project would 'float, no pun intended', Fulton thought he would punch him.

Fulton had to constantly switch between contractors so none would have enough information to piece together the nature of the ship they were building. When the Prometheus reached the finishing and armaments stage, he would use exclusively CIA technicians.

Fulton's plan was a little risky, but if it went well, he could stack the balance of power in the world for the next century. His father endowed him with a strong dose of patriotism from an early age. Crossfire could do two things for Fulton. First, he'd be fast tracked to DCI. Second, he would become chairman of the Oil Council - the first Westerner to hold that title. He would control the flow of billions of dollars. Of course, high rewards involved high risks, and Project Crossfire did have its down side. Starting a war often had its hitches.

"It's going fine," he finally answered, somewhat irritably. "I'm having a little trouble acquiring the special munitions, but it's nothing I can't handle." Fulton didn't intend to sound defensive, but he wasn't in the mood to be jibed.

"Hey, man. Don't get so sensitive," Peter said. He leaned in and lowered his voice. "You know nicknames bring good luck." He returned to his side of the booth. "Besides, we didn't meet to talk shop. Did you remember this year?"

"Remember what?"

"Your dad's birthday! I can't believe you forgot again." Peter sneered in jest.

"Is it past?" Fulton's eyes grew perceptibly wider.

"No, man, it's two days after Thanksgiving. How can you forget that? And you know how sentimental the old man is under all his gruff."

"No, you're right. How stupid! I've just been so preoccupied with the project lately. Man, he'd never admit it, but it would hurt his feelings if I forgot."

"Okay, listen. There's no time to get a card to him in 'Nam through his APO address, so I've got an idea. You send him a wire."

"A wire saying what?"

Peter leaned forward as he dug into the idea of finding a clever way out of this little dilemma. He rubbed his chin thoughtfully. "What's his favorite song?"

"Probably 'My Way'. He sings it all the time."

"That's perfect, you send him a wire with the lyrics to 'My Way'. The words of Paul Anka, traveling half way around the world to remind a weary soldier of home, it's perfect. The theme of triumph over adversity provides a nice touch, too."

"You are brilliant, Peter, simply brilliant. I'll pick up the sheet music right after lunch."

Peter raised his glass for a toast, "To Gunny Fulton, best damned soldier in the USMC." Fulton joined the toast with a smile.

* * *

The Kechla Citadel - Safi, Morocco

Amin gasped for air when Falon removed his hood. He had been traveling across the desert in the back of a jeep for over an hour with that hood on. He didn't realize that, despite the hot suffocation, the hood had prevented the choking dust from clogging his nostrils. Falon spoke a solitary word, indicating the massive stone fortress, "Kechla".

Kechla stood alone in a vast expanse of desert - a square edifice about sixty feet tall and roughly two hundred feet on a side. The windows were cross-shaped, eight total on the front face. Amin thought it an oddly Christian symbol to see in an Arab country, but then he thought about the age of the structure. He figured five hundred years easy, going back past the French occupation to the Portuguese. They built this – the Christians. It made sense. A four-foot wall encircled the roof. The entrance was a heavy steel door, ten feet by ten feet.

The surrounding terrain burgeoned with rock formations; keeping out heavy ground equipment - armored personnel carriers and tanks in particular, anything that could carry a gun heavy enough to penetrate the citadel.

Apparently, a single guard patrolled the outer perimeter. At least four guards walked a pattern hugging the walls of the citadel. All carried AK-47s and hand held radios. Pretty tight security, but the real trick was to figure out where this place was. When he returned to deliver the goods to Tartus, he'd need at least a platoon for the sting operation. He saw the whole thing in his head. First, launch Chemical Smoke grenades into the windows, then blast the door, throw in flash-bangs, followed immediately by Ranger sharpshooters. The instant the CS grenades were launched, they would signal four helicopters waiting just outside earshot. From that point, they could have men on the roof in just over sixty seconds, nicely timed with the ground level assault.

He estimated three minutes to capture and secure the facility. That meant three minutes to convince the bad guys of the benefits of immediate surrender. There would be sixty American soldiers, each with an M-16 capable of delivering eight hundred rounds per minute. A lot could happen in three minutes. Amin realized he'd need a second platoon to help clear the citadel room by room, after the primary assault. This was a pretty classic scenario. Estimated enemy casualties 75% plus. Estimated American casualties no more than 10%. All things considered, a good day's work. The problem was capturing Tartus alive. No living American knew what the man looked like, and Amin had no way to confirm the man he was about to meet was the genuine article.

Falon chose to use rough gestures rather than speech. He shoved Amin toward the large steel door. Amin almost lost his step because his hands were still bound behind his back. Falon, noting his oversight, slit Amin's ropes with a ten inch curved knife appearing from and disappearing back to nowhere.

The guard strained to get the enormous door open. Amin was amazed at the scale of the place. Just inside the door was an enormous room, whose walls bore authentic Portuguese tapestries dating from the sixteenth century. There was a fireplace so large that a man could easily walk into it without ducking. He took a quick headcount and figured about twenty, maybe twenty-five men on staff to operate the place.

Although there was an opulent wooden table of French design near the center of the room, the chairs had been removed. There was nowhere to sit. Tartus stood on the opposite side of the table with his hands crossed in front of him in a completely casual manner. His stance was relaxed and his expression was inviting. He was about forty years old, handsome, no facial hair. He wore typical robes, nothing ostentatious.

"Welcome," Tartus said. "I prefer to conduct business standing. I hope that does not inconvenience you."

Amin noticed that Tartus' Arabic didn't have the French accent so prevalent in the region - probably a result of extensive travel. Amin, however, deliberately kept his French drawl. "Not at all. Shall we get down to it?"

"You are direct. I like that quality in a man. Yes, please give me your proposal." Tartus hadn't moved a muscle yet. No fidgeting, no gestures. He was a speaking statue, one whose words delivered both life and death.

"I have a cousin in LA who runs a travel agency," Amin began.

"I fail to see how this involves me," Tartus said.

"You will, Tartus, I assure you. Now, you trade in women, many of your customers being sheiks stocking their harems. But, the market is flooded with inferior merchandise - all these Brazilian and Philippine junkies and whores, half of them diseased.

"Now, picture this - beautiful, young, blonde American girls, completely untraceable. I suspect such girls would bring a bountiful price, no?"

"And how do you plan to deliver such merchandise?" Tartus asked. Again, his tone was neutral.

"My cousin has a friend in Brazil, a country where the authorities are nothing more than a monetary nuisance. Also, it's a country where a lot of people disappear. When the right girl is traveling to Rio, the friend assists in the abduction and we deliver the girl to your people."

"Where?" Tartus asked.

"You would take possession in Brazil. I don't have the means to get them across the Atlantic."

"What you offer is of no value to me. I can already hire anyone in Brazil to do any kind of abduction. I choose not to because the risk is too high."

"But Tartus, the abductor is the tour guide. It's perfect!"

"Ah, so you *do* have an angle. That's what I've been waiting to hear. Perhaps we can do business, but such a conversation will take place at a different time."

Amin kept his poker face. "Of course."

Tartus abruptly changed the subject. "I am an intelligent man, so I am told." He smirked before continuing. "But, one must be especially wary of sycophants, don't you think?"

"They say that between flattery and admiration there often flows a river of contempt," Amin said. He knew he had Tartus. They were speaking as equals!

"Still," Tartus continued, "I am an introspective man." He leveled his gaze on Amin's eyes. "Do you believe truth and knowledge can be found within? Purely from contemplation?"

"All of the great philosophers found truth and knowledge from introspection," Amin responded. "Democritus reasoned out the existence of atoms in five hundred BC." Even as he spoke the words, Amin wished he could somehow retract them. Time slowed to a crawl as that tiniest little mistake flew through space at 350 meters per second toward one of the most dangerous men in the world. Part of Amin knew that he was already dead. The other part prayed for a miracle. His face revealed precisely nothing. In extreme conditions, his training always prevailed. The training provided the most important battle asset – confidence. With confidence, came calm.

"I agree with you perfectly, my friend," Tartus said. The words 'my friend' brought his men to full alert. To the casual observer, nothing changed. But fingers slipped inside trigger housings, thumbs subtly unsnapped holsters or eased safeties off. Most importantly, eyes came into sharp focus. Each man shifted his stare to cover his prearranged zone. In this manner, they collectively viewed every square inch of the room.

Amin saw Tartus nod his head once, subtly, and within three seconds two men had securely restrained Amin; a third placed a pistol to his head from behind. Two more guards positioned themselves ten feet out with their AK-47s trained on Amin's torso. Headshots were for the movies. In real life, victims frequently tried to avoid being shot, and they did this by moving fleetingly and erratically. If Amin had any surprises, the guards would be firing rapid shots at a moving target surrounded by friendlies. They would aim at center mass.

Four more guards had their rifles trained as well, but these men were invisible by design.

"Five hundred BC, huh? That would have been 1150 years before the Hijra, according to the *Arabic* calendar." He strolled around the table and stopped directly in front of Amin. His black eyes were like machines, emotionless recording devices. "The Hijra was Mohammed's flight to Medina. But, of course, anyone raised as an Arab would know this."

"I am well aware of our history, Tartus," Amin asserted, not backing away from Tartus' invasive stare. "I do most of my business with Westerners. Sometimes I find myself thinking in their terms. It was a mere slip of the tongue, mental confusion, if you will." Amin knew his death was assured if he panicked. His training allowed him to conceal all external signs of distress. His body language and tone of voice were casual, as if he were mentioning what he'd had for lunch. But, sometimes, not panicking simply isn't enough.

"There is only one truth. What reason does a truthful man have to become confused? As I mentioned before, I am an intelligent man." Tartus grinned, broke his gaze from Amin's, and walked around the French table. He turned to face Amin, placing both palms down on the table. "But, there is one thing that perplexes me, one concept I simply cannot wrap my mind around. Do you know what that is, my friend?"

"How to know when to trust someone?" Amin ventured.

"You see? You wear your heart upon your sleeve. That is exactly what a Westerner would say. You think forming alliances makes you strong, and that will be your undoing. Even your own Western philosopher, Friedrich Nietzsche said it, 'Friends weaken. Enemies strengthen.' The answer to your question is so obvious that a properly raised child could tell you. The answer is never. How could it possibly be anything else?"

"How can you go through life never trusting anyone?" Amin asked.

"Alive," Tartus answered. "My friend, you're missing a critical point. I didn't even suspect you were an American agent until that slip-up with the Christian calendar. But, even before that, I was planning to kill you. You were never destined to survive this transaction." Tartus said this with no emotion whatsoever. It was that calmness that frightened Amin the most. There was training, but there was also occupying a human body with a lot of nerve endings.

Amin knew all was lost, but denial is the most powerful force in the universe. He kept trying. "What you say makes no sense. How would a businessman profit from killing his associates?"

"What do you want – a lesson on how to be a businessman before I kill you? Let's just say there are legitimate reasons for everything I do. By killing you, I decrease the odds of there being a next you. I was going to tell everyone you were a spy anyway. By coincidence, it turns out to be true. What an amazing universe we live in! So much to learn!"

Tartus leaned close to Amin's face and whispered, "There's one concept I can't grasp and I think you can be instrumental in my education on this topic."

Amin knew from his training to prolong the conversation as long as possible. He needed every second he could buy to use for tactical analysis. One man was behind him at 5 o'clock with a pistol to his head. One man held each of his arms twisted behind his back. Two men with rifles stared menacingly from a range of about three meters. Plus, there were certain to be hiding gunmen. Scenarios ran through his head – none of them good. "And, what is that topic?"

"Masochism." Tartus paused for a long moment, preparing his quarry in much the same way a young lion toys with a wounded antelope before killing it. "You see, I have seen much pain inflicted in my life, and I've never seen any person enjoy it. Yet, there are self-proclaimed masochists out there. These people claim to have reversed polarity. They actually enjoy pain. The more pain they experience, the more joy they feel. What would cause a person to feel this way?"

"Low self esteem?" Amin asked.

"I disagree. I think these people have experiences that shift their perspectives. Some traumatic event, somehow connected to a positive result." Tartus turned his gaze directly into Amin's eyes. "Are you a gambling man, my friend?"

"Yes, I am," Amin replied, maintaining his composure. "Do you propose a wager?"

"Oh, the wager has long since been made between myself and Falon. I bet him I could convert a normal man into a masochist. You see, I have always had an interest in behavioral science. It is theoretically possible to reprogram the mind to love pain via a series of actions and reactions. You will be pleased to know that I have selected you to be the subject of this experiment. It is a great honor, yes?" Tartus gave one of the two rearguards a curt nod. The guard responded by walking to Amin and striking him in the solar plexus with the butt of his rifle. When Amin bent over in pain, breathless, the guard backed up a step and kicked Amin in the mouth as hard as he could. Amin spit several teeth to the floor along with about a half pint of blood. He saw one of his incisors protruding from the toe of the guard's boot. The guard returned to his position and his companion forced Amin to stand erect.

"You see? That was unpleasant, wasn't it?" Tartus asked in a conversational tone. "My hypothesis is that I can make you genuinely enjoy pain. Here's how I intend do it. Over the next seventy-two hours or so, my men will perform experiments on you, and these experiments will expose you to pain like no man has ever imagined. When you pass out from pain, they will inject you with adrenaline to keep the experiment moving along. Your extremities will be first mutilated, then amputated and fed to dogs. There's something enormously special about the look in a man's eyes when he sees his severed penis eaten by a ravenous animal. Through the use of adrenaline and antibiotics, we can keep you alive and awake indefinitely. When you have convinced me that you are enjoying the pain, when you are begging for more skin to be peeled from your body, for more tendons to be cut; when you tell me this and I believe you, two things will happen. First, I will shoot you in the forehead. Second, Falon will give me twenty American dollars." Tartus had a sparkle in his eye as if he were reminiscing about a family picnic. "But, I don't want to bore you with the details, nor do I want to spoil any surprises." Tartus turned to the rearguards and instructed them to take Amin to one of several torture chambers designed by the Portuguese in the 1500s.

Amin knew this was his best chance, with the two rear guards distracted. Either of them could incapacitate him non-lethally in less than a second. He had coiled his body into a spring. Now, he released that spring. In one swift movement, he kicked the guard behind him in the balls and propelled himself into a forward flip, painfully but effectively freeing his arms from the grip of his captors. He landed awkwardly on the small of his back, but the pain didn't matter. He had just one thing in mind. He scrambled between the two surprised guards and managed to get his hand on the downed guard's pistol before six jacketed rounds ripped through the center of his back. What surprised Amin the most was how long he actually lived. The men took every advantage of Amin's remaining time on this Earth. That gave them merely four or five excruciating minutes.

Chapter Eight

Beaumont, South Carolina

John squinted as Fat Jack drove into the morning sun toward Fort Jackson. Vast forests of pine trees lined both sides of the interstate. As John gazed across the blurring expanse of green, his thoughts wandered. What would the Army be like? Would he go to Vietnam? How could this be happening to him? His only solace was in knowing that Tammy would be waiting for him when he graduated Basic Training. At least their marriage would be an island of stability in an ocean of confusion and uncertainty. He noticed the sign 'Fort Jackson – Next Exit'.

John's head was bald as a result of his Mohawk bet. His father's kindly administered advice to cut off the strip of hair was probably a good idea. He doubted the Army would appreciate the humor in the mohawk. As they approached the gate, a corporal waved them to a stop.

"May I help you?" The corporal asked.

"Yea, I'm dropping my friend off for basic," Fat Jack responded.

"I need to see his papers."

John produced the appropriate documents. The corporal snatched the papers and studied them with some interest.

"You need to take the third right, then look for Administration Building B on the left. Go in the door marked 'Special Processing'."

"What's special processing, Sir?" John asked.

"I'm not a Sir! I work for a living. And special processing means you're a convict," the Corporal said, taking on a condescending tone.

Fat Jack drove through the gate and followed the Corporal's simple directions, passing between rows of Quonset buildings. They turned right on a narrow road running through an immense open field, populated with various structures used for training – rappelling walls, tires, jungle gyms, long cylinders as tall as a child, barbed wire over mud pits. There were scattered groups of soldiers in their battle dress uniforms negotiating the obstacles with varying degrees of success.

While Fat Jack was watching a soldier covered in mud being dressed down by a Drill Instructor, John was looking at the flashing blue lights in the rear view mirror. *What the Hell?* He motioned for Fat Jack to pull over. The two MP's jumped out of their jeep and approached the car aggressively. The first MP, the one with the most stripes on his arm, had a shockingly white crew cut with a unibrow to match. His partner was an enormous black man with pockmarks covering his face. John wondered if the man had had small pox or something like it as a child.

"What's the problem, Officer?" Fat Jack asked Unibrow.

"Get out of the car, both of you!" he barked.

"I don't understand..." Fat Jack stopped in mid-sentence when Pockmark produced his baton.

"Out! Now!" Pockmark truly had a way with words. His jaw was square, and his hair was cut in a flat top. His bristly five o'clock shadow at 10 a.m. reminded John of the GI Joe action figures he had enjoyed as a child.

Fat Jack and John immediately exited the vehicle with their hands up, as if they were in a stagecoach robbery. Without words, the MPs made their intentions clear. The two teenagers put their hands on the hood while they were frisked. John decided not to mention that the hood was burning the tar out of his hands. The MP's swiftly but thoroughly determined John and Fat Jack had no concealed weapons. Unibrow spoke. "Don't think I don't know what you're trying to pull here!"

Fat Jack drew a breath to speak, but John interrupted him at once, "What's that, Officer?"

"You will refer to me as Sergeant. And *that* is your attempt to go AWOL."

"What's AWOL, Sergeant?" John asked.

"Absent Without Leave, now put your hands on top of your head!" This was Pockmark. His eyes bulged with anger, as if they would leap out of his face and attack John themselves if he didn't comply. Having no military experience,

John didn't recognize the trademark hyperbolic rage the non commissioned officers used to express their wishes. He simply thought these were the two angriest men he'd ever met.

"Sergeant, I'm on my way to report to Basic Training."

"So, why is your head already shaved, smartass? Tell me that!"

"Our whole baseball team shaved their heads, as a prank."

"Bullshit! Hands on top of your head!"

Fat Jack opened his mouth to protest, but was halted by John's steely *Shut up!* glare. The John had taught John many things, not the least of which was the value of silence.

Unibrow cuffed each of them while Pockmark stood with his right hand hovering over his .45 automatic service pistol. He was in a slight crouching position. His left arm was protruding with the palm facing forward. *Like those magnetic football players on the vibrating field,* John thought. He noticed the gun-strap was unhooked. *These people take life a bit too seriously.*

Thus began John's first day in the service of his country. So far, he didn't like what he had seen of the new world. They detained Fat Jack and him for several hours before he was even allowed to tell his story. Once the MP's had verified his paperwork, he was taken to Administration Building B for special processing, where he was further admonished for his tardiness.

John had imagined that basic training would be action packed. Instead, it turned out to be an endless repetition of 'hurry up and wait'. For the next seven days, he was rushed from one place to another, only to spend hours waiting in line for supplies, shots, paperwork, and more shots. He wondered how long it would take his muscles to atrophy.

He was surprised to see the other recruits were almost exclusively teenagers. He was even more surprised that most were in terrible physical condition. There were kids who couldn't do five pushups. When he thought about it, the entrance physical wasn't exactly like the Olympic tryouts. He wondered just how tough this would be. Once you learned all Sergeants and Corporals were caricatures of rage by design, it wasn't so bad.

On day eight, he and fifty of his closest friends were herded into a bus for transportation to Ft. Benning, where the actual training would begin. John was one of the first on, so his seat was at the back, just ahead of the bathroom. The smell of chemicals and human waste made his stomach roil the entire trip.

There were no unoccupied seats on the bus, and two unfortunate recruits were forced to stand for most of the trip. They took turns sitting in the seats of those who had temporarily gotten up to stretch or to contribute to the stench of the bathroom. John wished for a book or magazine, but the only reading materials allowed to recruits were the Soldier's Handbook and the Bible. Three hours into the six-hour trip, John managed to doze off.

John was awakened by the sound of yet another cranky man's voice. "All right, you bunch of stupid shits! You've got exactly one minute to have your asses off this bus and in formation! Move it!"

He rubbed his eyes and tried to move forward, but the aisle was hopelessly blocked with panic-stricken teenagers. At times his feet lost contact with the floor as the viscous mass of human flesh and camouflage poured out of the tiny opening in the front of the bus.

Once outside, he saw there were hundreds of new recruits gathered in a large open area in the center of Sand Hill. The groups seemed to be divided into busloads, about fifty soldiers in each group. Drill Corporals herded them into formations roughly resembling platoons. In the center of the quad, four men stood in a square, each facing one group of recruits. John knew by their Smokey The Bear hats they were Drill Instructors.

The DI facing John's group was tall, about six-four or six-five. He was lean and hard. From the expression on his face, he seemed to have recently consumed a box of razor blades and enjoyed it. In his parade rest stance, his extremities defined a perfect pentagon. He snapped to attention and marched to the front-and-center of his new platoon. When he spoke, John noticed his voice was gravelly and hoarse, a condition possibly related to his habit of screaming every word he spoke.

"Listen up! My name is Sergeant First Class Peters. Welcome to Fort Benning, second platoon. There are a few things we need to get straight right now. Effective immediately, I am your new mama, your new daddy, your new priest and your new girlfriend. Hell, you might as well say I am your new God! And my first commandment is to forget everything that slick recruiter told you about Army life, because now Uncle Sam owns your asses. And for the next thirteen weeks, that means *I* own your asses!

"For instance, you were probably told you would be allowed one phone call per week. Second platoon, that is what we in the military refer to as a lie. You maggots won't even see a picture of a telephone for the next thirteen weeks.

Mail privileges are also revoked until you have earned them. So you will not be defiling our fine postal system with your pathetic, worthless chicken-scratch for at least a month. I have a message, and I want you to receive it loud and clear, so pull your heads out of your asses and listen up. There are just two groups of people in America who have no constitutional rights – felons and recruits. Keep that tattooed on your puny brains, no matter how tired or scared or angry you are. Combat has no room for emotion. You will learn to control yours or you will certainly die in combat, thereby depleting the enemy's arsenal by one bullet. I don't intend to spend the next thirteen weeks training you shitheads just so you can become walking, talking bull's-eyes. Do you understand me, second platoon?"

"Yes Sergeant!"

"Today, you each begin your journey from sniveling piss-ant to professional killer. And make no mistake, that's exactly what you are – hired assassins. There will be those among you who think you don't have what it takes to be a killer. You are wrong. The human mind is the most dangerous weapon ever devised by man or God. You were designed to kill. It's my job to teach you to kill better.

"Second platoon, you are one quarter of Charlie Company, 6th Battalion, 1st Infantry Training Brigade. Charlie-six-one. Repeat it back to me!"

"Charlie-six-one!" cried the frightened and confused group of teenagers.

"Down, get down, get your asses DOWN! Gimme twenty-five. Sound 'em off."

Although their alignment was not pretty, second platoon finally managed to synchronize. They began counting off their push-ups. When they had finished, most began to resume the standing position.

"Who told you to stand? Down, everybody back down and gimme another twenty-five!"

This time, after completion of the task, the platoon remained in what was called the 'front leaning rest' position, with their arms fully extended at the top of a push up. The name was intended to be cruelly ironic, since it was anything but restful. As their arms quivered in isometric exertion, their sweat dripping into the dusty Georgia hardpan, they gave Sergeant Peters their undivided attention.

"You will speak only when spoken to. When you are spoken to, every sentence will end with the rank of the superior you are addressing. And just in case you haven't figured it out yet, *everyone* is your superior. You will answer me only with: 'yes Sergeant', 'no Sergeant', or 'no excuse Sergeant'. Do you understand me second platoon?"

"Yes Sergeant!" the boys answered in unison.

"Company, a-ten-hut!"

Although they understood the command meant for them to stand, they did not know the correct procedure for moving from the front leaning rest position to attention. Of course, they were not supposed to know. The Army's method was to punish the entire group until they invented the correct procedure by trial and error. They had to learn to think under pressure. Eventually, second platoon rose in unison to attention.

John breezed through the physical challenges. *This can't be as serious as they make it sound,* he thought, *the entire experience must be a mind game.* Within the first couple of hours, John felt he had discovered the basic rules of the game. Do *exactly* as you are told, no matter how ridiculous the command. Expect to be punished for the mistakes of others. Most important of all, keep your mouth shut. Otherwise, the food was pretty good and the toys were certainly cool.

As second platoon endured their initiation rights into the US Army, John's attention kept wandering to the scrawny soldier to his immediate right. This boy had 'abuse me' written all over his face. He grimaced constantly, and reminded John of Ichabod Crane. When he wasn't whining under his breath, he was complaining to his neighbors. He was unable to do the twenty-five push ups that each punishment required. The penalty for not complying with a direct order was a 'grass drill'. Grass drills involved a tortuous non-stop regimen of running in place, push-ups, and sit-ups. Grass drills ended when the recruit collapsed. John noticed his name tag above his heart – Mastagiacomo.

"The man's a sadist," Mastagiacomo commented to John, not realizing Sergeant Peters had walked up behind him.

"Private Mastagiacomo, what exactly is a sadist?" Peters bellowed.

"Sergeant, a sadist is a person who enjoys hurting other people."

"And what do you call a person who enjoys hurting himself?"

"A masochist, Sergeant."

"That's what you are, Mastagee. That's what you are."

Three hours and hundreds of push-ups later, Sergeant Peters decided that second platoon understood his message for the day. It was time to form the squads.

"Platoon, a-ten-hut! Listen up, second platoon. Form a single line beginning here. Fallout! I will give each of you a number. Once you have your number, you will proceed to your assigned point. Second platoon will be made up of four squads. A squad is the smallest functioning unit in the US Army - the backbone of the organization. You will bunk with your squad. You will eat with your squad. You will shit with your squad. Your squad is your team, and you will function as a team. You will live as a team, and, if you are ordered to, you will die as a team.

"Squad one will form over there. Squad two there, three there, and four there," Sergeant Peters said as he indicated the four corners of the D&C (drill and ceremony) area, "As each of you moves out, I want the line to move up one step. Do you understand, Charlie Company?"

"Yes Sergeant!"

As John reached the front, he was assigned to second squad. Four soldiers later, Sergeant Peters assigned Isabue Gibson to second squad.

Once the squads had been formed, he gave them an afternoon of D&C (Drill & Ceremony) interspersed with punishment. When they broke for mess at eighteen hundred hours, even the weariest found a little extra pep getting into formation. John was first to arrive, so was at the front of squad two. Sergeant Peters named the first in each rank 'squad leader', figuring he had to start somewhere, and the hungriest was as good a place as any.

They marched the one and a half miles to the mess hall. As they stood at attention, their stomachs roiling with hunger, Peters paced down each squad. He squared off on John. "Soldier. Do you have a sewing kit?"

"No, Sergeant!"

Peters took out his pocketknife and cut John's nametag from above his heart. "Buy one. Second squad, gimme fifty for being out of uniform!"

At mess, John drooled as he passed through the line where PFCs heaped more and more food on his plate. Country fried steak, double mashed potatoes, green beans, and applesauce. He finished everything but the country fried steak within one minute of sitting down. He was leaning back in his chair, rubbing his belly, when he heard a commotion at the opposite end of the mess hall.

"Sergeant!" Private Gibson shouted.

"Drop and give me twenty-five, for not requesting permission to speak."

After succumbing to the inevitable, Gibson returned to the position of parade rest and shouted, "Sergeant, Private Gibson requests permission to speak!"

"Speak," Sergeant Peters replied.

"Sergeant, Mastagiacomo is trying to kill himself!"

Sergeant Peters flipped his folding metal chair on its back and sprinted toward Mastagee. He found the recruit standing behind his seat, his eyes wild with fear, furiously stabbing himself in the left wrist with a standard issue fork. He had a better chance of killing himself with his fingernails, but he had to be restrained nonetheless.

What Sergeant Peters did next took all of one second. He stepped to the left of Mastagee, leading with his right foot. He placed his right heel just behind Mastagee's right ankle. All the while, he was folding Mastagee's right hand against its palm, and forcing it between the subject's shoulder blades, exerting pressure with his thumb. Private Mastagiacomo involuntarily dropped the fork and fell backward. Peters turned him over to the MPs, who took him away. The boys promptly regained interest in their food and the incident was forgotten. The next time John saw Mastagee, the kid had a nice shiner, courtesy of the military police, no doubt.

Upon exiting the mess hall, John was stopped by the mess Corporal. "Boy, people in Vietnam are starving, and you are throwing good meat away!"

"Drill Corporal, I don't eat meat," Drake responded with military enthusiasm.

"And, why is that, Bone Head?"

"Because, Drill Corporal, the cow never did anything to piss me off."

The Drill Corporal could not restrain his laughter. He was so amused, in fact, that he only made the recruit perform one hundred pushups before he let him leave without eating the country fried steak.

Chapter Nine

Fort Benning, Georgia

John was jerked from a coma-like sleep by the sound of a baseball bat and a metal trashcan. He clawed at weary eyes that hadn't had time to crust over. He felt dizzy and disoriented. *Must start moving.* As he willed himself into action, he squinted from the bright fluorescent lights.

"OK, Bone Heads! Drop your cocks and grab your socks! Get your lazy asses out of bed. You heard me, UP! Beauty sleep is over." Sergeant Peters looked surprisingly fresh for a man who couldn't have had more than four hours sleep. His deep Georgia suntan was accentuated by the ruddy completion of his cheeks. When he screamed, large, crooked veins bulged in his forehead and neck.

The recruits, three weeks into basic, knew the drill by now. They had five minutes to shit, shower, shave, and be in formation. John rapidly ran a bar of soap over his grimy body, removing approximately ten percent of the dirt and sweat. No one spoke as they rushed through their new morning motions. The routines were disrupted this morning because two of the sinks were out of order. John was still waiting for a turn to brush his teeth and shave when Sergeant Peters blew his whistle. John grimaced and double-timed it toward the quad.

One of many difficult tasks the recruits had to learn was to fall into a perfect formation. They eventually figured out they needed a point of reference if they were to have their lines properly dressed. The point of reference became the squad leader for the first squad in each platoon. That man would choose a spot, and all others lined up relative to him. They efficiently assembled in the quad, standing at attention, awaiting their orders.

"Platoon, stand at ease!"

Every left foot moved eighteen inches to the side to form sixty uniform triangles of legs. Hands clasped behind backs, always with the right hand inside the left. Peters began his routine inspection, walking the length of each squad with his hands behind his back. He stopped in front of John.

"Well, look what we have here," he chided, "Private Drake thinks this is the Navy." Peters pressed the brim of his hat against John's forehead. "Do I look like some goddamned squid to you, Boy?"

"No Sergeant!" John shouted hoarsely, his voice weakened from stress and exhaustion.

Peters addressed the platoon, "Do we grow beards in the United States Army, like those rump ranger squids?"

"No Sergeant!"

"Private Drake must think you're all a bunch of faggots! Why else would he be growing a beard?" The platoon was silent, not knowing exactly what to expect, but quite certain it wouldn't be pleasant.

"Men, I'm offering you a chance to prove to Private Drake that you aren't queers. Wouldn't you like that, Second Platoon?"

"Yes Sergeant!"

Peters ordered John to retrieve his disposable razor from his rucksack. It took John no more than five seconds to produce the item. Peters snatched it and held it menacingly in front of John's face. As he addressed the platoon, he never took his eyes off John. John kept his eyes level and straight ahead, not looking the Sergeant in the eye, but not looking at the ground either. This seemed to elicit the least scorn from Peters, who tolerated neither confrontation nor fear.

"I want the entire platoon to drop and start sounding off pushups while Private Drake shaves - dry."

"Yes Sergeant!"

"You can thank Private Drake later, in private, if you like."

John scraped the hair off of his face, the only lubrication coming from his salty sweat and the blood generated by the task. For the next three days, his face would be raw and stinging in the Georgia heat. By the time he had finished shaving, the platoon was up to fifty-two pushups. John understood the idea behind pitting the recruits against each other. This practice ironically made them a more cohesive team. When one member of the team failed to pull his weight, the others would discipline him, usually in the form of a blanket party.

A blanket party takes place in the middle of the night. Four men restrain the victim on his bunk with a blanket while a few others take turns pummeling his belly with a bar of soap in a pillowcase. John had seen a few blanket parties, but didn't think the men would bother him. They usually preyed on the weak, like Mastagee. Once Peters relieved the platoon from the front leaning rest position, he discontinued the inspection, having found his mark for the day. He resumed pacing in front of them as he spoke.

"Today, we will be embarking on your first real test. Today, we begin your first bivouac. We will be spending four days in the woods, traveling an average of twenty-five klicks each day over variable terrain.

"You will do this in full gear, totaling seventy pounds in each rucksack. Each night you will make camp, and each morning you will leave no trace of your presence. You will be issued C-Rations, which I suggest you consume sparingly. Since today is PX day, our first stop will be there. Afterwards, we hump over to supply, and that will be your last contact with civilization for ninety-six hours. Drake, front and center. You'll be calling cadence."

"Yes Sergeant!" responded John as he snapped to attention and double-timed to his spot next to Sergeant Peters. He croaked in a hoarse voice, "Platoon, a-ten-hut! Right face! Column right – march! Left, right, left, right." The platoon began to echo John's words, "Two old ladies lying in the bed. One rolled over to the other and said, 'I wanna be an Airborne Ranger. I wanna live a life of danger.'"

The teenagers moved like some giant camouflage centipede. Cadence was not used merely to synchronize the steps of the platoon; it also passed the time and developed the lungs. Peters had made John platoon leader in the second week. Shortly afterwards, John had appointed Isabue Gibson first squad leader. Gibson, or Gip, as he preferred, was doing a five-year tour of duty with Uncle Sam for drug charges. John had taken a liking to him because they were both in for 'special processing'.

When they reached the PX, John had the squads enter one at a time, beginning with Gip's squad. Faces were pink from the exertion of the two-mile march, and it wasn't even six a.m. John took position next to the cash register because he was charged with the task of limiting each recruit's purchases to regulation. Gip was first in line. John took mental inventory of Gip's basket and noticed something strange. He spoke to Gip in a low voice.

"Gip, every week you buy the maximum allowance of cigarettes, but I've never seen you smoke one. How come?"

"Man, you never cease to amaze me."

"Me?"

"Whites. You white boys invented this capitalism shit, and after hundreds of years, you still don't understand it. You know what I'm saying? In fact, I'm here for that exact reason. Here I am, just a brother trying to make a living, but since my shit ain't taxable, I'm a criminal. Meanwhile corporations are ripping off the public, and fat cats are getting rich. Do you see any of them here? No way, Man, they're still out there gettin' paid."

"I guess you've got a point," John responded, gaining respect for his new compatriot. He reached into the nearby shelf and picked up a carton of Marlboros.

"Now you're catching on!" Gip jibed. "Okay, listen up. One smoke goes for a quarter on guard duty and bivouac. A pack goes for fifteen bucks. I can't have you undercutting me in the market, can I?"

"Fifteen dollars for a pack of cigarettes?" John asked.

"Supply and demand, Man. Never forget that."

John didn't.

After everyone had stocked up on boot polish and bug repellent, they reformed and marched to the supply depot where they were issued unloaded M-16's. For the three-mile march to the rendezvous point, they carried their weapons at port arms – a forty-five degree angle across the chest. Sergeant Peters marched silently behind John.

Once the unit reached the edge of the woods, John called them to attention and relinquished command to Peters. It took enormous self-control for John not to scratch and rub at his face. The Georgia heat was already inflaming his razor burns - dousing his face and neck with sweat. Sergeant Peters addressed his platoon.

"Okay, listen up! I'm giving Private Drake a map covering the pertinent area surrounding the Chattahoochee River. This is your one and only map. If you lose it, it will not be replaced. Keep that in mind. There are three rendezvous points, corresponding to the three days of this exercise. You will not bed down until you have reached the rendezvous point for each day. You are expected to reach the final rendezvous point by 1800 hours three days from now. For every hour you are late, you will be penalized one meal.

"Each of you has half of a standard issue tent. You'll need to pair up to shelter yourselves from Mother Nature's little surprises. Too bad there isn't an even number of you. Each night, one man will be sleeping under the stars with the mosquitoes.

"One last thing. I will be an observer during this exercise. I will not help anyone in any way. This exercise has begun. Platoon dismissed."

Chaos ensued as the youngsters scrambled to pair up, no one wanting to be the unlucky soldier left without a tent. During the scuffle, John and Gip formed their first official partnership by sharing a tent.

Not surprisingly, Mastagee was the odd man out. No one, including John, knew whether Mastagee's weakness and ineptitude were genuine or an elaborate sham. Either way, the truth would eventually come out. Such was the structure and purpose of basic training. Besides, as Sergeant Peters quipped, even a pussy can take a bullet for his country. Mastagee's contribution to the war effort may be to deplete the enemy's arsenal by one bullet. One thing was certain; he would not be washed out. The Army's criterion for acceptance was joked to be, 'If you can walk, with assistance, you are selected'.

Once the tents had been set up, John called formation. "Men, we're going to keep a fire-guard posted through the night." There was a huge, collective moan. Everyone had assumed fire-guard duty would be suspended on bivouac. "More specifically, we'll keep two fire-guards posted on opposite sides of the perimeter. That means thirty-six men – nine from each squad. Squad leaders, pick your nine men and give me a written list. I'll do the roster. Platoon, a-ten-hut. Fallout."

John thought he had done the right thing by instituting the fire-guard. It would free up tents to allow Mastagee indoor accommodations, but Sergeant Peters' menacing look conveyed a different message. John suspected the tent shortage was designed with Mastagee in mind, to toughen him up.

That evening, as the others slept somewhat uncomfortably in their tents, Mastagee jogged circles around the encampment with one hand holding his crotch and the other holding his M-16 over his head. He proclaimed at the top of his lungs, "This is my weapon. This is my gun. This is for fighting. This is for fun."

Mastagee had the misfortune of referring to his M-16 as a 'gun' within earshot of Sergeant Peters. The M-16 assault rifle, Peters had informed him, is a weapon, just as a shovel is an entrenching tool and a jeep is a truck. You have to talk the talk.

"Man, this is bullshit!" Gip told John as they lay inside their tent. The heat was oppressive, but zipping the tent shut was the only way to keep the mosquitoes out. They were both cranky and exhausted. "You piss off the entire platoon just to give the little guy a break, and Peters pushes him right back down!"

"No question it's bullshit, but what are we supposed to do about it?" John responded.

"I say we teach the Sarge a lesson," Gip replied. John saw the fury in his eyes. John knew Gip could relate to discrimination. Gip told him once that a gang of white bullies had beaten him with a section of water hose when he was thirteen for being in the wrong neighborhood. Now, Peters was telling Mastagee he was in the wrong neighborhood – that he was not welcome. John had a soft spot for Mastagee, even though the sad sack brought Peters' wrath upon on the entire platoon.

"What?" John asked. He sat straight up in the tent.

"Look, we're out here all alone with Sergeant Peters. If he gets his ass kicked by a bunch of recruits, you think he's gonna report it?" Gip said.

"Gip, you're a smart business man, right?"

"I do okay. So what?"

"So, what profit is there in taking out Sergeant Peters? What do we gain? As-suming he doesn't disable both of us in ten seconds, how would we be helping Mastagee? Huh?"

"This ain't about profit. I know his kind and I can't sit here and listen to this shit! There's just one way to deal with a bully – kick his ass." Gip removed a toothpick from his lower lip and threw it to the foot of the tent.

"Everything is about profit if you look deep enough. Gip, don't you see what's going on? Mastagee's gonna stay in the game until the last week. Then, he'll either wash out and restart basic, or he'll go to Vietnam. There is no option 'C', where he returns to his civilian life and becomes a librarian or whatever the hell his timid heart desires.

"Now, you know I do everything I can to help him, but getting us court-martialed doesn't improve anyone's situation."

"That's the problem with you white boys, you always think playing the game is the answer."

"Gip, you ever hear of changing the system from within?"

"I've heard of being an Uncle Tom, if that's what you mean."

"Don't even try to hand me that shit. What exactly is an 'Uncle Tom', by the way?"

"An Uncle Tom is a brother who denies his heritage, a brother who tries to learn and obey the rules of the white man's game."

"Gip, don't you think the real 'Uncle Toms' are the few bad apples who give all blacks a bad reputation? They are the ones holding you down, not the white man."

Gip grabbed John by the collar and shoved him hard. The tent collapsed, ripping most of the snaps open. Gip and John rolled for about five feet and came to a stop with John on top. John released Gip's shirt and stood over him.

"You finished?" John asked, breathing heavily.

Gip leapt up with the speed and agility of one who grew up on the streets. As he stood, he hooked his right fist into John's unsuspecting jaw, nearly dislodging one of John's molars. John fell flat on his back, stunned. He sat up and shook his head to dispel the vertigo. Then he did the last thing Gip expected. He spread his lips to reveal blood-covered teeth. He was smiling widely.

John remembered the last time someone laid a sucker punch on him. It was in ninth grade. The guy's name was Baby Huey. Huey was in eleventh grade and saw his mission in life to be disciplining those smaller than he was. At a party in Fat Jack's front yard, John had turned his back on Huey in the middle of one of Huey's boastful anecdotes. He couldn't listen to another word of Huey's insecure drivel. Huey punched John in the back of the head. Luckily, Huey was not a good biology student, so his blow landed on the crown of John's skull, rather than the delicate brainstem. John had bent forward and shot back into Huey, throwing him off balance at the waist. Huey grabbed John's shirttail to avoid falling over backwards. He yanked John straight up and wrapped his thick forearms around John's neck from behind.

John stood, lifting Huey entirely off the ground. John took two laborious steps backward and then fell back into freefall. His fall was interrupted when the tailgate of Fat Jack's pickup connected with the base of Huey's skull. Huey suffered a bruised brain. He missed school the next two days.

That was the closest John had ever come to getting his ass kicked. John did not like the feeling of helplessness accompanying Huey's attack from the rear. For a few seconds, he had been completely in that fat pig's control. Even during the worst times with his father, John had never been so helpless. With The John, because he controlled his own mind, he controlled the situation. He never once gave that bastard the satisfaction of seeing him flinch in pain.

The night of the Huey fight, he vowed never to be caught off guard again. More and more, he saw each day as a battle, each encounter as a confrontation. He remained compulsively ready for battle. While his classmates were thinking about whom they would sit with at lunch, John was calculating a tactical response to every movement around him. This was his way of dealing with negative feelings; he converted them into combat tactics.

John's paranoia had its coming-out the evening of the Huey fight. His father had nurtured it through the first few laps, but that day in ninth grade, John had taken the baton.

Now, despite his experience, he had dropped his guard for Gibson. *Why?* Because Gibson was not a schoolyard bully – he was a warrior. He fought for a purpose. John had found his first kindred spirit in this world. Tammy was his soul mate, of course, but to meet a fellow warrior was a distinct pleasure. His bloody grin erupted into explosive laughter.

Gip, poised in a boxer's stance, waited to see what this crazy person would do next. He did not let his guard down. He had seen more creative tricks than that. "Man, you're crazy!" he exclaimed.

"You're Okay, Gip. And I'm sorry about the Uncle Tom bit. Your people. Your problem. Your business," John said, as he extended his right hand, a symbolic gesture allowing a face-saving out for both of them. After a brief hesitation, Gip reached out and helped John to his feet. The two made eye contact, and like wild animals, came to an understanding of mutual respect without the use of words. Mastagee was still chanting in the background.

Sergeant Peters, who had been following their little scuffle, unceremoniously chimed in. "Gibson! Drake! Secure that shit! Save it for the gooks."

"Yes Sergeant!" John and Gip responded at full volume, their eyes never unlocking.

"Man, I'll never understand white folks," Gip said.

"Hey, I was just busting your balls," John responded, "That was a great shot, by the way. I'll take you by my side in a pinch anytime, and that's more than I can say for the rest of these punks."

"So, I punch you in the face, and you want me to believe you're not even mad?" Gip asked.

"You think that's the first punch I've ever taken? My fifty-two year old father hits harder than that."

Gip began to giggle. "You know, you're right about one thing. Most of these guys are punks." They laughed together.

In the background, they heard another recruit jibe at Mastagiacomo, "Hey Mastagee, one piece of advice. Don't ever try to crucify yourself. You'll never get the last nail in!"

The entire platoon erupted into laughter from their tents. John quietly put his hand on Gip's bicep, reminding him this was neither the time nor the place to make a stand. They both fell asleep a few moments later.

John awoke to a bright light in his eyes. He was disoriented, but realized someone was holding a flashlight inches from his face. "Get that shit out of my face!" he exclaimed. The light extinguished, leaving John completely blind. He heard Sergeant Peters' voice.

"Use that tone of voice with me again and I'll snap your neck like kindling. Now's the time for you to listen, not speak. I'll acknowledge that instituting a fire-guard schedule keeping a tent slot open was clever, but your brain is still put in backwards. You don't distribute the burden of the weak over the entire platoon. That's a good way to get sixty men killed.

"You cannot carry Mastagee through basic. It's not your job, and I'll bet he can pull you down more easily than you can pull him up. To be a leader, you have to be a nut cutter. Do you think the gooks are going to cut him any slack? Would you trust him with your life while he's on point or guard duty? Make him or break him, and I mean soon. Got it?"

"Yes Sergeant," John said.

"Good. Now, get some shuteye." Peters zipped the pup tent after exiting. John pondered what Peters had said for the few minutes he remained awake.

Chapter Ten

Langley, Virginia

Fulton was getting antsy. His appointment with the DCI was for 10:00am, and it was nearly 10:30. He forced himself not to look at his watch every couple of minutes. Not that he should have been surprised. The DCI was a notorious control freak that got a kick out of exerting his authority over others. Making Fulton wait was just his way of letting Fulton know who was boss.

"Special Agent Fulton, the DCI will see you now," the receptionist said.

"Thank you," he said as he entered his boss' office.

The DCI was an imposing man. His six foot three frame completely filled his luxurious leather chair. Just above his balding head, President Nixon stared intensely from a custom oil painting. The DCI did not stand when Fulton entered. He wasted no time with pleasantries.

"Have a seat, Agent Fulton. I understand Project Crossfire is proceeding according to plan."

"Yes Sir. We're nine percent over budget, but right on schedule."

"There's something we need to discuss. I want you to be crystal clear on this." He leaned forward on his elbows for emphasis. "I want this project completely sanitized."

Fulton didn't fully grasp what the DCI was saying. He hated the buzzwords of his trade. Why didn't the man just say what he meant in plain English? His quizzical look must have made this obvious, because the DCI elaborated. "What do you suppose would happen if one of these men talked to the press, or talked to a girlfriend who talked to the press?"

"Sir, that would be a disaster. That's why they won't be told the true purpose of their mission."

"Do you suppose they won't read the newspaper the day after? Do you also suppose not one of those men will realize he's sitting on a gold mine of information the US government would do or pay anything to conceal?"

"Sir, I see your point. I hadn't considered that angle." Fulton felt a little queasy at the thought of 'sanitizing' American soldiers, but the DCI had a point. If word got out, the US could potentially be ejected from the United Nations.

"These men," the DCI continued, "will be heroes. Men die for this country every day. They will be casualties of war. Are we perfectly clear on this?"

Fulton didn't speak. The DCI filled the void, "Agent Fulton, to be a leader, you have to be a nut cutter. You must come to terms with a fundamental truth of combat. Evil can only be vanquished by a greater evil. Now don't get me wrong. We're the good guys, but what makes us the good guys is not *what* we do, it's *why* we do it. Always remember the *why*. Are we clear now?"

"Yes Sir," Fulton responded without hesitation.

"Very well. Keep me posted," the DCI said, his tone indicating the end of the meeting.

As he walked along the hallway of CIA headquarters, Fulton was reeling from disbelief as what he had just heard. Killing American soldiers?

* * *

Fort Benning, Georgia

Mastagee rubbed his eyes and glanced at his watch. It was 0345 hours. *Fifteen minutes until I'm relieved,* he thought. With reveille at 0500, he would face a grueling day tomorrow. Such was the nature of fire-guard, an ancient discipline invented by the Romans, ostensibly for the purpose of guarding against fires. The real purpose of fire-guard was to teach soldiers to operate with precious little sleep.

At least he had a tent for the evening. If he'd been left outside, he couldn't have slept at all with the mosquitoes on a rampage as they were. Mastagee saw someone approaching in the darkness.

"Halt, who goes there?"

"Man, cut that shit out. You know who I am," Gip replied.

"What are you doing up? Are you my replacement?" Mastagee asked.

"No, Man. I set my watch to go off just before each watch. I'll be sound asleep again in three minutes, after you and I conduct a little business."

"Business? Uh, I've got twelve minutes left in my shift, then *I'm* off to sleep - for an hour, at least."

"Yea, and what're you going to have for breakfast?"

"I don't have C-Rats to cover breakfast. No one does."

"I do. I've got cigarettes, C-Rats, even a chocolate bar."

"Doesn't it bother you to miss sleep like this?"

"Hey, I grew up in the South Bronx. I've never slept more than two hours in a row in my life. Besides, business is about supply and demand. I've got to go where the demand is."

"Chocolate, you say?" Mastagee was interested.

"Hershey, an American tradition." Gip grinned.

"How much?"

"Five bucks."

"Five bucks! That's a rip off!"

"Another American tradition," Gip responded with a broad smile. His ultra white teeth seemed iridescent in contrast to his dark brown skin. The moonlight accentuated this effect. Mastagee knew that Gip was one of his supporters – he really didn't have any friends – so he didn't take offense at the price. He reached into his pocket and paid market price for the Hershey bar. Within a few minutes, both soldiers were sound asleep in their tents. One combat skill they had both acquired at Ft. Benning was the ability to fall asleep within minutes - anywhere, any time.

* * *

The next morning John looked over Gip's shoulder at the map, trying to locate just one landmark. After two days in the forest, they were tense and exhausted. As platoon leader, John knew he had to maintain a facade of complete control. By watching Sergeant Peters and the other drill instructors, he had learned that military leaders must be infallible. So, they either made no mistakes – unlikely - or displayed a good game face. The theme was calm. Calm begets calm. He asked, "What's our heading this morning?"

Gip replied, "Best I can figure, due west until we pass this point." He placed his finger on the map. "Then north until we hit the last rendezvous point."

"How far west?" John asked in a whisper.

"Uh, I'm not sure," Gip whispered in return, "I can't find a landmark to nail down our position, and I don't know what the landmark for the next turn is either. All I know for sure is we should be heading west."

John leaned close to Gip's ear, "You're sure about the west part? Or is that a SWAG?

"It's a genuine sophisticated wild assed guess."

"Shit. I guess that'll have to do. We hump in five minutes. You just find me that landmark. And act like you know what you're doing," John said. He knew leadership meant making fast decisions with imperfect information.

The day was just like any other – tedious, boring and hot. A jaunt through Sand Hill in August was like working out in a sauna, while wearing seventy pounds of clothes. Even with water breaks on the quarter hour, dehydration set in so rapidly that three soldiers passed out from heat stroke and were removed by the Safety NCOs. Those lads would have to start a fresh bivouac with another platoon. John was talking to St. George, a short, stocky kid with a mouth the size of Texas, when St. George succumbed to the heat. Right in the middle of a sentence, the guy's face went blank, his eyes rolled back in his head, and he fell flat on his face. John had never seen anything like it.

Gip eventually spotted a thick grouping of colossal oak trees. A landmark! At last! From there, the way became obvious. They turned north, moving at a brisk pace. John guesstimated that if the path was this clear all the way, they would reach the rendezvous point in time for their nightly four hours sleep.

John was dead on. They reached the campsite at twenty hundred hours. Weary young men shambled about setting up tents. Tonight, no one gathered firewood to heat C-Rations. Cold food and quick sleep was the silent consensus, except for those who pulled fire-guard duty.

* * *

Later, as John was unrolling his sleeping bag, Gip shook him and asked, "Hey, Man. I got a question for you. Why didn't you hit me back the other day?"

"Because I like you," John said. "Besides, I never hit someone unless I mean business."

"What the hell is that supposed to mean?" Gip asked.

"It means that a single punch can change the course of a man's life. A single punch can wipe out a bloodline. A single punch landed me here."

"Man, you are so full of shit!" Gip said, kicking dirt on John's boots.

"Okay, Jackass. See if those flaps of skin on either side of your head work. You don't understand. I'm not bragging. I was captain of my high school boxing team. They called me 'one punch Drake' because I have a unique way of fighting, that's all." John's tone was completely casual, but Gip detected the scent of bullshit.

"And I suppose you're gonna share this unique method with me?" Gip jibed.

"Look, in every fight, there will come an instant, just a fraction of a second, where a single motion will disable the opponent. I have the gift of recognizing that instant. I typically never throw more than one punch in a fight." John said this matter-of-factly, without the tone of boasting. "The down side is that hitting someone in that moment of vulnerability can seriously injure them. Now, most guys swing for the head. That's the worst target - it's highly mobile and encased in bone. The true weak points are the larynx, solar plexus, heart, groin and knees. A true blow to any of those places will incapacitate an opponent instantly."

John saw from Gip's expression that he was reassessing John. The two men shared a quiet intensity one rarely experiences.

Gip asked, "Hey, what are you in here for?"

"What do you mean?"

"I mean I know you're in for 'special processing'."

"You first," John insisted, even though he already knew Gip's story.

"What do you think, Man? Drugs! It was a real bitch too, 'cause it was just weed." Gip paused. "Man, I was all squared away before I got busted. I was on full academic scholarship to SC State."

"You were on academic scholarship?" John responded with a skeptical sideways glance.

"Yea, Man. They took one look at my grades and said, 'You're black and you made a D? Let's get this boy some scholarships and shit!' "

They both burst into laughter.

"Manslaughter," John said. The laughter stopped.

"Damn, Man. What did you do?"

"I threw one punch."

Gip realized that John was not bullshitting him. He asked, "So, where did you learn this one-punch technique?"

"From my father. He taught me how to focus all my physical and mental energy into one movement."

"Well, that was mighty sweet of him," Gip said. "Let me guess, he imparted this lesson by beating the shit out of you, right?"

John tapped the tip of his nose with his finger.

"I never knew my dad," Gip said. "He skipped out on my mother before I was born. Now, I guess you're thinking that I missed out on a lot of ass whippings, but I got my fair share."

"Most of the violent crime in America is black on black, they say," John responded.

"Well, whoever 'they' are, they're full of shit. When I was growing up, my mother had always told me that we had to stay in a certain area of the city. She never said why. Well, like most teenagers, I was curious and fearless. I crossed 47th Street and made it two blocks before six white dudes popped up out of nowhere. They roughed me up, tore my shirt off, but I got a few solid licks in. Then, four of them held me while the other two whipped me with pieces of garden hose. We didn't have hospital money, so I spent two weeks laying face down on my bed while my mamma kept my wounds clean. That was the best she could do for me. No pain killers, no antibiotics, nothing."

"Man," John said, "You have no idea how closely I can relate to that. And I'll tell you another thing, it makes me ashamed to be a white person."

"Forget all that white and black stuff. Be proud that you're a warrior. Life has made us both hard, like steel. And once you've got the steel, you'll always have it. Hey, I gotta know one thing. This one punch you threw, did it kill somebody?"

"Yes."

"Did you mean to kill him?"

"When I was twelve, I took a vow never to kill another living thing. It was an accident," John said.

The two sat in silence for several minutes. John paid close attention to the nature surrounding him. Bullfrogs were croaking in the swamp, almost drowning out the constant hum of mosquitoes. John grinned as he recalled the joke that the state bird of Georgia was the mosquito. Gip constantly swiped and slapped at them, but the mosquitoes did not seem to have an appetite for John's blood. Then, John saw a rarity. A white dove perched on a nearby limb. He was transported back in time to his first and last hunting trip. It struck him that what the world considered a symbol of peace was to him a symbol of cruelty.

John laid his head back against a tree and rested his eyes. Less than thirty seconds had passed before he felt an unidentified object pressed aggressively to his throat. "You're dead," Sergeant Peters said in an icy tone. "I just cut your throat." He removed the pine branch from John's neck. "If this had been combat, I'd have me a brand new American M-16 to use on your comrades." He stared into John's eyes, waiting to see his reaction.

"No excuse, Sergeant!" John responded, keeping his eyes straight forward.

"Drop and give me a hundred," Sergeant Peters said before receding into the darkness.

* * *

Langley, Virginia

Special Agent Fulton sat alone on the couch in his apartment, his head in his hands. He was revolted by what the DCI had told him. The initial shock had worn off and been replaced with anger and confusion. Murdering American soldiers was unthinkable to him. All along, he had known that Project Crossfire would result in collateral civilian losses, but that was an inevitability of war. His mind swirled like a tornado.

During his career with the FBI, he had clearly been one of the good guys. Now, the DCI had thrown him a curve ball he wasn't sure he could hit. He stood and paced his living room. The shag carpet felt pleasant to his tired, bare feet.

Whenever Fulton faced a dilemma, he tried to break it down into bite-sized pieces. First, he must decide whether he was capable of executing this mission. If that answer was no, then his career with the CIA was over. Maybe the FBI or DEA could find a slot for him. If the answer was yes, he had to personally select a commander for the mission. He would have to look that man in the eyes and recruit him for a suicide mission. That man would in turn unwittingly recruit a group of dead men. The thought made him nauseous.

Fulton paced for hours, occasionally trying to sit, but jumping up every time his rear touched the couch. This was by far the most difficult decision he had ever faced. He was disillusioned. How could he have been so naïve as to think he'd have a successful CIA career without getting his hands dirty? He knew that the price of liberty was the blood of patriots, but the murder of those patriots by their own government was an entirely different matter. Or was it?

Pete Townsend had once sung, "There's no easy way to be free." That simple, but powerfully insightful statement washed over Fulton's mind. Deep inside, he knew the DCI was right. He understood that the needs of his country outweighed the lives of a few dozen soldiers. Still, he viewed himself as a cannibal.

This was the pivotal point in his career. The decision he made today would be permanent and irrevocable. Either he possessed the ability to do whatever was necessary for the greater good, or he didn't. Once he crossed that line, there would be no turning back. *The end justifies the means*, he tried to convince himself as he paced.

Fulton plopped down on the couch in exasperation and lay on his back rubbing his temples. His tension headache had begun at the base of his skull and worked its way progressively forward. *The end justifies the means.* Was that the rationalization of an evil man or a fundamental truth of the universe? The path of righteousness wasn't as clear to him as it had once been. The older he became, the more corrupt he realized the world really was.

Could he face the corruption? Embrace it? Make it a part of him? He was fighting for the greatest nation in history.

"I can do it," he spoke aloud. Fulton repeated the statement again and again. Eventually, it became true. Speaking the words somehow hard wired the thought into his mind. He was decided.

In the right frontal lobe of the cerebrum was an area called the executive complex. This region governed Man's fundamental sense of right and wrong. Fulton had permanently stretched his executive complex, making it flexible, adaptable. Sometimes good people must do evil things to defeat an even greater evil. It wasn't a rationalization. It was simple logic.

With that epiphany, Fulton became what he needed to be – a monster. Now, all he needed to do was select a commander. He knew just the right man for the job. He lifted the phone and dialed the DCI's secretary.

Chapter Eleven

Fort Benning, Georgia

"Charlie Company, a-ten-hut! Right face! Column right march!" Sergeant Peters was barking orders at Charlie Company for the last time. They came to him as boys, and after thirteen weeks, they left him as men. Through two wars and almost twenty years, Peters had led his nation's youth along the path to manhood. His was a thankless job. The recruits never appreciated the sacrifices he made for them. They didn't notice that he slept exactly when they slept, and that he ran every mile they ran.

But Peters did not need their validation. His performance was measured in pushups, miles run and standardized test scores. If his recruits improved in these areas, he knew he had done his job; that their chances of surviving combat were improved. He was particularly proud of his miracle transformation of Mastagee. The kid had eventually toughened up enough to pass the exit physical.

He was also happy with his decision to endorse Drake and Gibson for Ranger School. Though both were full of piss and vinegar, they were smart enough to harness and channel their energies. There was great potential in these two. They were the only two recruits in second platoon that picked up on the game. They kept their chins up and their emotions off.

He surveyed them for the last time, marching in perfect cadence, in full dress uniform, on their way to the ceremony that officially declared them combat-ready soldiers.

"Charlie Company, eyes right! Present arms!"

In unison, two hundred soldiers saluted General Dalton and his staff of senior officers.

* * *

As he peered into the crowd, John caught his first glimpse of Tammy in thirteen weeks. Just then, she was the most beautiful and welcome sight he had ever seen. Her face glowed when she caught his eye. She waved frantically, a gesture he was not free to return. Both her parents were with her, showing support for Tammy and John.

His parents were also in the crowd, sitting nowhere near Tammy's family. This was no surprise. It merely solidified his resolve to never revisit Beaumont. This vow would become the first of many John would reassess in the months that lay ahead.

Throughout the graduation ceremony, John daydreamed. Although the thought of combat was terrifying and even repulsive to him, he knew Rangers received preferential treatment, and Ranger School was his best shot at not being separated from Tammy for extended periods of time. He had given a great deal of thought to fighting in Vietnam, and had decided joining Special Ops was far superior to living in the jungle for a year as a grunt. Most Ranger missions were surgical in nature, with periods of respite between. The war showed no sign of ending soon, and he just knew Vietnam was his destiny.

* * *

The next day, the Justice of the Peace married John and Tammy in a ceremony lasting no longer than five minutes. Tammy's parents attended, but the Drakes, as expected, did not. On the courthouse steps, they threw the obligatory rice, and wished the young couple a happy honeymoon and life together. Beer cans jingled behind the car as John drove their Challenger toward the national forest, where they enjoyed a modest camping honeymoon.

* * *

Fort Benning, Georgia

"Gentlemen," Master Sergeant Hicks announced, "Welcome to Zero Week. Sixty two days from now, roughly one half of you will be declared United States

Army Rangers, the highest honor an infantryman can receive outside of combat. Those who can withstand the rigors of the course will become members of the best-trained combat force in the entire world.

"The Ranger Course is sixty one days in length with an average of 19.6 hours of training each day, seven days a week. The emphasis during the course is on practical, realistic, and strenuous field training, designed to develop skills relevant to fighting the close contact, direct fire battle. You will be exposed to conditions and situations closely approximating and often exceeding those encountered in combat. Fatigue, hunger, the necessity for quick, sound decisions and the requirement for demonstrating calm, forceful leadership under conditions of mental and emotional stress are all essential elements in the Ranger Course.

"You will be trained to effectively function under conditions of simulated combat stress. Frequent and unexpected enemy contact, reduced sleep, difficult terrain and the constant pressure of operating within restrictive time limits will all contribute to this atmosphere of stress.

"At any point during the course, any student may be dropped on request. Ranger School is not mandatory. If you're not committed, we don't want you. When I dismiss you from this formation, you will proceed directly through the OD doors behind me in an orderly fashion for processing. Tomorrow, the fun begins. Company, dismissed!"

John and Gip couldn't believe they had ended up in Ranger School together, much less in the same platoon and squad. They had no idea their coupling was at the order of Major Briggs, who took his directive from General Dalton.

* * *

Langley, Virginia

Special Agent Fulton stared across the DCI's desk into his boss' foreboding eyes. The DCI's heart pumped ice water through his veins. Fulton realized he needed to develop that same coldness. The hard part of that transformation was behind him – making the decision to execute Project Crossfire.

"Well?" The DCI snapped.

"Sir, I've identified a commander for the mission. Lieutenant Commander Rymes – a squid. He's currently a desk jockey, but has combat experience in Viet Nam. Rymes had his own ship, held the rank of full Commander, and was on the fast track to Captain until he made a critically bad command decision. American soldiers were killed and maimed as a result and he was given a desk job." Fulton paused to let his words sink in. The quintessential bureaucrat, Fulton was attuned to his boss' mood and thought process at all times. He saw that the DCI recognized the name and waited for some subtle reaction from this stoic man.

"This tragedy you mention. Wasn't that the USS Burke incident?" The DCI inquired.

"Yes Sir, exactly. I believe Rymes would undertake any mission to regain his honor. He will jump at an offer to redeem himself. He'll accept the assignment without question. Plus, how many O-5's do we need sitting behind a desk? Rymes should have been court martialed. I think we owe him one, or more to the point, he owes us one."

The DCI sat quietly for several minutes, rubbing his chin. Fulton knew not to speak until he was invited. Eventually, the DCI responded.

"Excellent work, Agent Fulton. I want you personally to recruit Rymes. Work the redemption angle and emphasize the importance of discretion in selecting his crew. Tell him he's on a 'need-to-know' basis, but we need his full commitment up front. Understood?"

"Yes Sir," Fulton replied.

Chapter Twelve

Fort Benning, Georgia

Tammy knew the time had come. She could not continue to live with John without revealing her secret. He had graduated Ranger School with honors and had quickly risen to the rank of E-5, Buck Sergeant. Their lives together in the modest but clean house provided by the US Army had been wonderful these last months, but the splinter in her soul needed removal. She braced herself as she prepared to share her dark experience with another human being for the first time. Her lips trembled as she spoke. "John, there's something I've got to tell you, and you're not going to like it."

"What is it, Sweetheart? What's wrong?" John asked. Her tone instantly put him on edge.

"John, you are the most loving and wonderful man in the world. But, I need you to listen to me for a few minutes without interrupting."

John joined her at the dinner table and gave her his undivided attention. "Take your time, Honey," John said. Tammy's hands were trembling. She noticed his hands were trembling too.

Tammy was terrified. She had played out this scenario in her mind a hundred times, and every time the outcome was different. Sometimes, John went into a rage. Sometimes, John receded from her, turning to stone as surely as if he had gazed at Medusa. What man wanted a scratch-and-dent wife? She almost lost her nerve, but realized it was too late to turn back now. Better to have him leave her than to keep living a lie. If she could get this out, perhaps the nightmares would stop. There was also the chance her life would become a nightmare. If

John left her, whatever was left of her self esteem would evaporate. After some hesitation, she began her tale.

"John, you know how I'm afraid of water? Well, I haven't always been. My phobia started the summer after ninth grade, and it's related to my bad dreams. Remember, let me finish without interrupting me, or I may not be able to get this out."

Tammy proceeded to tell John the source of her demons. As the story progressed, John's body temperature dropped. By the time Tammy finished, he had become a block of ice. Tammy talked for over thirty minutes, often having to stop to cry. Neither of them would ever know the real reasons behind what happened all those years ago in Beaumont, but knowing the reasons would not have affected John's response. These are the events Tammy described to the best of her ability.

* * *

Tammy, Fat Jack, Patch and Skeet were celebrating ninth grade graduation at the river defining the northern border of Beaumont. Against the express wishes of the power plant upstream, they walked out across the rocks to their traditional spot. All the kids knew the sound of the gate release siren, and respected it immensely. It didn't take many drowning fatalities to hammer the lesson home.

The white water was breaking all around them, and they even had a mini waterfall with about an eight-foot drop. Behind the curtain of water was a cave of sorts that seated six comfortably. Of course, the first one in had to check for Water Moccasins, but even so, the kids universally considered it the coolest place on the river. John and Tammy were not yet dating. They were in the extended flirtation stage pubescent teens seemed to need.

Patch was still in convalescence from the car crash that had claimed both his eye and his license. Although a heavy drinker since the age of twelve, he blamed his addiction to narcotics on his postoperative treatment. He did, however, work diligently to augment his prescriptions with the most recent illicit drugs.

His latest discovery was a drug used in the 1950's as a general anesthetic for humans, but its use had been promptly discontinued due to its severe psychotic side effects. Since 1960, veterinarians had been using it to anesthetize animals. Apparently, the animals did not possess the higher brain functions necessary to suffer the side effects. Luckily, Patch knew the town vet, and had coaxed him into sharing a little of this uncontrolled substance for a nominal fee. The vet had some fancy name for the powder, but Patch just remembered its abbreviation, PCP.

Patch and Fat Jack hoisted the cooler of Budweiser across the rocks until they reached the right spot. Mother Nature had even been kind enough to provide a flat, high rock, providing safe quarter for their cooler. They basked in the warm sunlight, enjoying the contrast between the sun's heat and the water's extreme cold. Several hours passed without much conversation. Skeet had not yet had his life changing experience, and was sucking down beers with the rest. Tammy was immersed almost entirely in the water, and her body had become numb. Not a heavy drinker, she didn't realize she'd had seven beers until she tried to stand. The chilly water induced some sort of sensory deprivation making her feel sober until her departure from that frigid womb. Once standing, she staggered, almost falling before Fat Jack grabbed her arm.

"Hey guys, it's about time for a joint," Patch contributed to the sparse conversation.

"Patch," Tammy responded, "There are people all around!"

"Please, step into my office," Patch said, pretending to hold the waterfall back as if he were holding a door for the lady.

"Whose turn is it to look for snakes?" Tammy asked.

Snake reconnaissance was no light matter. A bite from a Water Moccasin could cost a person a limb unless they reached a hospital within forty-five to sixty minutes. Aside from the fifteen-minute walk to the car, the hospital was twenty miles away.

"I'm up," Skeet admitted, as he summoned his courage. His courage turned out not to be far away, as he had drunk nearly a twelve pack in two hours. He dove into the water curtain. For dramatic effect, he waited a couple of minutes before sticking his head back out.

"All clear!"

"Next time you take that long, we're gonna have a serious talk; the kind that doesn't have any words. You dig?" Fat Jack said.

"Okay, Man. I was just foolin' around."

Once inside their private chasm, Patch opened a series of plastic bags, eventually revealing his hidden treasure - the special veterinary joint. Patch had an evil grin on his face as he fired it up. He had never sampled PCP and wasn't sure what it would do when burned. The vet had told him it was injected into animals before operations. He took the first three hits, then offered it to Tammy. Tammy waved it away.

"Patch, I'm already a little too drunk. I don't need anything else."

"Come on, it's graduation. And besides, this is the best grass I've gotten my hands on, ever."

"Patch, I said no."

Patch begrudgingly passed to joint to Fat Jack, who was more than happy to accept it. Fat Jack followed the agreed upon protocol of three hits per turn before passing it to Skeet.

Marijuana typically begins its psychotropic effect within five minutes of inhalation. PCP, however, takes a little longer. For the first half-hour in the cave, the three men enjoyed the mild effects of the grass.

Skeet noticed the change first, when he felt a sensation of moving at infinite speed, although his eyes told him he was sitting cross-legged underneath a waterfall.

Patch followed soon after, with the vision of a purple child. This child was about ten years old, but with a huge cranium shaped like an inverted pear. His lidless eyes stared at Patch. Patch tried to look away, but the child followed his gaze everywhere. He noticed the child's eyes were all pupil. Occasionally, the purple child would lean near Patch's ear and whisper something unintelligible.

Fat Jack found it interesting that there was a naked cowgirl in the cave with them. Well, naked except for the boots and hat, otherwise how would he have known she was a cowgirl? His cut off jeans bulged in response to his hallucination. Fat Jack reached for his cowgirl.

Tammy slapped Fat Jack's face in response to his jerking at her tube top and exposing her left breast.

"What the hell do you think you're doing?" She screamed.

Patch experienced an epiphany. Tammy was the purple child. He realized that his mental anguish could be quenched by only one method. He ripped Tammy's tube top off and tossed it into the water. Tammy, horrified, covered her chest, but by then it was much too late. Patch began molesting her with his hands. She slapped him as hard and as fast as she could, to no avail. Patch seemed impervious to pain.

Fat Jack and Skeet were quick to follow Patch's lead. They held Tammy while Patch yanked her cut off jeans down. Tammy screamed, kicked, and punched at random. Some of her blows hit human flesh, but most contacted with rock.

Her assailants soon tired of her resistance, and held her head underneath the waterfall, nearly drowning her, and not really caring. She caught occasional gasps of breath by vigorously shaking her head. Meanwhile, her three best friends took turns at raping her.

Tammy blocked out most of what happened next, but when she awoke it was dark, and she was underneath the waterfall, naked and bleeding. She stepped out, humiliated at her condition, only to discover she was alone. The solitude was both a blessing and a curse.

Judging by the moon, she guessed it must have been ten or eleven at night. She certainly was in no mood to face anyone, but was facing a ten-mile walk home, naked, bleeding, and traumatized. How could this have happened? What did she do to provoke such an attack?

Tammy stumbled aimlessly through the woods for an indeterminate time, humiliated and confused. Her salvation came in the form of a couple of poachers named Bubba and Jimmy.

Bubba and Jimmy were men of many hobbies, but their favorite pastime was spotlighting deer.

"Sweet Mother of God!" Bubba exclaimed, "Jimmy, get a blanket from the truck!"

Tammy was in the early stages of shock, and did not speak as Bubba gently wrapped her in a blanket.

"It's okay, honey, we won't hurt you," Jimmy assured her, "We're gonna take you to the hospital."

Tammy shook her head vigorously. She coughed, hacking up some more river water. She managed one word.

"Home."

"Okay, Okay! Can you tell us the way?"

Tammy nodded.

When Bubba and Jimmy stopped in front of Tammy's trailer, Bubba offered to walk her to the door and talk to her parents.

"Please don't. I don't want anyone to know."

"All right, sweetheart, we won't tell nobody, right Jimmy?"

"I swear," Jimmy replied.

Tammy sneaked into her home and showered until there was no more hot water. She scrubbed herself until her skin was raw, suppressing her urge to cry, knowing that if she started, she'd never stop. She silently heaved as racking waves of revulsion pulsated through her body.

* * *

As Bubba and Jimmy drove home, they were sickened by what they had seen.

"Whatever bastard did that has gotta pay," Bubba said.

"Yea, but she didn't want nobody to know about it."

"I ain't talking about the law, numbskull. Mr. Drake will know what to do. Besides, he pays good money to know stuff."

* * *

As he sat at his kitchen table that day, John's mind raced with conflicting thoughts. Childhood memories made with friends. Growing up together. Friends being there in his times of need, when his family wasn't. Those friends destroying the woman he loved. Images flashed through his mind: violence against Tammy, violence against his friends, himself at twelve standing over that freshly shot dove.

Fortunately, the mind had a shut-off mechanism to protect it from trauma. John retreated into a merciful blanket of nothingness. At the simplest level of existence, emotions were separated from thought. Thoughts became crisp and logical. The area where emotions reside remains vacant. John had to face this shocking development. He needed a simple path to follow.

So, as John floated in icy emptiness, a thought eventually formed. It was a voice from the past. *There is no right or wrong. There's simply whose side you're on.* The John's insight interrupted the nothingness of John's thoughts. That phrase led John to the simple path he so desperately needed, drawing John inexorably into its gravitational pull. The universe suddenly shifted into focus.

Just as he had done so many times before, John became a machine – cold steel forged for a singular purpose. John remembered his training. There were many preparations to make, but his path was already beginning to gel in his mind. He had negotiated a new equilibrium with the world.

He and Tammy spent the rest of the day lying in bed, comforting each other while John constructed a game plan that would transform him into the thing he most despised. He neither showed nor felt any emotion whatsoever. He was in shock. Part of him had died.

* * *

The Prometheus

Commander Rymes stood on the deck of his new ship, Prometheus. Before him, twenty-two men stood at attention in platoon formation. The Prometheus was in dry dock, still under preparation, but Rymes felt it important to have this briefing on deck. He paced back and forth with his hands clasped behind his back, inspecting his crew. This assignment was an opportunity he never expected to receive. He was uncomfortable not knowing the details of his mission, but understood that such was the nature of the CIA. The smell of salt water filled his lungs with a passion he hadn't felt in years. He began his kick-off speech.

"Men, I have hand picked each of you for this mission. You should be proud to be a part of something this significant. The details of our mission are strictly on a need-to-know basis. Today, you need to understand that you will be serving your country and your president on a mission with extremely significant implications. The lives of thousands of people rest upon our shoulders.

"You're probably curious. That's only natural. I have no answers to give you except this. If you execute your orders properly and to the letter, you will all be heroes."

Rymes scanned the young, enthusiastic faces before him. He hadn't experienced the sensation of command in years. It was exhilarating. Second chances were rare in this life, and he was grateful. When Special Agent Fulton had recruited him, he could barely contain his enthusiasm. He knew little about the mission at hand – only a set of coordinates to reach. Once there, he would receive further instruction. Rymes felt a knot tighten in his stomach as he remembered the USS Burke, but that was the past. He had no intention of letting any harm come to any member of his crew. That was his top priority.

Chapter Thirteen

Beaumont, South Carolina

John looked upon his hometown with new eyes. He had learned things he could not unlearn. He was a man on a mission – one that superseded all the emotions and beliefs he had ever possessed. As he drove past the pecan orchards on the periphery of town, he hardly noticed the majesty of nature that typically engrossed him. He passed the old "haunted house" he and his friends had dared to enter on teenage Saturday nights. Only the bravest had ever ventured upstairs, where John & a few close friends knew there was a chair, just like the one from All In The Family. The significant difference was that this chair was missing a half moon from the area designed to comfort the occupant's head. This chair's final occupant had known no comfort. The dark brown stains on the chair and floor were a testament to that fact. The locals said Old Man Sisko had used his toe to pull the trigger of the twelve-gauge shotgun, thus ending one set of problems and beginning a new one.

Past the orchards, he was now driving through a seemingly infinite expanse of cotton. There were single lots of land larger than New York City. Two miles past the crossroads, he turned left on a country road having no designation other than S-9-63. After a quarter of a mile, he pulled into the dirt road leading to Fat Jack's trailer.

Fat Jack's front yard was littered with beer cans, some in trash bags, most not. His push mower was partially disassembled and beginning to rust. Judging from the height of the sparse weeds and even sparser grass, it had been out of commission for months. Rain had splattered mud up on the lower three feet of the once white trailer. The only object of any potential value was the '57

Chevy Fat Jack claimed he was restoring. Apparently, he hadn't gotten around to the wheels, unless he intended to use cinder blocks. Three dogs looking like they had vacationed at Auschwitz were hungrily tearing at a small mountain of trash bags.

John made his way through the refuse, wondering what he had ever seen in such an undisciplined slob. When he knocked on the edge of the screen door, it took Fat Jack several minutes to show his scraggly face. Fat Jack, like so many things in Beaumont, defied the laws of nature by not changing over time. He was wearing a sleeveless undershirt, stained with various bodily fluids and foodstuffs, a pair of cut off jeans, and bare feet. John strained to conceal his revulsion as he gazed into the hovel. Again, he wondered how this person had ever been his friend. Regardless of his business here today, John was still confused how such a morally and physically weak organism could ever have been his buddy and confidant.

"Fat Jack!"

"Soldier Boy, how you been?" Fat Jack bellowed, punctuating his salutation with a stentorian belch. He was on his second twelve pack of Budweiser. But, hell, it was almost three p.m. And it was Saturday, for crying out loud.

"Good, but I'm going to be a lot better in a couple of hours," John said, dangling the bottle of Jack Daniels in front of Fat Jack's face, "Up for some shots?"

"What kind of stupid question is that? Come on in Buddy, tell me all about the Army."

John walked in and sat on one of the filthy couches, spreading out so that even an idiot like Fat Jack would get the message to sit on the other. He placed one fifth of bourbon in front of Fat Jack, and produced another fifth from his satchel for himself.

"Why two bottles?" asked Fat Jack.

"I'm challenging you to a drinking contest. One thing the Army taught me was how to drink, and I think you're losing your edge." John winked.

"Okay, you're on," responded Fat Jack, not possessing the faculties to notice the label on John's bottle had already been broken.

They drank toast after toast, reminiscing about every event that had transpired between third grade and graduation. John told Fat Jack all about the Army and Fat Jack told him all the town gossip. Apparently, John's friends were proud of his escape from Beaumont, a rarity in their social circle. A weaker man, a man without a mission, might have become sentimental at this rehash of the past, but not John. He never lost sight of his objective. There was no more anger. Where anger had been, now there was simply the mission. The part of his mind that generated emotions had gone dormant that day in the kitchen with Tammy, like boiling magma encased beneath frozen stone.

As the afternoon progressed, the stories became less interesting and the bottles became emptier. When Fat Jack began to forget what he was talking about in mid sentence, John decided the time was right. "Fat Jack, you want to know the most important thing I've learned in the Army? Loyalty. That's it, plain and simple. You see, when you have to go into combat with a group of people, you learn to depend on one another, just like we depended on one another all the way through school."

Fat Jack, not quite sure where John was heading with this, merely nodded.

"I could always depend on you, just like you could always depend on me. You know what the penalty is for betraying that trust in combat? Well, do you?"

"Uh, they shoot you, don't they?"

"You're damn right. But it's not like in the movies, where there's a court martial and a firing squad. Your buddies do it – the same people whose trust you betrayed. And you won't see it coming. You'll just be on patrol one day and when your turn comes to take the point, someone's weapon will accidentally discharge. And the next thing you know, you're laying there gushing blood from a perforated bowel while your squad leader removes your dog tags to give to the Lieutenant. You'll be screaming because you know you won't die before the gooks find you; but your buddies will just casually stroll away."

"Man, that's cold," Fat Jack said. Despite his stupor, he felt intensely uncomfortable with this conversation.

"Yea, it is. It's cold to violate a sacred covenant." John emphasized the word 'violate'.

"Oh man, I'm really getting sleepy," Fat Jack mumbled, trying to change the topic. "The Army must have really taught you how to drink."

"Like I said, you're getting soft," John replied, as he poured himself another shot of iced tea from his personal bottle. One of the many interrogation techniques the Army had taught John was that many drugs, such as heroin, had a toxic dose that rose with usage. The unique attribute of alcohol was that, although one's tolerance rose over time, the lethal dosage remained constant. According to John's calculations, the time was right. "So, you gonna match me, or what?"

Fat Jack poured one of the last three shots from his bottle of Jack Daniels. Before he was able to slam the shot, he had to perform the Self Heimlich Maneuver on himself; to induce what John considered oral flatulence. After making room for another shot, Fat Jack raised his blood alcohol content to 0.40%.

"Fat Jack?"

"Yea?"

"It's your turn to take the point."

"Wha…"

"You got point," John said, staring directly into Fat Jack's dull, bloodshot eyes. Fat Jack was drunk, but not too drunk to recognize the Grim Reaper.

John saw a part of Fat Jack was relieved that his hour of atonement was at hand. Overcome with drunkenness and apathy, Fat Jack lay flaccid on the couch and closed his eyes for the last time.

John lit one of Fat Jack's cigarettes, taking a few puffs to build the cherry. There was a pillow on the couch next to Fat Jack's unconscious hand. John placed the cigarette between Fat Jack's pudgy fingers, making sure the business end touched the pillow. He waited to make sure the chemicals and cheap materials used to build and furnish trailers were as flammable as the clichés. Once the couch was completely engulfed in flames, John strolled out to his Challenger. Taking a quick glance to ensure he was alone in the country, John fired up the V-8 and embarked upon phase two. He neither smiled nor frowned. He merely marked an item off his list.

* * *

As John entered the Beaumont Saloon, he paused just inside the door to allow his eyes and his mind to adjust to his surroundings. Little had changed about the place. In the front room, there were two pool tables, each with approximately seven ashtrays. A Budweiser light, the working class chandelier, hung above each table. Along the perimeter were wooden booths, with heavy wooden tables, designed to extinguish cigarettes with little aesthetic loss. Even though the booths were littered with ashtrays, the clientele tended to crush their butts into the nearest convenient surface, having little respect for anything other than the pool tables.

John scanned the booths. The crowd was light for a Saturday night. There were perhaps twenty patrons, most from the local cotton mills, the rest farmers.

"John!" cried Ron, the proprietor of the one and only white bar in Beaumont, "Soldier Boy! The first Bud's on me."

John waved to Ron and maneuvered toward the bar.

"How've you been, Ron?" John asked.

"Same as always. You know the story."

"That I do," replied John.

"So, how's Army life? I heard you were Special Forces or something."

"Ranger."

"Oh, yea. So, you going to 'Nam?"

"Not if I can help it. Word is we may begin withdrawing troops any time now. If I'm lucky, I'll dodge that bullet." Even as he spoke it, John knew the pun was wasted on Ron. "Where's Skeet?"

"He's in the back, playing table hockey with Ann. You know, I still can't figure out why he hangs out here. Kool Aid drinking bastard. And I don't even sell that shit. He's the only guy I let bring his own drinks in here. I probably make about ten dollars a week in quarters off him. That's it."

"Ron, you've got a heart of gold. The good will alone should make you sleep better at night."

"Shiiit!" Ron replied; his most sincere attempt at wit.

John gave Ron an obligatory smirk, and walked into the back room. The back room had no seats; it's primary functions being foosball and table hockey. In the unlikely event of overcrowding, the back room could also provide additional space for locals who couldn't quite face their doublewides yet. One of the things John hated about Beaumont was the redneck conundrum. The money the average citizen spent on beer and cigarettes each month could easily have bought them a middle class lifestyle, thereby eliminating the impoverished conditions that they blamed for their vice.

"Skeet, you ugly sonofabitch, how've you been?"

"John? Holy shit! When did you get back in town?"

"Today," John replied, closely studying Skeet's wiry frame, the filthiness of his lanky hair, and the complete lack of discipline and motivation in his pathetic but short life. He had the ever-present bottle of cherry Kool Aid in his left hand. He looked into Skeet's eyes, trying to catch a glimpse of the monster he knew lurked within. There was none to be had. John mentally recorded the exact shape and size of Skeet's Kool Aid bottle.

"So, how's the Army treating you?"

"Skeet, I'm about up to here with the Army. Let's talk about something interesting. Hi Ann. Long time no see."

"Hi John. Aren't you supposed to be in uniform?" Ann asked.

"Only within fifty miles of base."

"So, what is this interesting thing you have in mind?" Skeet inquired.

"I gotta take a leak. How about you?" John asked.

"I'm drinking two gallons of Kool Aid a day, what do you think?" Skeet replied as he walked toward the bathroom with John.

Once they were alone, John asked, "You still think that Duster can take my Challenger?"

"Think? Shit, I know it can! You know, it's not so much the car as the driver," Skeet replied with a challenging smirk, "Besides, you've never raced me when I'm sober."

"Skeet, I'm not up to it right now. I think we should both be sober." John lied. He couldn't be the last person seen with Skeet, "Are you still working Sundays?"

"Yea, Man. Can't pass up that time and a half."

"Okay, how about tomorrow, right after you get off work? I-77?"

"Okay," Skeet said, "Just don't tell Ann about it, all right?" Skeet spoke the magic words.

"Well, if you don't want Ann to know you're racing, you ought to keep your mouth shut at work tomorrow. You know how small this town is."

"Good point. I'll meet you at five fifteen, at the head of I-77. How about a hundred bucks?"

"A hundred sounds fine. See you then, Skeet. I've gotta get some rack time. I'm still a little tired from the drive. We'll catch up tomorrow after I smoke your ass."

John and Skeet zipped their pants and parted ways for the evening.

* * *

"So, do you plan to join us for church?" Gloria asked John over the traditional Sunday breakfast of scrambled eggs, grits and bacon, with homemade buttermilk biscuits on the side.

"Mom, I'm twenty years old now, with a family of my own. You know I don't like church."

"Well, like it or not, it's the right thing to do. When you have your feet under my table, you should abide by my rules."

John wished he had stayed at a hotel. He had vowed never to set foot in Beaumont again, much less his parents' house. But he knew the appearance of a family visit was essential to his cover. Witnesses would place him in Beaumont at the time of his friends' closely spaced deaths, and he needed an official purpose to be there. His parents certainly didn't mind that he was visiting without his wife, who thought he was at Fort Bragg. As he considered it, being seen in church wasn't such a bad thing.

"Sure, Mom, I can wear my dress uniform."

"I'll be so proud of my boy." Gloria smiled.

* * *

Sunday afternoon, John waited at the head of the I-77 construction site. For those who were willing to move a few pylons, there was highway access about five miles before the public traffic began to merge. John knew Skeet despised reading, especially newspapers, so he was confident his old friend hadn't learned of Fat Jack's untimely demise.

Skeet showed up at five twenty. John figured he had two options. He could hand Skeet a complimentary bottle of Kool Aid, or separate Skeet from his own bottle for just a few seconds. One thing the Army had taught John was that combat was a highly fluid situation, requiring contingency plans and the ability to adapt. Sergeant Peter's mantra was that no battle plan ever survived contact with the enemy.

"Hey, Man. You ready?" Skeet asked John, as he pulled up alongside.

"You bet. But I gotta take a leak first." John knew Skeet peed constantly, a side effect of the Kool Aid habit that had replaced all his other oral fixations.

"Oh man, I'm with you!" Skeet proclaimed.

After they had romped into the woods a bit, they unzipped their pants and voided their bladders. John finished first, and walked rapidly toward the cars. *Now for the tough part*, he thought, *I just need five seconds.* When he reached Skeet's Duster, he hopped behind the wheel, noticing peripherally that Skeet was trailing him by about fifty feet. *Perfect,* John thought as he switched the Kool Aid bottles. As a cover, he turned over the engine and revved it up to eardrum shattering volume.

"Hey, Man. Take it easy on my car!" Skeet joked.

"I just wanted to get a feel for it. It's been a while, you know."

"Are we gonna do this, or what?"

"She's all yours," John said, opening the driver's side door. John walked around to his car, grateful for the existence of Isabue Gibson. That guy could get his hands on anything, from black market cigarettes to the special chemical he had requested. Apparently, there were those who extracted the pure compound from rat poison, and Gip somehow knew at least one of them. Last night, after seeing what type of bottle Skeet had been using, John had bought an exact match. The sole difference was that Skeet's new bottle contained one gram of a white, granular substance. The Potassium Cyanide was odorless, tasteless, and would produce the desired effect within sixty seconds of consumption.

The race began just before six p.m. John knew Skeet would be chugging the Kool Aid as a conditioned response to stress. As John looked to his left, he saw Skeet knocking back half of the bottle in one swig. *Good old Skeet, as predictable as a Swiss watch*, John thought. *Race time.*

John had modified his emergency brake to lock only the front wheels of his Challenger. He yanked the brake and stomped the accelerator, causing the rear wheels to spin as the car fishtailed slightly. When he released the brake, he shot out in front of Skeet's Duster. Skeet, a savvy racer, dumped his clutch and closed most of the gap. Within seconds, the white needle on John's dash had passed 100mph. John deliberately remained parallel to Skeet, keeping the race tight to egg him on to higher speeds.

* * *

At first, Skeet thought it was adrenaline. Sweat gushed from his pores, soaking his shirt and stinging his eyes. After a few more seconds, he noticed he couldn't catch his breath. He heaved his chest, trying to take in great gulps of air, but it felt as if a python was wrapped around his ribcage. Looking over at John, Skeet saw he was gaining ground. For the first time, he was actually about to beat John's Challenger! He risked a quick glance at the dashboard – 120mph. Just a touch of nitrous and his victory would be complete. Skeet flipped a switch, dumping nitrous oxide into the carburetor. Seconds later, his lungs collapsed. His heart would continue to beat until the residual oxygen in his bloodstream was exhausted, perhaps as long as four minutes.

As Skeet's Duster passed 140, he began to convulse. Every synapse in his body was firing uncontrollably. He felt like he was on fire, but this was no ordinary fire. More like being bathed in the flame of a giant welding torch. His chest was concave. Now, a dancing elephant had replaced the python squeezing his chest. He was in a universe devoid of oxygen. Although his eyes were open, the world went black. As he fell onto the steering wheel, the car lurched sharply to the right. John braked hard enough to avoid collision, but not hard enough to leave skid marks. Skeet's speed gradually declined from 140 to 105 miles per hour over a period of six seconds. From 105 to zero took less than a millisecond.

The medical examiner would later determine that Skeet was alive at the moment he wrapped his Duster around a South Carolina pine. Since the cause of death was obvious, he ordered the lowest level blood work, screening only for marijuana, heroin, cocaine and alcohol. All tested negative.

* * *

John knocked on Patch's door for the first time in nearly two years. Patch answered the door with an incoherent, bewildered look on his face. He stared at John with his one good eye, obviously surprised by John's presence. After a few seconds, Patch had to look away. John's eyes expressed a hardness forged by pain.

"Well, are you going to invite me in, or what?" John asked.

"Sure, Buddy, come on in," Patch responded in a stilted tone.

John stepped into Patch's house, and surveyed his environment as he had been taught. He noticed a steak knife on the kitchen table. He walked over and placed the knife and the three glasses on the table in the sink. Now, all potential weapons were centralized, and away from the living room area.

"What are you doing?" Patch asked.

"Habit. Army trained me to be a neat freak," John replied casually, "Got any beer?"

"Does Beaumont suck?"

"You know, Patch, you should have gone into stand up comedy," John responded with a broad grin that belied his intentions.

As they sat in the living room, sipping Budweiser long necks, Patch eventually brought up the dreaded topic of their friends' deaths.

"Man, I can't believe what happened to Skeet and Fat Jack. They were my best friends, and just like that." Patch snapped his fingers, "They're gone."

John watched Patch closely. He couldn't discern whether Patch knew why he was here.

"They were my best friends, too, Patch," John said in a broken voice, his head buried in his hands. As he looked up, a tear sprung from his left eye. This he had accomplished by rubbing salt into his hands in Patch's driveway. "I just can't believe that they're gone! All you and I have is each other." John began to sob.

Patch's body language loosened. John saw he was beginning to relax. He was convinced he could maneuver Patch into a state of even greater relaxation. Three beers later, Patch excused himself to the restroom to recycle some Budweiser. John acted speedily, opening the plain wooden box on Patch's coffee table. John knew this was Patch's hiding place for his heroin. Heroin, as the Chicago song emphasized, was diluted at a ratio of twenty-five or six to four. He opened the baggie and replaced the contents with 100% pure, uncut heroin. This would multiply Patch's dose by a factor of six. He had completed the switch and was returning from the kitchen with two fresh beers when Patch came out of the bathroom.

"Patch, you and I go way back. I'm really going to miss you."

"What does that mean?" Patch asked, with a slight tremor in his voice.

"It means I'm probably going to Vietnam," John responded after a dramatic pause. He didn't want to rattle Patch too much. All he had to do was be patient and let nature take its course. He already saw the subtle signs that Patch would need a fix soon. Patch probably was oblivious to his external symptoms of a running nose, sweats, chills and minor muscle spasms. John knew no force in the universe could prevent Patch from utilizing the contents of the wooden box on the table between them.

John neither enjoyed nor regretted watching Patch squirm. It was simply data indicating the mission was on track. He was in the zone of ultimate calm that lay on the other side of rage. He was nothingness itself. At some level, he knew his childhood had been a series of reactions to The John. It was as if his father were a solid object and John merely a reflection. Now here he was - a reflection again. This time, he was the reflection of three monsters.

"Hey, Man. Mind if I shoot up?" Patch spoke the words that would finally balance the ledger of an old account.

"Do I ever?" John smirked.

"Well, I didn't know if you, you know, being in the Army and all..."

"There's more horse in the Army than even you could imagine, Patch."

"Cool, Man," Patch said, eagerly opening his little box of life. Patch loved his box. He and the box owned each other. He rationed what he thought was the appropriate amount into a spoon, added a touch of citric acid, and held a cigarette lighter underneath until the white powder had become a clear liquid. Then, he meticulously drew the liquid into a used syringe. He wrapped the rubber cord around his bicep, flexed his fist a few times, and thumped the most obvious vein to cause it to swell. Then he injected himself with justice, released the rubber cord, and withdrew the needle.

Within seconds, Patch appeared immensely sleepy. John knew time was short. "Tonight, Patch, you face your court of demons."

Patch was semi-coherent, but he nodded weakly at John. He knew he and John had just become even-Steven. When he shit his pants, he couldn't tell whether it was from the fear or the heroin. His last thought was the realization that he'd spent his entire life escaping from reality. Now, he wanted all those years back. He promised God that he would live them this time. God wasn't listening. Patch drifted into oblivion.

* * *

The John sipped his weak coffee, reading the obituaries in the Beaumont Times; a habit he had developed in his late forties. He scanned for the names of all his friends, and couldn't resist confirming his name wasn't listed.

Wait! What was that? His body temperature dropped by several degrees as a spark ignited in her mind. As The John read the brief list, connections buried for half a decade reappeared. All three of the rednecks that soiled John's working class wife had died in mysterious accidents since John had returned home. Since only he and Gloria knew the connection, no one, least of all the police, would suspect a thing. Maybe that was the boy's calling – to be a soldier, a killer. He lifted the phone and called his old friend General Dalton.

* * *

"Sir, there's a retired Brigadier General John Drake on line one for you."

Drake, that old son of a bitch, Dalton thought. He picked up the phone with anticipation, simply from being able to talk to his old friend. If nothing else, a conversation with Drake would be a pleasant distraction from his worries.

"Dalton here."

"Jerry, how are you?"

"John, you know I hate that nickname, especially since my claim to fame was killing Jerries in WWII."

"Well, if you don't like it, tough. I've whipped your ass more than once, and I'll do it again if I have to. Come to think of it, I seem to recall saving your ass on more than one occasion," The John rebutted.

"Touché. Ouch," Dalton winced in mock capitulation, even though The John couldn't see him. "To what occasion do I owe this honor? Checking up on your boy? Fine lad, he is."

"Jerry, I'm not calling to check up on the boy. I'm calling to give you vital information about him. I think you have much more in your hands than you know."

Dalton's ears perked when he heard this.

"Jerry, you and I know how the world works. I know you're not running a Boy Scout troop there. I've got to tell you something about my son off the record. And I mean *really* off the record. You need to hear this. Do I have your word?"

"John, I'm insulted you would even ask, but yes, you do have my word."

The John relayed all the details he had pieced together, flavored with a touch of theorizing. It was a tale of improvisation, ingenuity and persistence. The boy stayed true to his path even after his first kill. He crossed the line and didn't hesitate or look back. This character was cool.

As Dalton listened intently to his old friend, he solidified the idea he had contemplated for some time. What if there was another way to run Operation Sierra? He thought about it and decided he had nothing to lose, given a few precautions. He recalled Einstein's definition of insanity – repeating the same thing and expecting different results. Dalton thanked General Drake for his insight, and assured his old friend that Sergeant John Drake Jr. would be appropriately utilized.

Chapter Fourteen

Langley, Virginia

Fulton sat at the head of the conference room table. All the CIA technicians who were involved in the final stage of Project Crossfire were in the room. Besides this small group, only Peter and the DCI even knew the project existed.

"Item one, encryption. Where do we stand?" Fulton was known for being somewhat direct with his subordinates. He didn't waste time with small talk.

"Well, Sir, I've developed a double blind system no computer in the world could crack within thirty days. You will have a choice of two transmissions – one to execute the mission and one to abort. In the first case, an encoded set of coordinates will be sent to the Prometheus. The captain and first officer will have booklets to break the code, but the solution will be a set of dummy coordinates. When they enter the dummy coordinates, the missiles will further decode them to acquire the real coordinates. Simply put, only you and the missiles will know the actual target sites."

"Excellent, and if I transmit the abort code?"

"It's also double blind. When decoded aboard Prometheus, it will be a set of dummy coordinates. When these coordinates are entered, the self-destruct sequence will be activated. Again, only you and the missiles will know what is going to happen."

"Good work. Thank you. Item two, self destruct sequence."

"Sir, as you specified, if the abort code is transmitted, the missiles will be detonated before the outer doors are opened. This will initiate a cascade effect among the shaped charges we've placed between the primary and secondary hulls. Of course, you'll need to wait at least thirty minutes for the crew to safely abandon ship before you transmit."

"Understood," Fulton said without emotion. Fulton had contemplated the fates of those unfortunate soldiers a thousand times, always arriving at the same conclusion – the DCI was right. Even if the mission were aborted, the crew of Prometheus must go. They knew too much. They knew a commercial vessel had been modified into a warship. They knew the missiles were not American. They knew which targets they could reach from their position. They would read the newspaper the following morning and connect the dots. It wasn't a difficult equation to piece together. Yes, the crew of Prometheus would make the ultimate sacrifice for their country.

"Thank you. Item three, munitions."

"Sir, I've had a hell of a time getting my hands on the specific missiles you requested. I nearly exhausted my Eastern Bloc connections before I found them."

"You found them?"

"Yes, Sir. Every one."

"Excellent! How long for installation?"

"Well, with the skeleton crew I have, they could be ready by the end of February. I'll have the men get started tonight removing the markings."

"No. You will not alter the missiles in any way – any way. Got that?"

"Yes, Sir."

"Very good. Now, let's get to work."

* * *

Fort Benning, Georgia

"General, Major Briggs to see you," the intercom buzzed.

"Send him in," Dalton replied. He didn't like the sense of deja vu.

After the obligatory salutes, Major Briggs sat and delivered his news. "Sir, we've lost another one."

"Shit!" Dalton shouted, slamming his fist on the mahogany desk, "What happened this time?"

"Sir, we're not sure, but Lieutenant Amin was confirmed dead at 0300 hours. He had been tortured pretty badly, Sir. We don't know what he might have compromised."

Dalton was displeased in the extreme. He was running out of options. So far, two highly trained field agents had been lost in Operation Sierra. Two years had passed, and they were no closer to Tartus. He needed a different approach, something unique. But what? His crazy idea about Drake and Gibson? He needed time alone.

"Dismissed, Major."

"Yes Sir," Major Briggs said as he stood at attention, saluted, performed a surgically precise about face and left the office.

* * *

Rio de Janeiro, Brazil

Lupe Hernandez awoke to the soft click immediately preceding the dull hum of her alarm clock. It was six a.m. in Rio de Janeiro, and she and her friends had vowed not to waste a single minute of the time they had there. Before the alarm had a chance to begin its obnoxious call, she flipped it off and rolled her bare feet to the floor. The hard wood was cold, in contrast to the already sweltering heat of the day. She padded to the restroom to begin her morning routine. She brushed her teeth with bottled water and showered, remembering not to open her mouth and invite the unfamiliar microorganisms of Latin America into her body. The desk clerk had assured her that the Rio Marriott was a world-class establishment, with filtered and purified tap water, but she was leaving nothing to chance. Just five months ago, her friend Becky had contracted a vicious stomach bug from a salad that had been rinsed in local water. As Becky described it, she could 'shit through a screen door from twelve feet'.

Lupe giggled at her friend's quip while she toweled off. By six thirty, she was dressed and ready to begin the adventures of the day. As a junior business major at UCLA, she knew she would soon begin the gradual descent into the blissful stupor of mediocrity that all children of successful people faced. Sure, she would never want for financial security, but she would also be denied the freedoms that came with independence. She would spend her adulthood in the most luxuriant prison on Earth - success.

Many would consider Lupe spoiled, since she came from an obscenely wealthy family. She saw things differently from most. Today, Lupe craved adventure, and she would get her wish. Not telling her father where she was going only served to increase the intensity of the adventure. Susan and Becky were waiting for her in the lobby.

"Buenos Dias, Lupe," said Susan.

"Susan, they speak Portuguese here, not Spanish," Lupe chided, "In fact, I'm pretty sure they'd resent your attempt to speak the incorrect Latin language."

"Hey, we're tourists. These people wouldn't exist without us. We can do no wrong!" Susan joked, catching the attention of the hotel concierge.

"Bom Dia, young ladies. May I be of assistance?" Hector asked. "Is this a first time visit for you?" Hector's English was impeccable. His accent was almost undetectable. But then, Americans were the tools of his trade.

"Yes, good morning," Lupe said, glancing at his name tag, "Hector. This is our first time in Rio, and we have three days to make the most of our experience. If you could provide some guidance, we'd be most appreciative." As she spoke, she dug through her purse for her wallet.

"Well, ladies, first you may be interested to learn that most businesses in Rio de Janeiro do have English speaking people on staff, and almost no one will refuse American dollars. This may help eliminate any concerns you have with translation of language and currency, and allow you to focus on the enjoyment of your stay."

"Hector, your English is excellent. Are you a native of Brazil?" Lupe asked.

"Yes, I am. In fact, I have never left this country. And, if you don't mind my saying, your English is excellent as well."

The girls all chuckled nervously at Hector's joke, not knowing whether or not he was being sarcastic. Hector was quick to add, "I have a friend who drives a taxi. He knows the city quite well, and will be in your exclusive service for the day if you are interested. He can show you the popular tourist sites, as well as some hidden treasures we have."

"Wow, that sounds perfect!" Becky exclaimed. "What does he charge?"

"Ma'am, it is customary for you to pay a flat rate for the entire day, about thirty dollars. In addition, the driver will expect to accompany you for meals, at your expense. Taxi drivers in Rio become much more personally involved with their clients than their counterparts in America, I am told. One other thing, you must never hail a taxi on the street. They are hustlers and enormously dangerous. Your taxi should always be arranged by an airport, hotel, or restaurant."

"What is your friend's name? We'd like to hire him for the day," Lupe said.

"His name is Felipe. And who shall I tell him his benefactor is for the day?"

"Lupe, Lupe Hernandez."

"Ah, what a beautiful name. I will make the necessary arrangements," Hector said as he departed for his office. When he returned, he said "Felipe is available for the day, and will meet you out front in ten minutes."

"Wonderful," Lupe said, "Hector, I have one question, what time will Felipe expect to be relieved? What I mean is, how long will our thirty dollars last?"

"Miss Hernandez, the days in Rio are quite long. We don't live by the clock. Trust me, you will know when the day is finished. I believe Felipe will outlast you."

"Thank you, Hector," Lupe said as she handed him a five dollar bill.

Within fifteen minutes, Felipe's cab pulled up in front of the Marriott. He was a short man; no more than five foot six. His hairline was receding and he compensated with the comb-over technique. Like most of the men in Latin America, he had a thick black moustache. His English, like Hector's was practically flawless. They spent a few minutes making polite small talk. That was one thing Lupe especially liked about Latin countries. People were polite to a fault. It was impossible to conduct the simplest transaction without discussing the weather, health, etc. Eventually, Felipe got to business.

"Where can I take you lovely ladies this morning?"

"Well, what do you suggest?" Lupe asked.

"Miss Hernandez, there are many beautiful sights in Rio, but one of the best is the Botanical Gardens. It would be my honor to take you there."

Lupe, although accustomed to the red carpet treatment, was still awed at Felipe's courtesy. He treated them not like VIP's, but like royalty.

"Yes, Felipe. To the gardens please."

Felipe drove through the crowded city streets with an aggressiveness that frightened the girls. He kept one foot on the gas and one on the brake, constantly pumping both. When changing lanes, he did not look over his shoulder because he already knew there would be a car in the way. When Lupe asked Felipe to slow down, he explained that his method was the safest because it was what everyone expected. If he hesitated or used turn signals, he would confuse the other drivers.

Fifteen white knuckled minutes later, Felipe parked near the entrance to the gardens. He turned to face the girls and said, "I will wait here as long as you like. If you lose your way, just ask for the northern entrance."

The Botanical Gardens were even more beautiful than Felipe had claimed. Each of the 141 hectares sheltered stunning examples of plant life from Brazil and all over the world. As Lupe spun, taking in The Imperial Palms, planted in 1809 by Prince Regent D. João VI, she was awed by the sheer size of the trees. It reminded her of childhood Easters. Her parents had a huge, knotted tree that she climbed to pick the enormous white blossoms it sported each spring. She learned quickly that the beauty of the flowers was offset by the monstrous spiders that lived in each bloom. She would use a stick to run the spiders away and steal their homes.

She rounded another corner and was awestruck by the landscaping. Huge trees decked with orchids were contrasted with giant victoria-regia, lilies, bromeliads, royal poincianas and tropical foliage. Lupe breathed deeply, the mixed aromas evoking random memories from her childhood. Once, a dove lit on a branch just a few feet from her. It was the purest white she had ever seen. When she reached out to touch it, the dove flew away. After nearly two hours of exploring the local flora, the girls found themselves a bit disoriented.

"Where the hell are we?" Becky asked.

"I'm not sure, but come to think of it, I haven't seen another soul in a while," Lupe answered.

They were in a maze of hedges, and due to the height of the bushes, could not see the sun to get a bearing on direction. They decided to keep moving, taking a right at each juncture. This method was unlikely to take them to an exit, but at least it was consistent. The girls figured they would reach either the center or an edge eventually. Besides, they would certainly come across other people in the process.

"What was that?" Becky asked.

"What was what?" Lupe replied.

"I swear I heard someone walking nearby."

"Hello! Can you help us please? We're lost. Hello!" Lupe's hails went unanswered.

"Becky, I didn't hear a thing, and no one is answering. I'm sure we'd get an answer, even if it wasn't in English," Lupe said. She was exasperated, hot and tired. Her sundress was soaked in sweat and she wanted a shower. She had no idea her next bath would be administered with a fire hose.

Even as Lupe spoke her words of reassurance, she heard the soft sound of leather-soled shoes on dirt just around the next corner of the maze. She ran toward the source of the sound, taking an abrupt left at the intersection. When she rounded the corner, she tripped on some type of branch or log. As she stood, she had several milliseconds to realize the log was actually a human leg. As she drew a deep breath to cry out, she detected a strong chemical odor. The last thing she saw was a dripping handkerchief converging on her nose and mouth. The world receded into blackness as the chloroform was carried by her red blood cells to her brain, rendering her unconscious within two seconds of contact.

* * *

Fort Benning, Georgia

"General, Sergeant Drake reports to see you," the intercom squawked.

"Send him in," Dalton replied. He had mapped out this conversation in advance. He knew where Drake's hot buttons were, and he intended to punch every one in sequence. Normally, he would have Briggs do the recruitment, but there was one change in the game plan that Briggs could never know about. Operation Sierra was beginning to make him indistinguishable from a fool. You don't come out of the rough with a putter. You use a wedge.

"Sir, Sergeant Drake reporting, Sir!"

"At ease, Sergeant. Have a seat."

John sat rigidly in the chair facing General Dalton, his hat in his left hand, resting on his leg. He kept his fidgeting to a minimum. For an E-5 to be summoned by the base commander was highly unorthodox.

Dalton fixed the young lad with a level stare that Drake returned in an unchallenging way. The general pushed his chair back and looked at the ceiling, steepling his fingers. When he spoke, it was in a softer voice.

"I grew up in Los Angeles, back before it became overcrowded. When I was a kid, no older than twelve, I responded to a newspaper ad. Three local kids were forming a jazz band and needed a sax player. My father didn't like the idea, of course. You have to bear in mind that the saxophone was the electric guitar of the 1940s.

"Well, we formed a group – The Jazz Club. Years went by - years of playing weddings and proms, but also the occasional nightclub. It was in one of these nightclubs where we crossed paths with fate. To make a long story short, at the age of eighteen I found myself in the office of a record company executive. He promised to make dreams I didn't even have come true. West Point was about to become irrelevant. Family tradition was about to become irrelevant.

My agent kept telling me there would never be another chance like this one. He was right. There wasn't. Thirty years later, I'm sitting in this chair with two stars on my shoulder because I made a decision that day.

"What I want you to understand is this, Sergeant: every decision brings an opportunity to do the right thing. You may not like how the right thing looks, but you'll see it, every time. And once you've seen it, it's a hard thing to ignore. When my hour came, I did the right thing. The right thing for me. The right thing for my country.

"Now, you are standing at a juncture not unlike the one that gave shape to my destiny over thirty years ago. The choice remains the same - man or mouse, hero or coward? And I'll warn you up front. You will become what you decide. That is a proven, scientific fact. They call it a self-fulfilling prophecy. So I suggest you give it serious consideration. As a man once quite correctly told me, there will never be another chance like this one. One chance to take action, to make a difference. Once chance to do the right thing.

"I have a mission worthy of a United States Ranger - dangerous and voluntary. But, once you're in, you're in for the duration." Dalton leaned forward and bored his steely gaze into John's eyes. "Your actions in Beaumont demonstrated resourcefulness, cunning and courage. Can you perform at that level every time?"

Drake concealed his shock that the General knew what he had done. There would be time to figure that out later. He remained in the moment, "Sir, I'm in. One hundred percent!"

"Good." Dalton reclined in his chair. "Major Briggs will contact you for briefing. Before I dismiss you, there's one thing we need to discuss, and I want you to listen with every cell in your body.

"This whole business in South Carolina needn't ever be revisited. I'm happy, and as long as I'm happy, it's a dead issue, so to speak. Do you completely fathom what I'm saying, Sergeant?"

"Yes Sir," John answered, bracing himself for whatever was coming.

"Now, here comes the part where you make me happy. Major Briggs will tell you about a man. He is a dreadfully bad character - one of the worst in the world. I'm quite sure you'll agree once you've been briefed. His name is Tartus. I want this man killed, by whatever means necessary. I do not want an apprehension. I want a kill. I'm placing this responsibility on you and you alone. I trust you are comfortable with this?"

John hesitated. He felt overwhelmed by this responsibility, but he knew he was perfectly capable of killing. If he had the capacity for emotion at that point, he would have been ashamed of himself for becoming that which he despised.

"Drake," the general said in a less formal tone, "We're talking about an utterly vile man. You are one of the good guys. In our business, good guys kill bad guys. It's a job – nothing more. Never become emotional about performing your duty to your country. Am I getting through to you?"

"Yes Sir." John nodded. He certainly had the no-emotion part down pat. He wondered if he would ever get his feelings back, or if he would spend the rest of his life dead inside. He tried to take himself back to that hunting trip, to remember how he felt standing over the dying bird. That incident had been his first defining moment. At that instant, his identity was hard wired into his brain. That dove was innocent. His targets in Beaumont were not. Something also told him that a long and treacherous path lay between him and his true self.

"Good. Obviously, if anyone were to hear even a rumor of this conversation, I would become profoundly unhappy. I trust we're clear on the matter?"

"Yes Sir."

"Dismissed."

Drake stood, saluted, and left the room with crisp movements.

* * *

Moving zombie-like down the hallway outside Dalton's office, Drake reeled from the disorientation. What had just happened? How much did Dalton know? What was this mission? John felt the blood leave his face. Icy perspiration broke out on the nape of his neck. He was having a delayed stress reaction, having spent his life honing the skill of concealing his emotions.

How could Dalton know? As he ran through the possibilities in his head, he kept coming up with the same answer – his father. The John and General Dalton had served together as Army fighter pilots in World War II, and John knew they kept in touch.

But still, how could his father possibly know what the police and coroner's office did not? He went through the events of that week in his head, searching for some clue that The John was aware of his activities. He found none.

Granted, it was common knowledge that Fat Jack, Skeet, and Patch had died in accidents the week he was in town, but who would suspect John in the deaths of his three best friends? What was the common link? Tammy. But, that would mean his father somehow knew about her rape. This simply made no sense. Even John Drake Sr. wouldn't sit on such information so critical to his son. Perhaps there was more to his father than even he thought.

One thing was clear; the General had him by the short hairs.

Chapter Fifteen

Fort Benning, Georgia

When John arrived at Major Briggs' office, Gip was already waiting outside. He wanted to ask Gip if General Dalton had approached him, but the receptionist rushed them in the instant John arrived.

Now, here they sat, each apparently hand picked by General Dalton for some covert mission - a mission so covert the base commander would recruit them personally, without uttering a single word regarding its nature.

"Men," Briggs began, "for the record I am stating that you have each volunteered for a highly dangerous and sensitive mission, one critical to our national security." He stared at each of them, looking for any lack of resolve. Seeing none, he continued, "Trafficking in women and girls has become one of the fastest growing criminal enterprises in the world. The media refers to this industry by the misnomer of white slavery. In reality, most of the victims are non-white."

John understood at once why he had been chosen for this mission. So, The John did know about Tammy. John's contemplated the coldness of a man who would hold such information for years, waiting for a time to use it to his own advantage. For once, he actually related to The John. He still felt nothing – no anger, no sense of justice, no satisfaction. He expected to become angry when he killed his friends, but he hadn't. He expected the anger to be quenched with a sense of justice, but there was nothing to quench. Someone had stolen all of his feelings. It never occurred to John that he was that someone.

Major Briggs continued, "This increasingly serious problem impacts all nations, including the United States. An estimated one to two million women and girls are trafficked annually around the world, typically for the purpose of forced labor, domestic servitude or sexual exploitation. White slavers lure victims with advertisements and false promises of jobs as nannies, waitresses, sales clerks, and models. The bolder ones sometimes even take their victims by force from tourist sites in second and third world countries. It appears trafficked women come primarily from the following countries: Ghana, Nigeria, Morocco, Brazil, Colombia, the Dominican Republic, the Philippines and Thailand.

"These girls flow towards industrialized countries, particularly those where the prevailing social status of women is one of servitude. The Department of State and the Department of Justice are training foreign immigration and law enforcement personnel to effectively implement border security. This approach, men, has proven to be entirely ineffective. Questions at this point?"

"Sir?" Drake gestured with his right hand, as if he were still in school. "What can two men do against such a large network of crime?"

"Not men. Rangers. And you can do quite a bit. Your primary mission is to locate and retrieve the daughter of a US Congressman from California. Ever heard of Juan Hernandez?"

"The civil rights advocate?" Drake asked.

"I like you Drake. You make a great straight man. As Sergeant Drake pointed out, we have a minority congressman and civil rights leader with a missing daughter. God knows our government does not need any more bad press in light of this Vietnam fiasco.

"The victim is Lupe Hernandez, age 20, long brunette hair, brown eyes, five foot six, one hundred thirty five pounds, UCLA business major. She disappeared eight days ago without a trace. Her father thought she was spending a long weekend with a friend in San Diego. When Lupe did not return to school, the FBI eventually determined she and two other friends had used each other as alibis and had motored off to Rio de Janeiro for a little R&R. At that point, the CIA became involved. They had an operative in Rio do a little nosing around.

"We know they had reservations at the Rio Marriott. They were last seen with the hotel concierge, Hector Enrico. He was helping them into a taxi. This Enrico character is a minor league player in the Brazilian black market. We don't think he's into anything as serious as trafficking women, but he has an associate, Felipe Palatzo, who may be. Palatzo operates a taxi service as a front for his more nefarious activities. Our best information says the girl was last seen entering Palatzo's taxi."

"Sir, a question please. What makes you so sure they were kidnapped by white slavers?" Gip asked.

"Because, Sergeant Gibson, Brazil is the kidnapping capital of the world. In fact, if you were to be kidnapped, Brazil would be the ideal place. The kidnappers infesting Brazil are among the most professional in the world. When the ransom is paid without the involvement of the local authorities, over 80% of kidnap victims are returned unharmed. That is considerably better than the US track record.

"In this case, no ransom has been demanded, even though all three girls were from substantially wealthy families. That means one of two things: the kidnappers for some reason killed them all, or they can make more money with less risk by selling them on the open market."

"Sir, I don't quite follow the leap of logic," Drake interjected.

"It's extremely unlikely the girls are dead," Briggs said. "They're worth too much alive. Although the trade is called white slavery, the victims are seldom Caucasians. American girls bring a premium to these sick bastards. This has the classic stamp of white slavers."

Briggs walked over to his wet bar to allow time for these concepts to sink in. "Coffee?"

"Yes Sir, please," they responded in unison.

As Briggs poured, Drake and Gip exchanged glances. Their faces shared the same expression, *why us?* While sipping his boiling hot, thermonuclear US military coffee sludge, Drake ventured a question, "Sir, permission to speak freely?"

"Speak."

"If there is a globally organized crime syndicate, why isn't the CIA looking for her? And if this is a kidnapping, what about the FBI?"

"Legitimate questions. Operation Sierra is CIA sanctioned. However, contrary to popular belief, most CIA agents are not combat trained. Their expertise is more in the collection and interpretation of information. A CIA field officer living as a native in Rio brought us the information about the concierge and the taxi driver. He cannot take any action or he would risk blowing a cover that took years to establish. When combat is required, the CIA typically contracts professional soldiers, which is why we are having this conversation.

"Operation Sierra was begun over two years ago with the objective of taking out the central hub of this network. Thus far, we have been unsuccessful, but we know a few things. First, the buck seems to stop at a man known as Tartus. This

Tartus character is among the most dangerous and elusive men in the world. The Hernandez kidnapping can be thought of as a separate mission from Sierra, but the odds are that Tartus is ultimately behind this.

"Now, as for the FBI, they are officially in charge of the investigation of the Hernandez kidnapping, but they can't make a move without a ransom demand. They have nothing to go on, and their jurisdiction is restricted to the US."

John and Gip both nodded, still a bit shocked by this entire affair.

"You two are not to speak a word of the mission to anyone. Your families will be told you are in Viet Nam. Understand?" Briggs stared each of them in the eye.

"Cry havoc, and let slip the dogs of war," Drake said softly.

"Oh, you know your Julius Caesar," Briggs said. By Briggs' tone, John guessed he had just been raised a couple of notches on the scale.

"Yes Sir. It seemed appropriate. I believe 'dogs of war' was a reference to the many soldiers whose anonymous accomplishments summed up to make a victory."

"General Dalton told me you were a clever one," Briggs responded. "Not many noncoms read Shakespeare." His gruff expression loosened into a slight smile.

"One more question, please," John asked. "Why us? Surely there are more experienced people who could undertake this mission."

"Another good one. The answer is simple. In the Middle Ages, it was said that the greatest swordsman in Europe did not fear the second greatest, but he feared the worst, because of the unpredictability. This will be the third deployment of Operation Sierra. I want it to be the last. It's time for a fresh perspective. Drake, you will be promoted to the combat rank of Staff Sergeant, E-6. You will be in charge of all aspects of the mission while in the field. You will receive your orders directly from me - no one else. Gibson, you will have the combat rank of Munitions Specialist, Grade 5.

"The two of you will be given three hundred thousand dollars cash and will travel as civilians. You will take no US military equipment or identification with you. You will have to rely upon your own ingenuity and cash supply to meet the objectives of this mission. You are on your own. The US government will disavow any knowledge of you if you are captured or killed. Should this end badly, your families will be notified that you died as heroes in Vietnam.

"And let me share this with you. I hate writing those letters, so if either of you gets killed, I will personally resuscitate you so I can kill you myself.

"Once you have ensured the safety of the Congressman's daughter, you will focus your efforts on the elimination of Tartus' operation. Shut him down permanently. Am I making myself perfectly clear?"

"Yes Sir."

"If you run out of cash, send a wire to this address." Briggs slid an APO address across his desk. "You will get the instructions on where to pick up your cash within seventy-two hours. All good?"

"Yes Sir," they chimed in unison.

* * *

Langley, Virginia

Fulton sat at his kitchen table, poring over schematics. Time was short, and he still hadn't solved the incompatibility issues. When Peter rapped on his door, Fulton almost jumped out of his skin. *Damn*, he thought, *I need to loosen up. I'm no good to the project like this.* As he walked to the door, he paused to dump the rest of his coffee in the sink. *Better switch to decaf.*

"Hey, Robert."

"Hey, Peter. Come on in," Fulton said, rubbing his eyes, "What can I get you? I was just about to make a pot of decaf."

"Decaf? Why would anyone want to drink that stuff?"

"I'm a little edgy. That's all."

"Well, it sounds like you need a cold beer."

"You know, that's the best idea I've heard all day."

Robert's every action conveyed stress. Normally a neat freak, wearing his tie right up until bedtime, Robert now appeared disheveled. His tie was lying across the back of the couch. His shirt was untucked - his hair mussed. He had even removed his shoes. Robert returned from the kitchen with two Michelobs, downing a third of his before he took his seat at the kitchen table.

"Work got you down?" Peter asked.

"It's these goddamned missiles. Just when we thought we had the hardware compatibility issues resolved, the software started to crash. This Eastern Bloc technology is crap. I just can't integrate their technology with ours. It's like the two systems were developed on different planets."

"Well, would the SS-18's have the capability to carry out this mission if the launch tubes and software were Eastern Bloc?"

"Sure. This is a cakewalk as far as SSM's go."

"Well, what if you dumbed down the American software? Strip it down to the basics."

"I can't. The self-destruct sequence is already coded. It would take weeks to rewrite and debug it."

"Then take the self-destruct sequence offline. If you have to abort, have the crew do it manually. A little strategically placed C-4 with a simple timer can work wonders."

"Peter, I can't do that."

"Why not?"

"Peter, it's not an option. Just leave it at that."

Peter raised his hands in mock capitulation. "Okay, Man. You're the boss."

Robert finished his beer in three swallows. He knew Peter must think he was crazy, integrating the launch system with the self destruct system, but he was limited in what he could tell even Peter. He had only told Peter that the Prometheus, an oil tanker converted into a warship, was to launch SSM's with conventional payloads in some sort of sneak attack. No one, however, but Robert and the DCI knew at whom.

"Robert, you're the best engineer I know," Peter said. "If anyone can work this out, it's you. Have a couple more beers, blow off some steam, and I'll bet the answer will jump off the page at you."

Fulton raised his bloodshot eyes to meet Peter's face. He ran his left hand through his hair. "Thanks, Peter. You're a good friend." They drank in unison.

Later that evening, when exhaustion overtook frustration, Fulton lay in bed, wondering whether he should have crossed the line regarding killing American soldiers. He could still hear the DCI's words, *It's not what we do that makes us the good guys. It's why we do it.* Deep down, Fulton knew that he was more afraid of failure than of betraying his conscience. He hardened his resolve and drifted off to sleep.

* * *

Somewhere off the coast of Brazil

Lupe couldn't tell whether her eyes were open or shut. When she struggled, she discovered her hands were bound behind her back with worn and smelly leather straps. Her legs were joined at the knee in an extremely uncomfortable manner. She let her concentration flow over each part of her body, starting at the soles of her feet and scanning to the top of her head. She sometimes used this yoga technique to help her get to sleep. Now she used it to convince herself that she still existed. Aside from her bonds, she felt little else. She was lying on her left side, on a cold, hard floor. The floor surface was smooth – metal.

As time passed, she became aware of a gentle disturbance in her inner ear. Lupe was so disoriented that it took her a while to notice it. The floor was gently rocking. A boat. She was on a boat.

She was restrained with well-used devices designed explicitly for that purpose. What had happened to her? The last thing she remembered was being in the Botanical Gardens in Rio. She had been kidnapped - no question about it. But, if she were being held for ransom, why was she on a boat?

"Where am I?" She was surprised at the sound of her own voice splitting the void of darkness and silence. Except when it came out, it sounded more like "Hmmf hm hmi." A cloth - not a full sized handkerchief, but one cut down to lessen the danger of choking, gagged her. It was a sick world, but even so, the market value of dead women was limited.

Lupe strained to hear or see or feel any clue as to her whereabouts. The only new thing she discovered was a sticky wetness in her crotch. She had peed herself sometime during her drug-induced sleep.

Chapter Sixteen

Norfolk, Virginia

Special Agent Fulton stood on the dry dock catwalk, overlooking the Prometheus. Project Crossfire was near its completion. The Prometheus was a masterpiece by any measure. Silos for 440 SSM's were invisibly installed below the deck of the apparently commercial vessel. Her flat deck with 166,000 square feet had the densest missile population of any ship ever built. The lower storage compartments were so crowded that the missiles could not be reloaded outside of dry dock. But reloading would not be necessary. Once the leviathan ship had fired its entire payload - in evenly dispersed launches of twenty-two missiles each – its mission would be accomplished. Shame the ship and crew had to be destroyed.

Prometheus would depart in less than eight hours. Fifteen days into its mission, it would fire the missiles, precipitating a cascade effect culminating with the USA in control of the world's power supply.

Peter quietly walked up beside him, "Thought I'd find you here. Nervous?"

"Believe it or not – no. Somehow I feel calmer than I ever have in my life."

"So, I guess you got the bugs worked out?" Peter asked.

"Yea. I followed your suggestion and took the self-destruct sequence off line until we resolved the launch codes. Once the two systems were operational, it was fairly easy to integrate them."

"One question, Robert. I've been with the Agency for over ten years, and I've never been given a project of this magnitude. What's your secret?"

"Peter, Bob Hope once said he'd rather be lucky than good. Well, when I was stationed in Vietnam, I saved the life of a boy who turned out to be the godson of the DCI. It was really no big deal. Over there, lives are saved and lost every day. But, I was the one who shot the gook sneaking up behind David, so I got the prize. That single bullet has opened a lot of doors for me. You know, the DCI personally recruited me from the Bureau."

"I always heard it was because of some big drug bust," Peter said.

"Well, that is true, but how often have you seen someone enter the Agency at the Director level? I skipped the ten years of groundwork to prepare me for the role of Director of Middle Eastern Operations."

"You lucky son of a bitch," Peter jibed.

"Hey, what can I say?"

Fulton turned to face his masterpiece. He inhaled deeply, taking in the fossil fuel odor that was Prometheus' signature. His hands tightened on the rail as he looked over his shoulder and said, "Peter, these are the greatest years of our lives. Just think about it. Half the world is at war, and here we are, in covert ops. I know I'll never be in the history books, but I'll be dead before they're written, anyway. This way, I have the satisfaction of knowing every citizen of the United States will owe me their freedom for the next hundred years."

"A little dramatic, aren't we?"

"Peter, the DCI sanctioned me to end the oil embargo by whatever means necessary. Well, my proposal took it a step further. If things go as planned, the US will control the world's oil supply well into the next century."

"Robert, I think there are better ways of solving problems than starting a war," Peter said.

"I'm not starting a war, I'm ending one. Syria started the Arab-Israeli war, in case you haven't read a newspaper lately. Now, Saudi Arabia is tacitly allied with Syria, but is officially neutral in the conflict. They give lip service to their relationship with the US, and the UN eats it up like candy. All the while, they're gouging us with crude oil price increases and production cuts.

"As it stands, we can't take direct action against Saudi Arabia because of U.N. sanctions. As long as Syria and Israel continue with their minor tactical battles and posturing, the conflict will drag on forever. If I bring the US into the war, it'll be over in a matter of months. I won't be costing lives. I'll be saving them."

Robert gleamed with patriotism, proud of his grandiose plot. His sole regret was not making the time to tell his father. Fulton's father had been the ultimate patriot. He actually fought at Iwo Jima, climbing the hill with a flame-thrower;

ensuring that no under-cooked Japanese occupied the many caves along the attack route.

Robert remembered his story about the famous raising of the flag picture. It turned out that the original photo was deemed un-press-worthy, due to the disheveled appearance of the soldiers and the flag. So, the press liaisons had arranged another photograph with fresh soldiers and flag, not even the original men!

Knowing the whole country had rallied behind a staged photo had burned his father's ass, and the man was not shy with his opinions. He had preached his purist views about the supremacy of the US to both Robert and Peter in their youth. But still, being raised a patriot was a far cry from being a warmonger. Robert had crossed a line that Peter would not.

"So, exactly how do you plan to turn this squabble into a full blown war?" Peter asked.

"Peter, I can't give you the details, but I can tell you to watch the news on March 18th."

"Robert," Peter said, "I'm happy for your success, but I don't condone interfering in the politics of other countries."

"If not us, who?" Fulton asked.

Peter didn't answer him. He turned slowly on his heel and left as silently as he had arrived.

* * *

Guanabara Bay, Brazil

Fejo appeared relaxed as he reclined in the Captain's chair of his tramp steamer. Although he always had the jitters about getting out of port, his face and posture projected complete calm. Years of making a living by his nerves had taught him to reveal nothing in front of the crew. If he looked nervous, they would surely panic. There were many preparations to make before The Lady and the Tramp set sail in just a few hours. She had nearly a full hold – thirty-eight of forty guestrooms filled.

Jorge, his first officer, entered the cabin noisily. "Captain, we're cleared for departure at 0800."

"Good. Set heading to 31.7 degrees. Once we clear port, all ahead full."

"Aye, Captain."

"And how are our guests?" Fejo asked.

"Resting comfortably, Captain. There are a few toilet accidents, but nothing major."

"Good. Once we hit the open sea, begin changeover," Fejo replied, referring to the procedure of untying the girls and cleaning those who needed it in preparation for the eighteen day journey to Tarfaya, Morocco. They were kept gagged and tied while in port to avoid any unnecessary noise. Invariably, there were those who soiled themselves out of fear or simply the inability to wait until the Lady and the Tramp was cleared by the Guanabara Bay Shipping Authority. Fejo closed his eyes and began mentally spending the money he would make for this haul.

* * *

A US civilian airplane flying south

Drake was completely relaxed in his airline seat, swirling a cup of iced Coke while reviewing his game plan in his head. Drake and Gip were traveling as civilians, with nothing linking them to the US military. They had no tools to aid them in their mission except their carry-on bag full of cash. Major Briggs had made it clear that if they encountered trouble, they were on their own. Being young and arrogant, Drake paid this statement no heed. It didn't occur to him that life in a Third World prison or violent death were realistic outcomes of this mission. He was focused on facts; trying to pick up Lupe's trail.

Gip interrupted his thoughts. "Man, this is fly. I've never flown first class before," Gip said, "As a matter of fact, I've never flown any class before."

"Compliments of Uncle Sam," Drake replied.

"Okay, let's go over this again," Gip said, "The girls were last seen talking to this guy Hector."

"The hotel concierge." Drake said.

"Right, and Hector is a black market sleaze bag."

"You were there. You heard what Briggs said."

"And because Hector is connected to a cab driver named Phillip..."

"Felipe," Drake interrupted Gip.

"Yea, whatever. Do you honestly believe this Felipe will lead us right to the girls? That shit seems thin," Gip said.

"Look," Drake said, "I know it's thin, but it's all we've got. Briggs said Brazil is the kidnapping capitol of the world. I don't think it's that much of a stretch. Besides, do you have a better idea?"

"Okay," Gip said, "So we just walk up and ask this Hector dude 'Excuse me, but we were wondering if you recently sold any American girls to white slavers,' and he'll tell us where he sent them."

"Depends on the way I ask," Drake said, smiling broadly.

"I still say that shit is thin."

"We'll just have to be..." Drake paused, searching for the right word. "Persuasive."

"Hey, can I ask you a question?"

"Go right ahead," Drake responded.

"How'd you get roped into this assignment? Briggs sold me a line of shit about me having a talent for making black market connections because I was a drug dealer. That, plus he said a munitions specialist was essential to the mission."

"I have a strong conscience," Drake replied.

"What the Hell does that mean?"

"All the most effective killers have strong consciences. They all do it for a reason."

"So, what's your reason?" Gip asked.

"That's heavy, man. I don't even want to go there," Drake replied as he reclined his seat. He recalled the image of Tammy standing in their front yard, crying at the thought of her husband going into combat. Life had dealt her some heavy blows, and now the one person she leaned on was in harm's way. Drake promised himself he would make it back, not for himself, but for her. He contemplated Gip's question of exactly what he would do with Felipe when he found him. The answer was obvious. Gip didn't know because he couldn't face the answer.

* * *

The Kechla Citadel

Tartus was startled out of his light nap by the sound of footsteps in the hallway. Keeping his eyes narrowed to a slit, he quietly freed the holster strap from his Glock 9mm. He immediately began forming contingency plans. If the door opened without a knock, he would feign sleep until he got a head count, then he would either shoot or run. When he heard the knock, he relaxed slightly. He waited until he heard his faithful servant speak.

"It's Falon," the voice whispered in Arabic.

"Come in, my friend," Tartus answered, knowing Falon would have referred to himself as 'me' if there were any trouble.

Falon, recognizing the code phrase, 'my friend' = 'all clear', entered without his weapon drawn.

"Falon, it's good to see you," Tartus said graciously. He knew a visit from Falon meant one thing – money. He wasted no time getting to business. "You have news for me?"

"Fejo has a shipment of thirty-eight. The ship is due in Tarfaya in eighteen days. They should be here in Safi in nineteen," Falon said, adding a day for the three hundred mile drive.

"Please, sit. Tell me about the shipment." Tartus made a sweeping gesture with his hand.

"Thank you. Tartus, Fejo may have what we've been waiting for. The recruitments were all made in Brazil, but there was an unexpected boon. Three of the girls appear to be Americans. They are light skinned, and Jorge heard them speaking to each other in English."

Tartus stroked the stubble on his chin. Of course, everyone spoke English. But in situations of extreme stress, people tended to revert to their native tongues.

"What race are they?" Tartus asked.

"One is slightly Hispanic, but mostly Caucasian. The other two are pure white," Falon said.

"I'll want to see these three first."

"Of course, Tartus."

Three American girls would bring a premium greater than the other thirty-five combined. Because they were exceedingly difficult to acquire, American girls went exclusively to Tartus' most elite clientele. Even in Brazil, Americans were hard to come by. They seldom traveled to dangerous places without the protection of bodyguards or at least large groups. In fact, Tartus knew Fejo avoided Americans like the plague. They were much too dangerous.

If Fejo actually had three American girls, it would most likely be by accident. Then again, Fejo was already posturing to elevate his price for this shipment.

Why else would his mate Jorge have made it a point to mention the Americans to Falon? Well, business meant money, and Fejo had brought Tartus considerable revenues over the past eight years. If the smelly little man wanted a taste of the big league, Tartus would grant it within reason, considering the difficulty of making trustworthy partners in his line of work. He dismissed Falon and picked up the telephone. After making the international connections, his grip tightened as King Fahr answered.

"Hello, Honorable One," Tartus said in Arabic, "I believe I have something that will interest you."

"I'm listening," said the man able to inspire fear even in Tartus.

"With my next shipment, I'll have some rare merchandise - three units from America. I thought perhaps you would like to discuss the matter in person."

"Three? These are quality?"

"The highest quality, Honorable One." Tartus knew it was dangerous to promise something he hadn't seen himself, but this was the opportunity of a lifetime. King Fahr had purchased dozens of girls from him in the past decade, but all were from Third World countries.

"When can we meet?"

"Twenty days, Honorable One."

"Very well. We'll meet for lunch on the seventeenth at Kahlid's in Riyadh. You will have the merchandise nearby?"

"As you wish, Honorable One." Tartus smiled as he replaced the receiver. He knew he could command almost any price for three clean, middle class American girls. He suspected King Fahr al-Azon Al Saud would love showcasing them in his harem.

Chapter Seventeen

International Waters, East of Norfolk, Virginia

Commander Rymes stared blankly over the deck of the Prometheus. The sea was choppy. White-capped green mounds slapped against the hull with relentless effort. He was nervous about his new command. When Fulton had recruited him, Rymes was given the barest of details. He was to navigate the oil tanker to a certain set of coordinates just northeast of the Suez Canal and await the transmission of double blind launch codes. Neither he nor the technician who transmitted the codes would know the missiles' targets.

Fulton had told him the encoded launch codes would be transmitted a few moments before the launch. Rymes would then translate the message into another code that only the missiles could decipher. Until they received the transmission, he and his crew had a boring assignment - posing as commercial sailors.

As a career Navy man, Rymes was accustomed to waiting. 'Hurry up and wait' was a common slogan among the armed forces. Still, he couldn't help but speculate. He looked out over the deck at his men. They were a good group of soldiers. Many had combat experience in Vietnam, and all were expert sailors.

Their mission was a simple one - sail, launch, and return home. Although not particularly challenging, this mission could restore his good name and get him back in the game. But why was he here? He wasn't aware of any Middle Eastern activities warranting a sneak attack of this magnitude.

Although he considered himself lucky to be given another crack at command, something just didn't add up. He felt the familiar sting of guilt that always accompanied his memories of his last combat mission.

The one question that perplexed Rymes most was why his ship's missiles were all Soviet SS-18's.

* * *

Rio de Janeiro, Brazil

Drake stood at the Marriott Rio desk. Gip was two meters behind him, broadening his line of sight.

"Good Morning, Sir. How may I help you?" the desk clerk asked.

"My friend and I are new to Rio, and we'd like to arrange a tour," Drake replied. Drake and Gip were dressed in 100% Armani - casual slacks, T-shirts and sport jackets; basically like the perfect marks for conmen. It didn't take Hector long to slither his way into the conversation.

"Mr. Drake," Hector said, having instinctively filed away his name, "I am Hector, the hotel concierge. I'm sure I can help you gentlemen with whatever arrangements you'd prefer." He turned his gaze to Gip as he spoke. Gip met his eyes levelly.

"Well, we're sort of taking an unofficial vacation. Neither of us has been to Rio before. Money is not an issue. We'd also prefer a little female companionship, if you know what I mean," Drake said, producing a hundred-dollar bill. "Do you think you could fix us up for couple of days?"

"Well," Hector began, "I do have a dear friend who owns a taxi. This is extremely important in Rio, Sir. If you hail a taxi on the street, you never know what you're going to get. My cousin, who grew up here, by the way, hailed a taxi off the street once. He was taken to a remote place where other men were waiting. They beat him so badly he permanently lost the hearing in his left ear."

"What's your friend's name?"

"Name? Uh, his name is Felipe."

Bingo! "How much does Felipe charge?" Drake asked.

Within moments, Drake and Gip were in the back of Felipe's cab pretending to listen to his tour speech. John paid careful attention to the driver, and although the man did have a seedy air about him, he gave no clear indication he was a kidnapper. Drake decided any approach was better than no approach.

"Felipe."

"Yes, Sir."

"My friend and I are interested in something that is not on your tour."

"Sir, I am a man of many talents and connections. All you need to do is ask," Felipe responded with a grin.

"Felipe, we are interested in girls."

"Well, Sir, who is not? If you are looking for girls, you have come to the right place. Rio has many girls."

"Felipe, we want a special type of girl. The type we can take off your hands with no questions asked." Drake let the statement sink in. "Permanently."

After some thought, Felipe responded, "Mr. Drake, I know just the place."

Felipe made a U turn at the next light, and drove to the nearest pay phone. When he returned, he said, "Mr. Drake, Mr. Gibson, the arrangements have been made. The cost to you will be ten thousand dollars each." Felipe anxiously waited for his mark's response. This was a risky business, selling to strangers.

"That won't be a problem," Drake responded. Felipe had progressed from seedy character to prime suspect in Drake's mind. He scratched at the duct tape strips encircling his arm, and thought of the full-contact conversation he planned to have with Felipe.

When Drake returned to the cab, he said, "We'll be ready in one hour. We'll meet you in front of the Marriott.

An hour and a half later, they pulled into a small hotel, about twenty minutes drive out of Rio. Felipe turned to face his guests. "My friends, this is where we part ways. Your girls are waiting for you in room one thirty two."

"Felipe, do I look foolish to you?" Drake asked. "I'm not about to hand you twenty thousand dollars for merchandise I haven't seen. My friend and I will require your accompaniment to the room. Once we are comfortable with the situation, You'll get the cash. Understand?"

"I understand," Felipe said, without surprise.

Felipe entered room one thirty two first, quickly followed by Drake and Gip. Two young girls, no older than their late teens, were naked and hog-tied on the bed. Standing at the foot of the bed was one of the largest men Drake had ever seen. His obsidian, soulless eyes panned from Drake to Gip. Shark's eyes, flat, black and hungry. The giant wore a tacky rendition of a business suit. His jewelry was gaudy. Gold chains hung from every extremity.

The bathroom door was closed, suggesting the presence of at least one other man. The giant roughly frisked Drake and Gip. They were not surprised. Drake remembered his Ranger training – no one was more relaxed than immediately after they searched you.

Gip slowly worked his way around the perimeter of the room toward the bathroom door while Drake casually looked for a weapon. His eyes registered but did not linger on the ink pen on the desk. He calculated his move to take about two seconds. The giant, with his gun still holstered, could not beat that time. He split the difference between Felipe and the girls in his field of vision, studying each in the periphery. When he saw Felipe catch his eye, he jerked his stare toward one of the girls. The feign worked. Felipe turned to face the girls. Time slowed to a crawl as the entire balance of two men's lifespans was compressed into the next five seconds.

Drake grabbed the pen, flipped off its protective top with his thumb, and promptly buried it in the giant's left carotid artery. The giant gurgled in the warm metallic soup of his own blood, staring at Drake in disbelief. Before he could reflexively draw his weapon, Drake had the man's .38 revolver. He immediately tossed it to Gip. When the second man burst out of the bathroom, Gip was ready.

"Hey!" Gip shouted, mainly to add confusion. Gip's hand was shaking slightly, but at this range the man knew he couldn't miss. The man froze for just an instant, but that was all Gip needed. Gip lowered the pistol to his victim's solar plexus, using the man's spleen as a silencer. The molten lead traveled upward at a steep angle, lodging between the second and third cervicals. The man was dead before his flaccid body slapped to the floor.

Meanwhile, the giant silently bled out on the carpet. When Gip turned to face the room, he saw Drake had Felipe in a sleeper hold. Felipe was unconscious in twenty seconds. The sleeper was an excellent hold. The old saying that the brain could live four minutes without oxygen was a myth. Actually, there were four minutes of oxygen left in the bloodstream once the lungs stopped breathing. When the carotids were pressed shut, unconsciousness ensued within seconds.

Two minutes after the door to the hotel room closed, Drake and Gip had secured the scene. Gip searched the pockets of the two dead men and came up with a switchblade and a set of Mercedes keys. Both would come in handy.

Having brought no weapons with them other than their special forces training, Drake & Gip had to improvise. They knew company could arrive at any minute.

"Gip, get us into the next room."

"Consider it done."

It took Gip less than fifteen seconds to pick the cheap lock to room one thirty three. Drake easily lifted Felipe and dragged him to the adjacent room. Any onlookers would simply think Drake was helping a drunken friend, if they thought anything at all. The room change would provide them with a tactical advantage should more company arrive. Gip hastily released the two girls, returned their clothing, and sent them off in Felipe's taxi.

Drake stripped his own jacket and shirt off, and removed several bands of duct tape from each arm while Gip undressed the interrogation subject. One difference between the regular Army and the Special Forces was the Army taught the art of killing a man. The Special Forces taught the art of keeping a man alive.

Drake sat studying his quarry. Two facts kept surfacing in his mind. First, he was limited to the tools in this room, plus the switchblade Gip had taken from the dead giant. Second, he didn't know how much time he had. This would have to be relatively quick, robbing him of the most valuable tool of interrogation – time. Given enough time, everyone cracked.

When pain was quick and severe, some had the wherewithal to die nobly. He would have to skip the fancy psychology. His one hope was that Felipe was what he appeared – a weakling. Whether or not this pathetic man knew anything about Lupe Hernandez, he deserved what awaited him. Drake was repulsed by what Felipe was willing to do to those two young girls. The image sickened him. He thought of Tammy and grit his jaw.

For the first time since he learned Tammy's secret, Drake felt emotion – anger, a blinding fury focused entirely on Felipe. Although he didn't realize it, John had possessed the anger all along. It was just inwardly directed. Anger directed inward becomes depression. Now, the coin had flipped. This pathetic man personified all the injustice in the world to John. Drake convinced himself that the more he hurt Felipe, the more his rage would be assuaged - the more justice would be served.

Drake looked from the knife in Gip's hand to Felipe, who was naked and bound to a wooden chair with duct tape covering his mouth. He thought of Tammy, and the ruin that rape had brought to her life. He still saw the haunted look in her eyes. He still heard the shakiness in her voice as she recounted the terrible event that would always follow her. He also remembered the day he stood over a dying dove and took a vow never to cause the death of another living thing.

Drake wished things were like the movies, where the lines between good and evil are clearly drawn. In his current situation, the lines were hazy, and Drake struggled to determine whether he was one of the good guys or one of the bad guys. He remembered his father's words, *There is no right or wrong. There's simply whose side you're on.* At first, this statement had appalled him, but now it was a convenient rationalization. He hardened his resolve.

Felipe awoke and immediately lost control of his bladder. Drake noticed the subject's breathing had become labored and panicky. He knew that every minute he waited, Felipe's will grew weaker, and he didn't want him to pass out from carbon dioxide buildup. When Felipe pissed himself, Drake thought the time was right. Drake stepped in front of him.

"Felipe, you and I are going to chat. If you tell me what I want to know there's no need for you to be hurt. Now, we'll start with a few simple questions, but I'm warning you, if you don't talk now, it will be a long time before your next opportunity."

Drake jerked the duct tape off of Felipe's mouth, tearing his lip slightly on the upper right side. As Felipe opened his mouth to cry out, Gip swiftly flicked open the switchblade and placed it in the corner of Felipe's eye. Felipe let his breath out in a hiss through clenched teeth.

"Try to scream and I dig your eye out of your face. Understand?" Gip asked, as calmly as if he were talking to a child.

"Yes, I understand," Felipe managed between huge gulps of air.

"Felipe," Drake said, "We want to talk about the girls. Where did they come from?" Drake had to strain to restrict himself to one question at a time, but he remembered his training and gave the subject time to respond.

Felipe responded, "I don't know where the girls came from. You killed the men who got them for me."

"Wrong answer," Drake said as he replaced the duct tape on Felipe's mouth. He had to impress upon the subject that he was in complete control of the conversation. He took the switchblade from Gip's hand and walked over to the desk. Drake knelt and cut a thin strip of wood from the leg of the chair. Without saying a word, he cut a two-inch strip of skin across the back of Felipe's left hand, just above the knuckles. Felipe quivered in pain as the four tendons snapped one-by-one. Drake then made two vertical cuts, each about an inch long, at the ends of the first cut. Felipe now had three quarters of a rectangle cut into his hand.

Drake placed the wooden strip on the back of the subject's hand and rolled the loose skin onto it. He then proceeded to roll past the pre-cut area up the subject's left arm, leaving a path of exposed muscle approximately two inches wide extending from Felipe's knuckles to his shoulder. The sound reminded John of bacon sizzling.

Felipe screamed through his nose, clenched his teeth, and flexed every muscle in his body in a futile effort to escape the horror. Stomach acid and bile came up through his sinuses and out of his nostrils.

Felipe closed his eyes and bit hard, snapping both of his upper front teeth. Once, when Drake was just below the elbow joint, Felipe passed out from the pain. Gip quite effectively remedied this by throwing steaming hot water from the sink into Felipe's face. Felipe sucked air in through his nose with such a fury his nostrils collapsed with each breath. The muscles in his face convulsed with agony as his head shook left and right, instinctively signaling *no, no, no!*

When he reached the shoulder, Drake cut the flesh croissant off and held it in front of Felipe's face. "Now, this conversation is getting boring. Felipe. Let me cut to the chase. You have plenty of skin left and I have all night, so you and I can both be certain you will tell me what I want to know. I am interested in your little business of buying and selling girls. I had a friend." He produced a picture of Lupe. "She disappeared ten days ago. If I don't find out where my friend is, I will become much more creative." Drake produced several salt packets from his pocket and set them within Felipe's sight. "You do believe I'm creative, don't you? Or should I demonstrate?"

Although Drake displayed the calm sadism of a seasoned combat veteran, he was acting. Inside, he was seething with rage. He pictured Felipe raping Tammy. This thought threatened to bring back the hurt and humiliation he had buried along with his friends. Drake suppressed all thought but the cold fury coursing through his veins – a slurry of ice water moving through frozen pipes. In that zone, there was no pain, no regret and no hesitation. In that zone, he was the good guy, operating on his most basic instincts.

Drake studied Felipe. No major vessels were opened. Felipe's capillary bleeding was bright red and copious, but not life threatening. He delivered a quick blow to the mouth before removing Felipe's gag for the second time. This time, the little sewer rat was most eager to share the details of his little enterprise. Before he spoke, Felipe spat out the jagged tips of his incisors. He took in huge, wheezing gulps of air.

"Pleath! I'll tell you everything you want to know. Just let me breathe!" Felipe's voice was weak and hurried. He had developed a pronounced lisp as the result of his broken incisors. When he spoke, Drake couldn't help thinking of Sylvester the cat.

"Don't worry, Felipe." Drake smiled, "The one thing you can count on is that I'll keep you breathing." Drake was pleased to hear Felipe use the phrase 'everything you want to know' instead of 'everything I know'; the latter being a sign of some remaining resistance. Felipe was not leaving himself the option of claiming ignorance. "Talk. You have three seconds to begin."

"Fejo. Hith name ith Fejo. He has the girlth. I am just a bithneth man. Pleath don't hurt me anymore! I, I, I deliver untratheable girls to him on occathion. I don't know what he doeth with them."

Without saying a word, Drake raised the duct tape to Felipe's mouth. Felipe jerked his head back. What he said next came out as a scream.

"No! Tarfaya! He takth the girlth to Tarfaya, Morocco. He deliverth them to a man named Tartuth. Fejo's ship is called The Lady and the Tramp. He thails out of Guanabara Bay. I think he just left two, maybe three dayth ago. Thith ith everything I know. You have to believe me!"

"I believe you," Drake said calmly.

Drake had made no promise to Felipe about releasing him or even providing a merciful death. Somehow, that distinction was important to him. He replaced the duct tape over Felipe's mouth. There was a faint glimmer of hope in Felipe's eyes. *This piece of shit thinks I'm going to leave him alive,* Drake thought.

With slight hesitation, Drake pulled another piece of duct tape from his arm and placed it securely over Felipe's nostrils. He then pulled a chair in front of Felipe, staring directly into his anguished and quivering eyes. Drake expected Felipe's anguish to soothe his own wounds like some magic salve. When Felipe died, Drake expected a spike of raw, healing power to fill the void left by his emotions. He wanted the power to change the past, but would settle for the power to restore justice.

But, none of these things happened. Drake's anger was not diminished, but amplified and turned inward. He had become that which he hated most. He was no better than the monster he had just killed. His mind reeled with confusion, blinded by an all-consuming rage. John Drake hated himself, and he didn't understand why.

Once the convulsions had stopped, Gip prodded Drake's arm and pointed at the door.

"Let's get out of here," Gip said, a little nervous about what he had just seen.

"I agree," Drake said in a tremulous voice.

After watching the parking lot for a full minute to make sure they hadn't attracted any attention, Drake and Gip slipped out the door and made their exit in the black Mercedes parked behind the motel. Only then did they remove the patches of scotch tape from their fingertips.

"Man, that was some cold shit you did back there," Gip said, "I don't remember them teaching any of that at Ranger school. Man, how do you even think up shit like that?"

"I've been thinking a lot recently."

"Man, you've got some angry thoughts," Gip said.

"You have no idea," Drake said in a deadpan tone.

Chapter Eighteen

Riyadh, Saudi Arabia

Fahr al-Azon Al Saud sat at the head of the table. As King and Prime Minister of Saudi Arabia, he presided over the Council of Arab Oil Ministers. He knew this would be a difficult meeting. Since the Fourth Arab-Israeli War had begun, tensions were high among the Arab nations. Syria, with support from the Soviet Union, had initiated the conflict during Yom Kippur in 1973, ostensibly over a territorial dispute. The sneak attack on the Jews' holy day was an insult of the highest magnitude to Israel. The flames were further fueled by the Arabs' refusal to recognize Israel as a nation. The Arab extremists saw the fight as a Jihad, a Holy War bringing religious purity to the Middle East. They referred to the conflict as the Ramadan War, named after the Muslim holy month.

Fahr knew it would be nearly impossible to keep religion out of this discussion. Although a devout Muslim, he was not a proponent of killing in the name of religion. Fahr's interests were economic in nature.

"This meeting will now come to order," he proclaimed, banging his gavel. "Our purpose today is to discuss our production schedules, as well as review our position relative to the United Nations."

The Syrian representative, Azul, was the first to gesture.

"The chair recognizes the Syrian representative."

"Thank you, Mr. Chairman. Gentlemen, these are historic times. Our solid support from the Soviet Union will finally enable us to reclaim that which is rightfully ours. For over seven years now, the Jews have occupied the Sinai Peninsula, the Gaza Strip, the Golan Heights, the West Bank and East Jerusalem.

At this crucial juncture, it is imperative that we remain united. The time is right for us to act. We cannot allow this disgrace to continue.

"There will be those who want to divide the Arab nations. We cannot let this happen." Azul, like many extremists, was a charismatic speaker. There were subtle nods of agreement around the table.

One man was not nodding - Rao, the Egyptian representative. He leaned into his microphone and interrupted the Syrian.

"Azul, we cannot ignore the power and influence of the United States. Although the Soviets have been generous with their weaponry and hardware, I think the US will be a more stable long-term ally. Look at the aid they have given Israel. They have superior weapons and financial stability. They even send their sons to die for their allies. Show me one Soviet soldier fighting for our cause." Rao was leaning forward on his elbows, his black eyes amiably unwavering from Azul's.

"Rao," Azul said, "We are all aware that the Americans have been courting Sadat since he rose to power. Why is Egypt so willing to betray its roots for these Westerners?" Azul made a sweeping gesture to the west. Muslims, who prayed five times each day facing Mecca, were always conscious of the direction. "Throughout their brief history they have demonstrated a complete lack of honor. They exploit their own citizens and the citizens of their supposed allies. They think they are the policemen, the conscience of the planet! The Americans are political and economic expansionists, and they will not stop until they own the world."

"Philosophical differences aside, the Americans have behaved with complete honor in our dealings with them," Rao said. "They offer substantial support, and in return all they ask is our acknowledgement of Israel's status as a nation."

"Never!" Azul slammed his fist on the table and pointed directly at Rao. "To those dogs, this is simply a political matter, one of national borders and UN status. We are fighting a Jihad. We fight for the glory of Allah!" Azul raised his fist in a gesture of triumph.

"You sir, who speak of honor." Rao remained calm, but his voice became firm. "Is a surprise attack on the holiest day of the Jewish year, honorable? How can we expect to live in harmony when we defile their religion?"

"Harmony is for bureaucrats. We don't need their harmony - a harmony in which they insult us with impunity, a harmony in which they take our lands. And who was it that violated the UN cease-fire directive? The Jews!"

"Azul, you miss the point." Rao had the tone of a man addressing a small child. "The UN resolution also called for Israel to return the Arab properties they took during the Seven Days War, the properties you so eloquently catalogued just moments ago. It is the UN, with the United States as the dominant force, whom we wish to befriend. We can regain what we lost and let the UN deal with Israel."

"What makes you think the UN has any control over the Jews? They have defied the UN Security Council twice in the past year. You want to place our fate in the hands of those hypocrites?" Azul took a deep breath, ready to continue.

"Order!" Chairman Fahr proclaimed. He instantly had the attention of the dueling diplomats. "You worry needlessly. We will never be slaves to the Americans or the UN so long as we control the world's oil supply. Let them run their armies without fuel, if they can. Egypt and Syria may have their differences, but we must never allow the Westerners to see this. We will handle our internal bickering amongst ourselves. We must present a unified front to the outside world at all times, is that agreed?"

"Agreed," Rao said.

Azul's face was dark and foreboding. "Agreed," he finally replied.

"So, I move that we further increase the price of crude oil by twenty percent, and cut production by an additional fifteen percent. This will increase our revenues while choking the West where they are most vulnerable. Let us remind the world who controls the power supply." Fahr grinned. "I call for a vote. All in favor?"

Azul immediately raised his hand, giving a challenging stare at each of the other members. Slowly Abu Dhabi, Iran, Iraq, Kuwait, Qatar and even Egypt joined the consensus.

"The price increase and production cut will be announced one week from today, March 18. I will make the press release personally," Fahr closed.

Fahr was pleased with the outcome of the meeting. He had further increased the wealth of his country while appeasing both the religious zealots and the military. He wondered how men achieved positions of such power when they wore their hearts upon their sleeves.

He looked at his calendar. He had a lunch meeting with Tartus on the seventeenth. He had a lot of politicking to do between now and then, but there was no way he would miss that meeting. *Tartus said he had a special surprise for me,* he thought, *I wonder if he actually had what he promised?* The greatest status symbol for a Sheik was his harem. And, with the help of Tartus, Fahr would have the ultimate trophy for his – an American girl.

* * *

Guanabara Bay, Brazil

Jao was relaxed with his feet on his desk as he read the New York Times. Being a shipping clerk for the Guanabara Bay Transport Service was a peaceful job. He received, proofed and filed the shipping manifests for all outgoing and incoming vessels. This required perhaps three hours per day of actual work. He spent the rest of his time reading or watching his black and white television. Jao liked to practice his English, and was quite good at reading the language. He did, however, have to concentrate to converse in the perplexing tongue. The teacher of his night class liked to joke that the Americans had rules to cover 55% of their language, and had to memorize the other 45% of exceptions.

The walls of his office were peeling and bare, except for a solitary ornament – a nude poster of Jane Fonda, taken from the opening scene of "Barbarella". He was deeply engrossed in an article about the OPEC oil embargo when he heard the bell above the door issue its distinctive ring.

A short, stocky white man entered, followed closely by a tall black man. Both were obviously Americans. They had a quiet intensity, immediately putting Jao on guard. The white man spoke first,

"Hello. Do you speak English?" His voice was calm as the dead.

Jao knew he would likely avoid work by claiming ignorance, but he was bored and could use the practice. He didn't have the opportunity to talk to genuine Americans often. He typically test-drove his English with other Brazilians who blended the Portuguese and English languages into an amalgam.

"Of course. What can I do for you?" Jao answered. His tone was cordial but officious.

"My friend and I were supposed to meet a man named Fejo on the tenth, but we missed him. He had work for us on his ship, The Lady and the Tramp. Can you please help us out and tell us whether the ship has left? We really need the work," Drake implored.

"Sir, I appreciate your situation, but I'm not allowed to reveal such information," Jao replied, concentrating on each word. He was quite proud of how well he was doing.

The black man stepped forward. Jao missed some of what he said, but he easily recognized the one hundred dollar bill in his hand.

"Of course, I didn't realize you gentlemen were from the Shipping Authority. I'll get the documents right away," Jao answered, deftly pocketing the C note. When he returned with the manifest, he laid it on the counter and began thumbing through the pages. Jao caught the briefest glimpse of a shadow speeding toward the left side of his jaw. Then there was blackness. When he awoke fifteen minutes later, the men were gone.

Trying to ignore the soreness in his jaw, he returned to his paper. *Crazy Americans,* he thought as he slipped back into the article, *they'll try to rob anyplace. We don't even carry any money.* He had a brief laugh as he imagined the look on their faces as they must have looked in vain for the cash register. He did find it a bit curious that they had left the hundred-dollar bill in his pocket, but dismissed the matter. He had forgotten about the manifest, and never noticed it missing.

* * *

The South Atlantic

By Lupe's reckoning, it had been two days since she had awoken, bound and gagged. Since then, she had been treated with relatively little brutality. She had not seen either of her friends since she woke, but heard the Hispanic cries of dozens of women from her stall. Every morning a man arrived with an empty bucket, exchanging it for her previous day's toilet. He also left a water bucket indistinguishable from her toilet bucket. Finally, there was a bowl of what appeared to be dirty grits. She ate greedily, using her grimy fingers as a scoop.

The sea had gotten progressively rougher, making her stomach buckle with each lurch of the boat. Lupe's body was covered with grime. She had never been filthier. Even as a child, she had been meticulous about personal hygiene, reading books in her room while the other children played outside with the heat and dirt and bugs.

One of the men came below deck, the same one who brought her the daily buckets. He was speaking Portuguese in a soft tone of voice, almost pleasant. When he appeared in front of her cell, she noticed he had no buckets. One look at his face told her all she needed to know. His eyes were full of lust, moving slowly up and down her body. Lupe curled into a ball, humiliated by the feeling of powerlessness this filthy lowlife gave her. She closed her eyes so tightly that she saw purple spots floating on the insides of her eyelids. He had stopped talking. *Maybe he went away.*

When Lupe mustered the courage to sneak a look, she saw he was still there. If there were any doubt as to his intentions, he removed them by inserting his left hand down the front of his pants. His right hand was behind his back. Deep down, Lupe knew what the beast wanted, but she couldn't accept that this was happening to her. She screamed and cursed at him, threatening him with her father's vengeance, but he just laughed softly. As he turned to face her through the bars, his right hand produced a cattle prod. When he grinned, his rotten front teeth emitted a stench easily detectable across the eight feet separating them. Lupe screamed again and crawled into the corner, hoping somehow to burrow through the steel hull and swim back to California.

She heard him lock the cell door behind him. She recoiled into the corner, holding her knees in her arms. She knew there was only one chance to avoid or postpone the assault, but wondered how well a one-hour self defense course would stand up against an armed, hardened criminal. The short but brutish man grabbed her by the arms and lifted her to her feet with ease.

"You lay one finger on me, and my father will have your balls in a jar on his night stand!" she screamed. Her voice was hoarse. "Do you know who I am, you filthy bastard?"

"My puta, I know exactly who you are. You are my lover for the evening. If you relax, it will be less painful, I promise you that."

Lupe knew the time for action had not come. She assumed a submissive posture, indicating that she would withstand his assault with little to no resistance. He began to kiss her face and neck, his fetid breath almost making her vomit. She opened her knees. Jorge responded by ripping her sun dress off in one quick motion. He placed the cattle prod on the floor and used both hands to remove her bra and grope at her breasts with his coarse and filthy hands.

Lupe knew she was going to vomit any second, but held it in, reaching between the monster's legs and clasping his erection. Jorge immediately dropped his pants, ready to penetrate her. As soon as she saw he was naked from the waist down, Lupe made her move. She grabbed his testicles with both hands, squeezing and twisting with all her might. Every human being aboard The Lady and the Tramp heard Jorge howl in pain.

Lupe dragged him by his testicles to the door of the cell, where she took his keys and began working at the lock. Her efforts were interrupted by a blast of stinging water. Fejo stood in the hallway with a fire hose, sweeping across both occupants of the cell in quick motions, careful not to remove flesh from bone with the tremendous pressure. He screamed something in Portuguese to Jorge, who was unable to stand.

Obviously frustrated, Fejo unlocked the cell, dragged Jorge into the corridor by his shirt and retrieved the man's cattle prod. After a lustful glance, he tossed Lupe's garments back to her. Neither Jorge nor any other member of the crew paid Lupe a visit for the remainder of the trip.

Chapter Nineteen

Langley, Virginia

Special Agent Fulton was covered in a light sweat. He smelled his own scent. The DCI's waiting room was luxuriant far beyond what one would expect. Instead of the wooden benches typical of government facilities, the DCI had plush leather couches. Fulton suspected the Renoir above the fireplace was an original. Despite these extravagances, the room felt tight and claustrophobic. In moments, Fulton would face the final administrative hurtle in Project Crossfire.

When the receptionist appeared, Fulton jerked slightly. His inability to conceal his stress made him angry. He was a CIA agent, and should have ice water in his veins. He resolved to calm himself. He imagined he had already been fired and accepted his former boss' standing offer at the FBI. Visualizing the worst-case scenario and realizing it wasn't so bad was a calming exercise for Fulton. This mental exercise firmed him up in about two seconds.

"Agent Fulton, the DCI will see you now." She was a pretty girl, just a little chubby. She wore a flattering skin-tight gray cotton dress-suit that accentuated the curvatures of her body.

Fulton stood, bathed in his new calmness. He dabbed the sweat from his brow before entering the office of the man who ultimately controlled the destiny of half the world's population. The DCI had the posture of a man accustomed to discipline. When he looked Fulton in the eye, he conveyed a sense of quiet urgency.

"Hello, Agent Fulton," the DCI said.

"Good morning, Sir."

"Coffee?"

"Water would be good, Sir."

"Very well." The DCI poured two glasses of iced water. He handed one to Fulton before he sat behind his mahogany desk. He came straight to the point.

"Agent Fulton, according to the schedule you submitted, Project Crossfire goes active on March 18th. Now, I gave you complete autonomy in developing a plan to end the OPEC oil embargo by March 1st. You have spent nearly a billion dollars and are coming in three weeks behind schedule. I need a complete report before giving you the green light. Walk me through it, and be thorough."

"Yes Sir." Fulton had been preparing for this moment for months. Explaining the mechanics of his project relaxed him. "The Prometheus is en route. This former commercial oil tanker has been completely retrofitted as a battleship, armed with Soviet SS-18 ICBM's, each packing a dozen conventional thousand-pound payloads. The crew is entirely military, mostly active and reserve Navy, with a few jarhead technicians. Of course, they are all posing as civilian oil workers.

"In one week, she'll arrive just northeast of the Suez Canal and drop anchor. The canal is a notorious bottleneck, and most vessels have to anchor for at least forty-eight hours in the waters just off the northern entrance. The Prometheus will take position in a direct line between Tel-Aviv and Saudi Arabia.

"When I transmit the double blind launch codes, the Prometheus will launch her entire complement of Soviet SS-18's, focusing on downtown Tel-Aviv. By the time they are in radar range, the missiles will be on their descent and it will be too late for counter measures."

"Continue," the DCI said without inflection.

"When Prometheus launches her missiles, two things will happen. First, based on the composition and last known vector of the missiles, the Israelis will assume they were launched from northwestern Saudi Arabia. Our intelligence indicates the Saudis have Soviet ICBM capability in that sector. Second, the damage to Tel-Aviv will decimate the Israeli government, leaving them helpless.

"With Israel near death's door, the US will have to come to their aid in defense of such an unconscionable attack by the Saudis. The UN would not consider standing in our way, given the circumstances. This will give us a legitimate excuse to attack Saudi Arabia and ultimately take control of the world's oil supply. This will ensure our country's independence well into the next century."

The DCI appeared pleased. Fulton knew the DCI had hired him because he owed him a debt of honor. He wanted to prove himself worthy of the honor.

"Agent Fulton," the DCI continued, "you can't expect an oil tanker to launch hundreds of missiles from a high traffic area and remain undetected. You do remember what I said about sanitation, don't you?"

"I do, Sir, which is why I designed shaped charges into the Prometheus' primary hull. They will be automatically triggered when the missiles are launched."

"And you have no moral issues with this? You are comfortable killing not only thousands of allied civilians in Tel Aviv, but a ship full of American soldiers?" The DCI had a challenging tone in his voice. Fulton knew the old man was just testing his mettle.

He remembered his vow to return to the FBI if this project collapsed. What Fulton didn't know was whether he was expected to regret the killings or not. Did the DCI want a heartless bastard as his successor, or a compassionate man who did what he must for the greater good? Ultimately, he went with heartless bastard.

"Sir, with control over the world's energy supply, the US will be completely independent. We'd answer to no one. Those men must die, but they will die patriots. The most unfortunate thing is that they will never be recognized in the history books. But, then, neither will we." Fulton was becoming animated, and had to remind himself to maintain a calm demeanor.

To Fulton, Project Crossfire was the ultimate challenge. This was exactly the type of ambitious undertaking he loved. He tolerated the tiresome and perpetual game of befriending traitors in the perpetual search for information so he could do the fun things like this.

"How do you plan to sink a ship of such size without someone coming to the rescue? It must take hours for a multi compartment vessel like that to go down."

Robert grinned, having received validation of his life's greatest accomplishment. The DCI was down to questions about minor details. "I have a man in the Suez Canal. He will direct traffic, ensuring that no other vessel goes near the Prometheus. He thinks the US is staging an extraction from Syria – a downed pilot."

"Two hours?"

"Remember, Sir, the Prometheus only looks like an oil tanker. It doesn't have the multiple compartments designed to keep it afloat. I specifically engineered it to sink in just under fifteen minutes."

"What about their SOS?"

"What SOS? The radio will detonate along with the hull."

"Lifeboats?"

"Sieves for hulls, with iron weights built into the keel. No trace of the Prometheus will remain."

"Life jackets?"

"Might as well be lead."

"You think those Navy guys ever heard of treading water?"

"Not in the vortex created when a ship with a displacement of three hundred thousand tons sinks in just under a quarter of an hour."

"This operative in the Suez Canal – he's a loose end."

"He won't be after we rendezvous in Norfolk. I'm meeting him personally to transfer the money he was promised. Let's just say he'll be a permanent component of the new bridge being constructed there."

"Well." The DCI smiled. "It looks like you've thought this out pretty well. By the way, I like the name 'Crossfire' - pretty cute. Congratulations on a job well done."

The men stood and shook hands.

"Thank you, Sir," Fulton said.

"I don't need to tell you that this conversation never took place, do I? If this thing goes south, you're going with it and I'm not moving a goddamn inch. Understood?"

"Yes Sir."

* * *

Tarfaya, Morocco

It was 9:00 a.m., and Drake was already sweating. "Damn, it's hot. I mean, I grew up in the South, where the temperature stays in the triple digits most of the summer, and I'm about to die here."

Gip didn't look much better. Large beads of sweat rolled down his bald head. Of course, the jet lag and sleep deprivation did not help improve their moods. Drake had managed a few hours sleep on the plane. He had heard that the airlines decreased the oxygen level in the passenger compartment shortly after takeoff to help induce drowsiness. Surely enough, despite his tension, he had dozed off. Still, this was their third continent in as many days. As they maneuvered the throngs, moving toward the port, he already felt his legs tiring.

The streets of Tarfaya were crowded and dusty. Drake saw a boy of ten standing on his head, with his hat laid out for tipping. He got the impression the boy maintained that position for hours on end. There was an old man with a white scraggly beard handling a King Cobra. As the man stared into its eyes and sang an incomprehensible song, the snake seemed to be hypnotized. *Pretty risky career choice,* Drake thought. He remembered biology class. One drop of King Cobra venom contained enough poison to kill thirty-two adult men.

An unbelievably thin young man was doing back flips, always landing in the same spot on his small rug in the street. Passersby occasionally tossed coins on the rug. He looked like he ate three crickets a day, whether he was hungry or not. Women were everywhere, their entire bodies covered except for their eyes and feet. They carried baskets of laundry balanced on their heads, using no hands. *How can they stand the heat wearing all that?* Drake wondered. He and Gip seemed to be the only ones sweating. One woman balanced an urn on her head with at least ten gallons of water. She never wavered. Her hands were relaxed at her sides. Drake saw constant muscle flexes in her feet as she plodded along, choosing each step carefully. She seemed to balance her load by minor motions of her ankles.

The air was hot and stagnant. Drake prayed for even a slight breeze. The stillness, however, was actually a blessing to the natives, since it kept the sand on the ground where it belonged. Hundreds of vendors sold every conceivable type of handcrafted souvenir. They shouted in Arabic, English and French at passersby.

The streets of Tarfaya reminded Drake of the state fair back home. That world, the one where children popped balloons with darts while ice cream melted and ran down their hands seemed light years away. Time and space were distorted for Drake because he had been through so much in such a short time. Three years ago, he would never have guessed that this day he would be walking the streets of a foreign land as a soldier, a murderer - an instrument of justice.

Drake was carrying a satchel full of US currency. He wondered what would happen if the natives knew this. In a country where a man will handle venomous snakes for people's spare change, what would a man do for three hundred thousand dollars?

"The manifest said The Lady and the Tramp has a crew of eight," Gip said, "She's due to arrive in Tarfaya tomorrow. That gives us roughly twenty four hours to acquire weapons and devise a plan."

"So, what happens now? If we let them dock, we'll never get on board. The boat will be crawling with Harbor Patrol agents," Drake replied. He was tense, and rubbed his knotted neck with both hands. He put his palm under his chin and twisted his head sharply to the side, cracking his neck loudly.

"Hey, didn't anyone ever tell you that causes arthritis?"

"Gip, we'll be lucky to live through tomorrow, and you want to preach to me about arthritis in my old age? Get real."

"Okay, so we know where they'll be and when. We also know how many men there are. So, how do we take the ship? When will She be vulnerable?" Gip asked.

"What procedure does a commercial ship follow when entering an international port? Can we get them in customs?" Drake asked.

"Customs? I don't think so. That's probably the highest security risk. Wait a second. I wonder how they do make it through customs? I'm sure they would be boarded and searched." Gip looked up and rubbed his chin. Both he and Drake drew a blank on that one.

They arrived at the port. The sea was teeming with vessels of every size. Sailboats loaded with rich tourists, tramp steamers full of merchandise, military boats, Harbor Patrol boats and fishing boats - both commercial and private - all shared the limited space, somehow managing not to collide with each other. They sat and watched the activities of the harbor, hoping inspiration would strike.

Drake noticed the ubiquitous sea gulls and was again taken back to his defining moment standing over that dove. He kept reminding himself he was still that twelve year old child at heart – that his history from that point forward was a succession of responses to his father's abuses. His violent outbursts were merely reflections of The John – baggage he must unload if he was ever to have inner peace. He thought of the sadist who tortured Felipe to death and tried to convince himself that the end justified the means, and that evil must be combated with an even greater evil. It wasn't working. His actions were not those of a warrior, but of a beast. He saw no honor in what he had done to Felipe. He owed himself more than that, and strangely, he felt he owed the dove more than that.

Drake shelved such thoughts for the moment and put on his game face for the upcoming battle. He and Gip sat in complete silence for almost two hours before Gip spoke.

"Hey, I've been thinking about how these guys move the girls through this port. Remember what the cab driver said? They always come through Tarfaya. I doubt they choose this place at random. They probably have Customs in their pocket. I mean, look at all the street hustlers here. This place has to be corrupt as hell. How else could they pull it off?"

"So what are you getting at?" Drake asked.

"Look, we're in a corrupt port and we have three hundred thousand dollars in American cash. Corruption and money go together like beer and ice. You do the math." As Gip spoke, Drake gestured to interrupt him. Gip raised his hand to silence his partner, "Hold on. Listen up. I have an idea, one that just might work."

"I'm all ears," Drake said.

* * *

The Lady and the Tramp – Tarfarya Bay

The sea was choppy, with ten to twelve foot white-capped waves. Fejo sipped his coffee. He cursed as it burned his lips. Jorge had been with him for eight years, and the idiot still couldn't remember he liked a little ice in his coffee. His anger fleetingly passed as he remembered the bounty he would reap from this shipment. Jorge was a fool, but fools came in handy when it was time to divide the profits. Besides, Jorge did have his talents. He had no fear. Whether this was because he was courageous or because he was stupid did not actually matter. What did matter was his calmness under pressure. So what if he liked to sample the merchandise? How could one expect such a base and ignoble creature not to fulfill nature's calling? At least he cleaned up after himself, and he never left a mark on the girls.

He looked out over the bow and saw Jorge smoking a cigarette with four of the crew, wasting time. As First Officer, he should set a better example, but there was no real harm done. Besides Jorge and himself, the rest of the crew of The Lady and the Tramp was comprised of temporary workers. Their work was menial and their average tenure was one or two voyages. Some even worked simply for one way passage, running away from debts or wives or whatever troubles they had created for themselves.

Off the bow, he saw the Harbor Patrol boat approaching. Fejo wondered why they were paying a second visit. They had already solicited a healthy bribe when they met him at the two-mile marker. The Tarfaya Harbor Patrol officers were notoriously corrupt and were some of the easiest men to bribe Fejo had ever met. In fact, this was the main reason he and Tartus had chosen Tarfaya, rather than a more geographically convenient port. Routing through Tarfaya caused them to have to transport the girls by truck over three hundred miles to Safi - a dangerous proposition. However, the risk was small compared to that of going through Customs in Casablanca. This visit would be nothing more than a small inconvenience, he thought. During his initial encounter with the Harbor Patrol, he had paid ten thousand American dollars for 'special treatment', meaning the Harbor Patrol would turn a blind eye to the transfer of the girls to Falon's private boat.

A dark skinned man was piloting the boat. The blackness of his skin and the prominence of his cheekbones looked Swahili. He obviously was new to the job. His approach was painstakingly cautious as he slowly maneuvered to come alongside The Lady and the Tramp. There was a light skinned man, probably Arabic, lazily manning the fifty caliber mounted machine gun.

The guns were more for show than anything else. Fejo suspected they were seldom loaded, and that even if they were, the officials who manned them were incompetent government bureaucrats, with no weapons training.

* * *

Gip was nervous behind the wheel of the boat. The twenty-five footer pitched and lurched on the rough seas. They were only two miles out, but the contrast between this water and that of the inner harbor was enormous. Every time he corrected his course, the waves threw him off. They pummeled the boat at a forty-five degree angle off the port bow. He increased power each time he turned into the waves, and was immediately forced to throttle back as he was pushed to starboard.

Drake had his hat pulled down over his eyes. He still had a deep tan from his time spent outdoors in Georgia, probably dark enough to pass for a Moroccan.

There were five men smoking cigarettes on the bow, paying them little attention. Gip made out the pilot or captain in the bridge. This man was looking directly at him.

* * *

The Harbor Patrol boat was about twenty meters out when Fejo saw something strange. The man behind the machine gun seemed to be studying the entire deck of his ship. The man had gone from apathetic to attentive, and Fejo did not like it. The effect was subtle, but something deep in Fejo's mind told him this was wrong. Just as he switched to ship's radio to public address, he heard the first shots.

Jorge was in the middle of telling a filthy joke to one of the new crewmembers when the man's right arm flew away from his body in a violent explosion of scarlet. Time crept to a near halt. Bright red arterial blood shot out of the man's shoulder in spurts. There was a pounding, staccato sound, similar to the hammering sounds of a construction site.

* * *

Drake held the butterfly trigger down, trying his best to compensate for the roughness of the seas. He had hoped to take all the men out in the first round of bullets, but the targets momentarily disappeared as the patrol boat crested a wave and faced Drake skyward. When his line of sight returned to the targets, three were running in panic. He remembered his training. Bullets go where they are aimed, not where they are willed. Muscles stood out on his face as he clenched his jaws. Every muscle in his body was tight, and he would feel a soreness like he had never imagined later. His concentration was so intense he didn't even notice he was biting his lower lip. Blood ran down his chin. His upper teeth were bared in a raging snarl. He cut the other three men nearly in half with a sweeping motion.

Gip roughly pulled alongside the larger vessel, almost bouncing away and necessitating another pass. He and Drake rapidly scurried up the webbing on the side of the boat, each with a tow-line in his mouth and an Uzi 9mm slung over his shoulder. Drake jumped over the rail first. He seemed to be able to move and see with extraordinary speed. His environment moved in slow motion. To his right, there were three bodies and one man screaming on the deck with a missing arm. He wouldn't survive more than a few minutes. To his left, he saw Gip tying off his rope. Beyond Gip the deck was vacant. Directly ahead he saw the starboard side of the bridge, also vacant. Just ahead of the bridge was a hatch leading to the lower decks.

Chapter Twenty

The Prometheus

Commander Rymes and his first officer, Lieutenant Commander Joe Killian, were alone on the bridge. It was past midnight, and neither could sleep. Rymes paced nervously.

"Sir, what are you so worried about? This mission can't fail. All we have to do is launch a sneak attack and cruise back home. What could go wrong?"

"Joe…" Rymes paused. "Every mission carries the potential for failure. Not being able to imagine a failure is exactly what worries me. I haven't had a decent night's sleep since we left."

"Well, if it will make you feel better, we can brainstorm about potential problems." Killian counted on his fingers. "Okay, there's mechanical failure…"

"Joe," Rymes interrupted, "This isn't a case of typical mission anxiety."

"Do you want to talk about it?"

Rymes thought for several minutes. Both were comfortable with the silence. Finally, he decided he could confide in Killian. The man was solid, and more importantly, not talkative. Although they had known each other for just two weeks, he sensed a quiet strength in Killian.

"It was 1971, my first command," Rymes began. "The USS Burke. She was a beautiful destroyer, five hundred feet of aluminum with a complete complement of SSM's. She could turn over thirty knots due to her lightweight design. I had served as her XO (Executive Officer) for three years when the skipper was promoted to Full Bird and transferred to an aircraft carrier. I remember kidding him about being a ferry driver for the pilots. Never in my life had I been more ready for the challenge of command. The day my orders came through, I was like a kid at his own birthday party. The crewmen were congratulating me and I was walking on top of the world.

"Five months later, I hit bottom. Not literally, of course. We were in the Gulf of Tonkin, twenty klicks east of Haiphong. Our mission was a routine missile launch, not entirely dissimilar to our current assignment. We had been running a blockade for three months, and the ship was overdue for routine maintenance. The missile launchers in particular were questionable.

"Now you know the Navy. They're ultra conservative when it comes to scheduled maintenance. I just knew those launchers were fine. My silver leaf wasn't even broken in and I already had my sites set on Captain. I wasn't about to let some pencil pusher stand between me and the Full Bird. I ignored the maintenance notice. I remember feeling... superior, godlike. I tell you, there's nothing like being at sea. My ship felt like my own country, and I was the leader.

"So, I ordered the launch. That strike would have been our twenty-first in thirty days – a new record. The men were exhausted, but spirits were high. I thought I was the most motivated commander in the Navy. But, the illusion didn't last long.

"One of the launchers malfunctioned. The man monitoring the pressure for that hydraulic unit was exhausted and didn't notice when the pressure began to build. A pump exploded, and damned near ignited one of our missiles. Had that happened, the statistics predicted 50% casualties and the ship lost.

"The primary explosion killed two men. Another suffered burns over ninety percent of his body. That man, Jenkins, is still in the naval hospital at Norfolk, and the odds are he'll never set foot outside a hospital again." Rymes' eyes welled with tears as he spoke. "I tell you, there're no words to describe how I felt when I had to write those three letters.

"I visited Jenkins' family. I cried in their living room as I explained how my ambition was the reason their son would spend the rest of his life in bed, a mutilated husk of what he was meant to be. To this day, I can still see the look in his father's eyes when he told me he forgave me. In a way, I think his forgiveness was more painful to me than the incident itself. If he had caused my son to become horribly disfigured, I don't think I could have forgiven him.

"I was reduced in rank to Lieutenant Commander and stationed stateside – Norfolk."

Though no human possessed the words to give solace to this tormented man, Killian felt like he had to try. "Sir, I can't imagine what you're feeling, but I do know the Navy has seen fit to give you another command. You won't make the same mistake again. Besides, we are at war. Over fifty thousand American boys have died in Vietnam. They all had families. You couldn't possibly have known. Who knows how many lives you saved by ordering the launch? Think of the infantry and cavalry troops stationed around Haiphong. Think of the NVA who couldn't get Soviet supplies because of your attack."

"Joe, you're right about one thing," Rymes said, "You can't imagine."

* * *

Tarfaya Bay, Morocco

Gip's senses were heightened as he scanned the deck for any signs of movement or hiding places. There were none. The only sounds were the occasional seagull squawks and the incessant slamming together of the two boats. Drake broke the uncomfortable silence.

"Gip, you go aft and look for a hatch. I'm going down there." Drake pointed toward the hatch that had saved Jorge from the barrage of bullets. Drake hurried to the hatch, but stopped himself short of the entrance, counted to three, and flung himself into the unknown.

Gip jogged down the side of the pitching and yawing boat, holding his weapon above his head with both hands to maintain his balance. Even so, his finger was pressed against the trigger guard. His training was ingrained to the fine-muscle memory level. His fingers knew exactly what to do with a weapon without conscious thought. They maintained the shortest possible, safe speed-to-draw.

When he reached the aft, he hesitated for a second before he swung into the opening of the hatch, leading with the barrel of his weapon. His eye detected motion and notified his finger even before his brain. He automatically aimed center-mass and pulled the trigger, spraying his bullets in a spiral pattern. Although he had extensive training with fully automatic M-16's, the recoil of the Uzi took him by surprise. The 'rise and run' effect was greatly exaggerated in the eight-inch mini-gun. The bright light of the muzzle flash assaulted his eyes, momentarily blinding him. Bullets flew wildly, ricocheting throughout the corridor below. He involuntarily blinked and backed away from the hatch.

* * *

Drake leapt into the fore hatchway, ready to fire. Seeing nothing, he relieved the two pounds of pressure he was exerting on the five-pound trigger, and moved his finger back outside the trigger guard. The day was overcast, so his eyes adjusted easily to the darkness below. He cautiously crept down the steel steps, his eyes darting back, forth, up and down. He was in a hallway, with rooms looking like the crew's quarters along either side. Adrenaline coursed through his system as he began the repetitive drill of throwing himself gun first into each opening, never knowing if each lunge would be the last action of his life.

* * *

Gip leapt into the doorway of the aft hatch. He braced himself by holding the left railing as he slid down the steep stairs. He pointed his Uzi into the darkness as he descended. When he saw something that was not steel, he almost fired again, but caught himself in time. There were two bodies lying at the base of the stairs. *That's six down, two to go,* he thought. *I wish I could let Drake know. We should have brought radios.* Forgetting the radios was a typical rookie mistake, and Gip was ashamed. He didn't want to let the General down.

As he descended the stairs he realized that the number of targets still alive was irrelevant. They must search every square inch of the boat in any case. Who was to say there wasn't a mistake or an outright lie in the manifest? He saw motion again, but knew he couldn't fire upon just anything that moved anymore. Drake was somewhere down here with him. Gip's eyes were still spotty from the muzzle flash, putting him at something of a disadvantage.

"Drake!" he called out. If he didn't have an answer within a millisecond, his finger was ready to send half a magazine of lead down the corridor.

"Gip!" Drake shouted back.

"How many down?" Gip asked.

"Four above deck. I haven't seen anyone down here yet."

"I got two just inside the aft hatch."

"Okay, just two left. I'll go down first. From here on, we stick together," Drake said, indicating the hatchway that led to the cargo holds.

At the bottom of the ladder, they found themselves in another corridor much like the one on the crew deck, except this time the rooms on either side looked more like horse stalls, or prison cells. Each room was barred in front, with solid walls between. Drake and Gip stood back-to-back and crept along the passageway. The rooms were all filled with greenish yellow cargo.

"Bananas! Damn it! Drake, we're on the wrong boat!" Gip exclaimed.

"Let's discuss this after we clear the deck, Okay?" There was just the slightest hint of tension in Drake's voice.

There were twenty rooms on each side of the hallway. They moved cautiously, backs pressed together, forming a gun toting, four-legged spider. Each cargo hold they passed brought the threat of instant death. Gip heard his heart pounding in his ears. He had to hold the Uzi with both hands to steady it.

Near the middle of the corridor, the bananas in cargo hold fourteen began to explode in Drake's face. Gip, once again blinded by a muzzle flash - this time not his own - opened fire into hold fifteen across the hall. He didn't release the trigger until his magazine was empty. Once the Uzi had spent its leaden contents, he couldn't see a thing, but he didn't need his eyes to reload. Fearing a double flank ambush, Gip kept his attention on the starboard hold. After a couple of extremely long and worrisome seconds, Gip looked over his shoulder to see a Hispanic man lying in a pile of badly ruptured bananas. He was barely alive. Gip was blinking madly, trying to force the giant purple spot out of the center of his field of vision.

"In, let's go!" Drake whispered urgently.

Gip entered cargo hold fifteen and turned to face the door, a new clip already inserted, locked and loaded. Although his vision was impaired, he still detected motion, and he didn't have to worry about shooting Drake by accident. Anything he saw would immediately be on the receiving end of a steady stream of 9mm lead.

* * *

Drake removed Jorge's .45 automatic and placed it squarely in the center of the man's forehead. He was badly hit. His shirt was soaked in organ blood that looked black in the poor lighting. He made a constant gurgling sound, accompanied by the signature whistle of a sucking chest wound – a punctured lung. Without immediate attention, the man's remaining good lung would collapse, rendering him instantly mute and instantly useless.

Drake took the man's cigarette pack out of his breast pocket and removed the cellophane wrapper. He then forced the victim to sit up, causing excruciating agony as the air trapped in the wounded lung was forced out through the bullet hole. When Jorge was almost able to touch his toes, Drake pressed the cellophane against the hole, sealing the lung in an airless state. He allowed Jorge to sit back up. The suction would hold the cellophane in place long enough. This crude first aid would buy the man a few minutes of life - of talking.

"Where are the girls?" Drake asked. His face looked unusually pale in the lighting, accentuating the effect of coldness he emitted. The combination of stress, fear and pain had blessed Drake with a partial neurological shutdown. This self defense mechanism kept his mind functioning. In this stripped state, Drake's mind was devoid of emotion. No fear, no fatigue, no remorse.

"Go to hell!" Jorge replied in heavily accented English. He tried to spit in Drake's face, but he didn't have the wind.

"Drake, what if we got the wrong ship?" Gip asked over his shoulder.

"We don't have the wrong ship. Why was this asshole shooting at us? Huh?"

"Because we killed everyone else, Man! What would you do?" Gip said.

"Well, I think our new friend wants to tell us all about the girls. Hey asshole! Where did the bananas come from? Where are the girls? You know what I'm talking about!"

"Brazil," Jorge sighed.

"The girls are in Brazil?"

"The bananas... are from Brazil," Jorge replied between wheezes.

"Where are the girls?" Drake repeated, knowing he didn't have much time.

"What girls? We are delivering bananas... Why is the Harbor Patrol doing this?"

Drake had forgotten the uniforms and boat they had acquired from the newly rich Harbor Patrol team.

"We're not Harbor Patrol. We work for enormously powerful people who want those girls." As Drake spoke, he hovered his left index finger above a bullet wound in Jorge's thorax.

"Please don't hurt me. I don't know... what you are talking about."

"Wrong answer," Drake said icily as he inserted his finger into Jorge's liver up to the knuckle and began to wiggle it roughly.

Jorge did not respond. The dead seldom do.

* * *

After a thorough search of the rest of the boat, Drake and Gip had found no traces of the missing man or the girls. They checked the identifications on the seven bodies and concluded that Fejo had been the man they saw on the bridge and he had somehow escaped. No lifeboats were missing, however. If this Fejo swam through two miles of ten-foot seas, he was one tough son of a bitch. Most likely, he had drowned. What was most baffling was the absence of the girls. Had Felipe lied to them, causing them to murder seven innocent people? The ship's log showed nothing unusual. They did find one bit of potentially important information, a name and a place – Falon, Shaqra.

"Well?" Gip asked, "Where the hell are the girls?"

"I have no idea, but whatever Falon and Shaqra are, that's where we're headed. Let's get the hell out of here."

Chapter Twenty-One

Southern Morocco

Lupe's eyes opened to complete darkness. She blinked, hoping to jump-start her vision. It didn't work. As the chemically induced stupor wore off, she became aware of movement. But, there was something different about this movement. It was bumpy; not like the gentle motion of the ship where she had spent the last week. She also noticed she could not move her arms or legs. The scent of unwashed bodies and excreta was strong. When she tried to stand, she realized she was hog tied with ropes that bit into the soft flesh of her wrists and ankles. After a brief struggle, she decided staying put was the least painful option.

There were bodies on all sides of her, and she heard the deep breathing of many people. A jarring bump lifted her several inches off the floor, causing her head to land on another person's hipbone. *A truck*, she thought, *now I'm on a truck*. The impact of the bump woke many of the other girls, some of whom began screaming in Portuguese.

For a time period that seemed about a week, she had paced her small cell on the boat, wondering where she was being taken and for what purpose. She had overheard the other girls, dozens of them, frantically discussing their situation. Unfortunately, there wasn't an English-speaking girl within earshot of her cell. She had no idea whether her friends had befallen the same fate as she. If Susan and Becky had escaped the kidnappers, the authorities might already be searching for her. What authorities, though? No one knew where she was.

With no clock and no window, it was difficult for Lupe to mark the passage of time. She had slept when exhaustion asserted itself over her nervous tension. She had eaten when her would-be rapist gave her bread, cheese and water.

There was nothing to remind her of life as she knew it – not even toilet paper. She was in a world so alien that she shut down emotionally. Lupe simply stayed alive, one minute at a time.

A child of a US Congressman, she had enjoyed a pampered life, keeping her virginity until her freshman year at UCLA. Even then, she had dated Bobby for three months before they made love. That day was special to her, and she had planned to cherish it forever. It was the first time for both of them, an unusual occurrence in an era when free love was sweeping the nation. Now, she associated the act of lovemaking with filth. Even the word 'lovemaking' disgusted her. She had been reduced to living as an animal, knowing that at any moment she could find herself at the sexual whim of a mindless and brutal monster.

The language barrier had prevented her from communicating with the girls around her. Now, they were all in the same compartment. She drew a deep breath and called out. "Susan! Becky! It's Lupe! Are you here?"

At first, there was no response other than the foreign chirping of the thirty-five Brazilian girls. After an unbearable pause, she heard the first friendly sound in over a week.

"Lupe! It's Becky. Where are you?"

"I don't know. I'm tied up and it's dark. Can you see anything? Have you seen Susan?"

"I can't see anything. What the hell is happening? Where are we?"

"I don't know," Lupe shouted. Becky heard the tension in Lupe's voice.

Just then, Lupe's body was thrust toward the front of the trailer as the driver locked up the brakes. She rolled; banging her temple on the metal floor so hard she had to strain to maintain consciousness. The entire front of her head immediately exploded in pain. By the time the truck came to a halt, all thirty-eight girls were piled on top of each other in the front quarter of the trailer. Everyone seemed to be awake and screaming in panic. Lupe wasn't sure, but she thought her right arm had been dislocated in the process.

She gasped for air, but the closeness around her face and the weight of bodies on her torso impeded her breathing. She developed instant claustrophobia. If her limbs had not been bound, she could easily have thrown all the other girls into the air. As it was, she violently flexed every muscle in her body in vain. Her wrists and ankles screamed out in agony as she struggled. She felt consciousness slipping away from her.

Abruptly, the back doors opened, flooding the trailer with bright light. A man shouted something in Portuguese and many of the other girls became instantly quiet. The man repeated himself, punctuating his sentence with the cocking of his gun. The trailer became silent.

Although Lupe was blinded by the sudden invasion of light, she discerned the speaker and one other climbing into the back of the truck. They spent several minutes roughly jerking the girls out of their situation. One of the men grabbed Lupe by the rope binding her wrists and yanked her free of the pile. Her injured arm screamed in pain.

Although she had felt no emotions other than fear and rage in the past week, she felt a gushing sensation in her body and mind – the sensation of gratitude. She wanted to thank the man for so kindly restoring something she had taken for granted her entire life – the ability to breathe.

Lupe took in enormous gulps of air. In the harsh light she saw dozens of girls, all hog-tied as she was. The one man she was able to see was fat and vile, with a huge black mustache extended below his lower lip. She heard the other man utter a phrase that was neither English nor Portuguese - possibly Arabic. The fat one stood inside the doors as his accomplice closed him inside with them. Although Lupe didn't understand what he said next, she got the message loud and clear. The man's gun was a good communicator. There would be no more talking. She lay quiet, more confused and afraid than ever.

* * *

The Kechla Citadel, Northern Morocco

"Tartus, the shipment is secured in the cellar – thirty eight girls in all." Falon stroked his goatee as he spoke. As usual, he had handled all the details of meeting The Lady and the Tramp to extract the girls and fill the cargo hold with bananas. This subterfuge worked flawlessly, preventing any potentially dangerous encounters with Moroccan Customs. The girls were put to sleep and tightly bound before being transferred to Falon's private boat, while well-bribed Harbor Patrol agents looked the other way. He then took them to his personal pier and loaded them into the back of an eighteen wheeler. By the time the girls began to awaken, they were usually at least halfway to Safi.

Once there, they were moved to the catacombs below Tartus' citadel. Built during the Saadian Dynasty by the Portuguese, the Kechla citadel was enormous. Including the catacombs, there were over sixty thousand square feet in

Kechla. The dungeon itself could accommodate over one hundred guests. Tartus' three thousand acre tract of surrounding property ensured complete privacy, enough privacy that they did not bother using the chloroform. With an empty cell between each prisoner, Tartus did not worry about communication among his girls.

Clients were welcome to visit and view the goods. Buyers came from far and wide to acquire household servants, wives, slaves, prostitutes, and of course, stock for their harems.

"And what about the Americans?" Tartus asked, his voice casual. Falon knew Tartus had been eager to inspect the rare new product. Nearly all of his merchandise came from third world countries. The three American women would bring him a premium much higher than the other thirty-five combined. Falon figured Tartus had already pre sold King Fahr, who would certainly pay the most generous premium for such a treasure.

"They are safe and sound," Falon replied.

"I want to see them right away."

After descending the stone steps leading to the lower level, Falon led Tartus to the right. They walked in silence past the heavy wooden doors on either side, hearing but ignoring the cries of the women who pressed their faces to the narrow barred openings in each door. Near the end of the hallway, they walked through an area barren of occupants for perhaps twenty meters. Finally, they reached the three cells containing the most precious goods.

Falon was proud that he had done his job exceptionally. Not only were the American girls separated from the rest of the group, they were evenly spaced among twelve cells. This ensured no communication between them. Tartus had told him the greatest threat to submission was communication. If prisoners were allowed to talk to one another, they redeveloped something that the trans-Atlantic travel had squashed – hope. A human being without hope was as malleable as a lump of clay in a potter's hand, something to be molded to the desired shape.

When they reached Lupe's cell, Falon gestured for Tartus to look through the slit in the door.

* * *

When Tartus stuck his face in the slit, he was surprised to see a woman's face right before his. She screamed at him in English.

"You bastard! I'm an American citizen! You can't get away with this shit! My father will see you rot in jail."

Tartus involuntarily withdrew, not accustomed to such boldness in a prisoner. Her stunning beauty also took him aback. She was American, all right. She had jet-black hair, with large brown eyes, and had slightly Hispanic features. But, her race would not matter. She was obviously of the finest stock. Her look and manner screamed upper middle class America. *I'll have to renegotiate price with King Fahr for this one,* he thought.

"My Pretty, you will fetch me a fine bounty," Tartus said in English.

The American promptly spat in his face. Tartus paused for a moment, and then belly laughed.

"My Pet, you have just increased your sticker price two fold," he said with a mile wide grin on his face. His calm demeanor served simply to further enrage Lupe, who tried in vain to fit her hand through the tight bars to claw his brown face. Tartus chuckled and strolled to the next occupied cell.

This one cowered in the corner. Her golden hair was dingy and matted, but her beauty was undeniable. She sat with her knees held tightly to her chest. The girl wore no jewelry. No big surprise there, since Fejo's crewmen tended to have sticky fingers when it came to such things. Tartus did not mind the pilfering. It was part of the economics at that level.

She was obviously upper middle class American as well. Tartus could tell by the look in her eyes. Most of the Philippine and Brazilian girls had accepted their fate by this stage. This girl was in denial. Tartus saw the gears in her head turning, imagining some American knight in shining armor coming to her rescue.

The third cell contained a brunette, pacing wildly on bare feet. She did nothing to suggest she was even aware of Tartus' presence. Again, she smacked of America. Although her clothes were dingy, they were obviously expensive.

"Be sure to clean these three by morning. They are earmarked for a special client."

"As you wish, Tartus," Falon replied. Typically, the girls were sold in their natural state, as Tartus' normal clientele did not make a fuss over such things, their own personal hygiene leaving something to be desired.

Tartus heard the soft noise of sandal clad feet approaching, the leather soles grinding the ubiquitous sand into the stone floor. He looked to see Shahid, his head of security, walking hurriedly toward them.

"Sir, Fejo is here to see you. He says it's urgent."

"With Fejo, it's always urgent," Tartus replied. He had little patience for Fejo. "Tell him I'll meet him in the great hall."

"As you wish, Tartus."

* * *

When Tartus entered the great hall, he saw Fejo pacing nervously, waiting for him. He paused to soak in the glory of his favorite room. With forty-foot ceilings, the ground floor of his home was impressive, even to his most elite clientele. Richly restored sixteenth century tapestries covered the walls. On the east wall, there was a twelve-foot high fireplace with an authentic iron cauldron hanging idly above the carefully stacked logs.

"Tartus, we have trouble," Fejo opened, speaking in his native tongue of Portuguese.

"English, Fejo. Or have you forgotten?" When dealing with people of other cultures, Tartus preferred English as the common denominator. Virtually everyone he knew spoke at least passable English. This was more an industry standard and professional courtesy than a necessity. Tartus had a facility for languages, being conversant in eleven tongues. "Now, what is this about trouble?"

"My boat was taken. My crew is assumed dead."

"What?" Tartus asked in surprise. The disgusting but profitable little man had quite efficiently acquired Tartus' undivided attention.

"I barely escaped with my life."

"Slow down, and start from the beginning."

"We met Falon as planned, in international waters. The transfer of the merchandise was routine. But, when we approached Tarfaya, the Harbor Patrol intercepted us. It seemed to be a routine pass by or inspection. I was unconcerned at first. It's my job to have such men in my pocket, and I'm exceptionally good at my job.

"But when they were just about alongside, they opened fire and killed at least four of my crew in front of my eyes. They maneuvered to board my ship, and I was lucky to escape with my life. I didn't even have time to lower a lifeboat. I had to swim over two miles through ten-foot seas to reach the shore. I can tell you, I nearly drowned several times. I heard automatic weapons firing as I swam for my life. I must assume my crew was taken or murdered. What kind of savages would do such a thing?"

"Fejo, the first thing you need to do is calm down. Serenity always precedes success. The more pressure you feel, the more slowly you must act. My people have an ancient saying, 'Adversity introduces a man to himself.' So, Fejo, whom did you meet when your ship was under attack? A man of courage, or a good swimmer?"

"Tartus, you don't understand! If I hadn't escaped, there would be no one to warn you of this threat!"

"How many were there? How many men?" Tartus asked.

"Uh, two that I saw."

"Two men? Against how many in your crew? Eight? Ten? What kind of imbeciles do you hire?"

"Tartus, the crewmen are sailors, not soldiers. We've never encountered anything like this before," Fejo said.

"You know what I think? I think if you hadn't escaped, you might have killed the attackers and I wouldn't be facing a threat to a multi million dollar business." Tartus' face was growing red with frustration and rage. Fejo's incompetence had placed his entire operation at risk.

Falon had maneuvered behind Fejo and was awaiting a signal from his boss. He had seen such confrontations before, and he knew Tartus never raised his voice purely for show. Something ugly was about to happen.

Other staff members quietly appeared along the periphery of the great hall, their hands resting on their weapons. Most carried modern semi-automatic or automatic firearms, but a few still brandished traditional knives and short swords.

Tartus' men were well trained in the art of war, and any of them would die for him without hesitation. That willingness was the true measure of an army in Tartus' opinion. The choice of weapons was merely a detail.

"Tartus, I am not the enemy here! We must work together to find out what is going on. We don't know who these men are or what they are after."

"And how have your actions brought us closer to knowing these things?" Tartus had to remind himself not to kill the man. He had made this promise to himself. His jaw was tight, and his eyes squinted. He leaned progressively forward into Fejo's face.

He forced his entire body to relax a notch or two. He nodded at Falon, who immediately knew to restrain Fejo. There was little danger that the man was armed, as everyone was subjected to a thorough search before entering Tartus' home.

"What is this?" Fejo asked in bewilderment as his arms were pinned behind him. Fejo looked around wildly as at least six other men converged on him. "Tartus! I am your loyal servant. I can help you find these men. I, I'm the single living person who can identify them. Please!"

"Fejo, I will not kill you, not this day. But, you must be reminded of your failure to serve me properly. Since you have demonstrated you are a man who runs away from danger, I'm going to help you with this problem. I assure you - the next time you are under pressure - you will not run. You will, by necessity, remain and have to think or fight your way through it. This will make you stronger by making you weaker, so to speak. Falon, please cut both his Achilles tendons." This last part Tartus spoke in Arabic.

"No! Please!" Fejo screamed back in Arabic, not being totally ignorant of the tongue. But, Tartus was done talking, at least for now.

When the other men arrived, they roughly threw Fejo on the banquet table, face down. Two men lay across the backs of his legs while three others restrained his upper torso. Falon, renowned for his lack of emotion, calmly drew his knife and sliced the rear of each of Fejo's ankles to the bone. The man was hobbled for life.

Although the quantity of blood was terrifying to Fejo, it was by no means life threatening. No arteries had been severed. He would live to serve another day, but would never run again. In fact, he would walk only with great difficulty and the assistance of a cane for the balance of his life. Tartus smiled.

Chapter Twenty-Two

Special Agent Fulton wrung his hands in nervous tension. The Prometheus was nearly in place. Soon, he would have to set the plan into action. Although he knew his mission was pure and righteous, he still had the normal human doubts. Like all great men, he was not concerned about his game plan. He was worried about Murphy's Law. He remembered the courage and patriotism of his father during WWII. The man had stormed a hill infested with the enemy – an enemy hiding in caves. Fulton's enemy was flagrantly in the open, but somehow more elusive. The Gulf Six had raised the price of Saudi crude by an additional seventeen percent. The rat bastards actually had the gall to announce further production cuts on the heels of the price increase.

Fulton's homeland was threatened by a superpower more insidious than the goddamned Japs. These people were actually taking his country with the full knowledge and consent of the American public. Blue-blooded Americans were waiting in line for two hours to purchase gasoline.

Well, let the Arabs have their fun while it lasted. The Nixon administration would go down in history as the greatest leadership of the twentieth century. With Israel's government all but destroyed by Soviet missiles coming from the direction of Saudi Arabia, the US could justifiably bring down the hammer on the Saudis. Massive air attacks would take out most of the major cities within a few months, beginning with the capitol city of Riyadh, and the oilfields would be America's.

Fulton was calmed by the knowledge that his was a superior vision. He relished his morning coffee, knowing he would be one of the unsung heroes in

American history. In fact, anonymity was something of a comfort to him. Nixon had the tough job. He didn't have the liberty of short cutting the system for the greater good. That was the job of the CIA. That was the job of Special Agent Robert Fulton.

* * *

The Prometheus

"Three more days," Rymes said to Killian. It was the morning of March 15th, and both men knew the waiting was almost over.

"Still got the jitters?" Killian asked.

Rymes simply stared at Killian through bloodshot, sleep-deprived eyes. He was exhausted from stress, and was afraid his judgment was impaired.

"Sir, all this worrying won't help. We need you at your best on the eighteenth," Killian said.

"Joe, I know you mean well, but trust me when I tell you to back off this issue." Rymes was curter than he intended to be, but he was struggling just to hold himself together.

"Skipper, I'm only trying to help. If you need anything, to talk, anything, you know where to find me."

"Thanks, Joe. I don't mean to be harsh, but men's lives are on the line here."

"Well, they couldn't be in better hands. I don't think you realize how rare compassion is in a commander."

"Again, thanks. Now go make your rounds. I want every circuit checked and double checked."

"Aye Sir," Killian said as he turned on his heel and headed down below deck.

* * *

Safi, Morocco

"So, did you find out?" Drake asked. Gip had been working the slums of Tarfaya in search of this Falon. Drake had expected him several hours earlier.

"What do you think, Man? Why would I come back without the answer? Falon is known to frequent a bar on the northern side of Safi – a real shithole, from what I hear, called Shaqra."

"So, that's it, huh? Let's just hope we have better luck than Sierras One and Two did," Drake said.

"Hope? Luck? Shit, man, we need better than that. What we need is to avoid the mistakes those other dudes made."

"We're not taking their approach," Drake said.

"I know that. What I don't know is what approach we *are* taking."

"I'm telling you, I've got it worked out in broad strokes. First, we go to Shaqra and find Falon.

"That's your plan?"

"That's the plan, until I hear a better idea. The way I figure it, we don't have more than a few days to find Lupe and her friends. If it takes much longer, they will already have been sold. I get the feeling that in this business, speed is essential."

"Hey," Gip said, changing the subject, "I've got to ask you something. I saw the way you iced Felipe, and I saw the way you dealt with that guy on the boat. I know you put on this stone cold act, but this almost seems personal to you. You're even calling the girl by her first name – someone you've never even met."

"Gip, have you ever been in love?"

"I've been in love plenty of times. Never for more than one night, though." Gip chuckled.

"What if Lupe was the girl you loved?"

"But she's not. That's the point."

"But someone does love her. That's the point."

"You know, for a cold blooded killer, you sure have a big heart. I mean I'm standing next to a man who can torture someone to death in the morning, then turn around and refuse to eat meat for lunch cause it's inhumane. What's up with that?"

"Like I said, the cow never pissed me off."

"Yea, well if I'm ever about to piss you off, do me a favor and let me know before you go pulling out my fingernails with some rusty old pliers." Gip grinned.

"Deal. Now let's find this Falon."

Chapter Twenty-Three

Shaqra

Initially, Drake had thought sparse clothing, such as the khaki shorts and short-sleeved white shirts worn by tourists, would beat the heat. But it hadn't taken him long to adopt the maximum coverage philosophy of the natives. The sun, sand and wind were brutal, and could sap the strength out of even a deep-south boy like Drake. They were traveling down a comically dusty road in the back of a taxi, just north of Safi, Morocco.

After the taxi dropped them off, Drake and Gip assessed their surroundings. They were in an ancient wooden building, with sagging eaves. The roof looked on the verge of collapse. They were in a remote section of Safi, where the streets were notably devoid of the vendors and beggars so typical in this strange country. The lack of traffic did have one major negative effect. The earth was not packed down. Sand bit into their faces and hands, carried by a perpetual cross wind.

Drake opened the door, and the contrast between the blinding sun outside and the pitch darkness within made the doorway resemble a porthole into another universe. He and Gip stepped inside. When the door closed behind them, they were momentarily incapable of seeing anything other than what Drake's mother called 'sun spots'.

They stood there for the better part of a minute, each pretending to be surveying the place, while they were actually praying their retinas had not been scorched beyond repair by the West African glare. As their eyes adjusted, they saw perhaps twenty or twenty-five customers, scattered throughout a two hundred seat bar. One bartender lazily read a magazine, apparently unconcerned about his clientele. The patrons did not seem to care. They had the look of men who valued privacy. Drake noticed the occupants were all men. Perhaps this was the Moroccan version of a gentleman's club. The principal difference was that, instead of exploiting women as their American counterparts did - gawking at naked specimens, the Moroccans excluded them entirely. Drake reminded himself that he was in a different culture, one he'd better learn quickly unless he wanted it to be the last he ever saw.

They took a table on the periphery, careful not to invade anyone's personal space. They were fifteen meters from the closest occupied table. The other patrons seemed to take no notice of them.

"Well, what do we do now?" Drake asked.

"We wait," Gip answered.

After fifteen uncomfortable minutes, a man appeared. He was not the bartender, and Drake had no idea where he came from.

"Do you speak English?" Gip asked.

"Of course. What are you gentlemen drinking today?"

Drake had to conceal his surprise at the waiter's sophistication. If Arabic speaking people dropped into a redneck bar in the States, would they be greeted in their native tongue?

"Bourbon," Gip said.

When the man returned, he placed an unopened bottle of Jack Daniels and two glasses on the table. No ice. Drake had to restrain himself not to treat him as an American, who would without delay have helped them find Falon for a generous tip. After receiving a more than generous tip in American dollars, the man left without a word.

"Man, why didn't you pump him for information?" Gip asked.

"Yea, that works. Two strangers show up and inquire about the local crime kingpin. Why didn't I think of that?" Drake smacked his own forehead with the palm of his hand.

* * *

After two days of nursing glasses of bourbon, Drake and Gip were getting bored. Against every instinct Drake had, he kept his mouth shut. They simply walked in and ordered their bottle and nursed it as long as possible, making small talk about sports and old girlfriends. At ten fifteen p.m. on the second day, the break they were looking for occurred.

A man they had not seen before entered. Unlike Drake and Gip, his eyes seemed to adjust from the piercing light of Safi to the dismal lighting of Shaqra in seconds. He didn't hesitate in the doorway like most did. He had the rough look of the desert. His skin was weather beaten and taunt. He was lean beyond American standards. His black eyes scanned the bar slowly. Drake saw the muscles in the man's jaw flexing as he assessed his environment. The stranger's eyes scanned the room and came to rest on a scruffy looking group of men on the opposite side of the bar from Drake and Gip. One of the men at the table called out, "Falon! Over here."

Drake instantly knew they would save Lupe. On some level, Drake had convinced himself that saving Lupe would in some way balance the cosmic scorecard. He didn't distinguish between the two women – the one he loved, and the one he had never met. Falon personified Drake's childhood friends who had so thoroughly betrayed him. Bad guys were bad guys. They all must pay. His moral confusion was behind him. He felt nothing but icy rage.

The two of them sat for several more hours, nervous but patient, knowing their moment to shine was at hand. Falon was in an animated story about God knows what for what seemed like eternity. Finally, Falon stood to leave. Drake's heart quickened, knowing the mundane task of waiting had come to an end. His actions over the next hour would decide the success or failure of the mission. He could not fail. He owed Tammy that much. He owed the dove that much. *Game time.*

* * *

Safi, Morocco

Falon put a teapot on the burner and filled his steeping spoon with his favorite Moroccan mint tea. As he sat, he exhaled, surveying his Spartan apartment out of habit. In his line of work, there was no such thing as excessive caution. Nothing seemed to be out of place.

He kicked his sandals off and extracted his .45 automatic from its holster in the small of his back. The damned thing itched incessantly, and he was glad to be rid of it. He held it before his face and looked at the weapon. The smell of gun oil and the weight of the weapon were pleasantly familiar to him. He gently placed it on the coffee table directly in front of him.

Allowing himself to relax, Falon focused on each muscle group in his body, beginning at the soles of his feet and working his way upward. Clarity of thought was slow in coming, but eventually arrived. His mind was a vessel completely devoid of content - no stress, no worries, no thought. His eyes, though open, were unfocused and unmoving. He maintained this meditative state for ten minutes, then stood to stretch.

He reviewed the day's events. Someone had taken Fejo's boat, killing all hands on board. So, they were serious. Just two men to take eight? How was such a thing possible? Even if they surprised the crew, surely someone had been left to retaliate. And what was this business with the Harbor Patrol? Falon knew the HP granted him certain liberties, such as turning a blind eye to his comings and goings for a generous donation. But who would assist in murder and hijacking? Piracy was a capital offense in Morocco.

Whoever these men were, they were exceptionally powerful. They had either the boldness to kill the HP officers, or the money to bribe them. And it would take some serious cash to interest government officials in a beheading offense. This whole thing smacked of American agents. Was this related to the American Tartus had killed a few months ago? Of course, there was no evidence that the man had been American, much less an agent. Still, who else would have the effrontery to expect immediate entrance into Tartus' enterprises? Every question begged more questions.

He finally decided that trying to solve this mystery by sitting alone asking himself questions was like battling the mythical Hydra. For every head he chopped off, two more appeared. Falon heard the telltale chirp his clock made upon each hour. Six o'clock. He unrolled his mat toward the east and knelt. He gently placed his palms and his forehead on the mat and closed his eyes in prayer.

If Falon had opened his eyes just then, he might have seen the eye peering back at him from beneath his door. As it was, he was fortunate in one sense – he was at peace with his maker.

Falon was shaken out of his trance by the concussion of his door being kicked in. He jumped to his feet with catlike speed just in time to receive Drake's powerhouse blow to his jaw.

When Falon awoke, the first thing he noticed was the array of wires cutting into the bridge of his nose. The next thing he noticed was his nudity. His jaw screamed in pain and he felt it swelling already. It felt broken. When he tried to open his mouth, he realized it was taped shut. *Oh Shit*, he thought, *this isn't good*. He took inventory of his parts and concluded they were all still attached, albeit uncomfortably restrained. He recognized the floor of his apartment, but he didn't remember it being this dusty. As he strained to see his periphery, his situation became clearer.

He was tied to his own bed frame – nude, spread eagle, facing the floor. The bondage and the broken jaw did not inspire optimism. What Falon saw next caused his bowels to void involuntarily. His teapot was sitting on his hotplate beneath his stomach. The spout pointed toward his crotch. He saw the burner was turned off for now.

"How'd you know he was going to do that?" He heard two men having a conversation in English. "Pray like that? I mean, it's not like the guy's a model citizen."

"Know your enemy, Gip." This was a different voice. *The deeper voice belongs to Gip,* Falon thought. "Religion is different for these people than it is for Americans. Everybody prays five times a day, facing Mecca. Even scum like this."

"I think he's awake," Gip said.

"Yea, I bet he's ready for a little pow-wow," the other man answered." The speaker, who Falon nicknamed 'Boots', chambered a round and placed his pistol against Falon's temple.

Falon's mind rushed through every conceivable way he might survive this experience and came up with naught. A firm believer in Allah, he was not afraid to die. He was willing and able to accept certain death. Within a few seconds, Falon was at peace with his imminent mortality.

What he could not come to terms with was the possibility that these men may let him live. There was no glory in being tortured, broken, disgraced and left alive to occupy a mutilated body for the rest of his life. The spout of the teapot was just a few inches from his exposed manhood.

Boots appeared before his eyes. Although he strained, he could not see anything above his captor's knees. Not knowing the face of his enemy was painfully disconcerting. If he could just get a glimpse of the man's eyes, he would be able to see his fate in them.

"Falon, we need to talk," said Boots. Just as Boots spoke, a black hand reached from the side and ripped the tape from his mouth. *So Gip is black,* Falon thought. Falon saw two options: he could remain quiet and let the men do what they would, or he could taunt them, provoking them into killing him.

The quiet and relaxed demeanor of the man in boots suggested the coldness of a professional – a man who had spent years perfecting his technique. This man would not lose his temper. Silence was said to be the best response to give a professional interrogator. That would be Falon's approach to this predicament, which, Allah willing, would be his last.

"Not feeling chatty, huh? But of course, where are my manners? It's impolite to rush the conversation before we enjoy a treat. Would you care for some tea?" Boots kept his voice level. This man was trained and sadistic – definitely elite military. When Falon did not answer, Boots added, "It's no trouble. I was preparing to make some anyway. Perhaps you'll change your mind. Meanwhile, you just relax and don't worry about making conversation."

Gip returned the tape across Falon's mouth. Falon saw Gip reach down and activate the burner below the teapot. Sweat stung his eyes as he closed them tightly to pray for a swift death and the strength to remain silent. The seconds stretched into minutes. Neither Boots nor Gip said a word.

The heat from the burner itself was already causing Falon's stomach to redden as it rose in a column. Although it hurt, he knew this was nothing compared to what lay ahead. As the teapot began to announce its impending boil, Black Man ripped the tape off again.

"Pardon me for asking," Boots said, "But, would you like to have a talk and forget about the tea? I seem to have lost my thirst." Gip stood out of sight, never speaking as he carried out Boots' instructions. These men were definitely professionals, and Falon had met enough professionals in his life to know they always got what they wanted.

Sweat now gushed down Falon's face, rhythmically dripping off his nose into the forming puddle below. His midsection was beginning to blister. But, worst of all, he heard the intermittent whistle of the teapot. Within seconds he would be experiencing pain like he had never known. With each noise, the teapot spat a preview of coming attractions into Falon's groin. He closed his eyes and tried to disappear.

"You know, upon further consideration, I believe I *would* like some hot tea. We'll have to continue this conversation later," Boots said. His mockingly cheerful tone unnerved Falon. Gip replaced the tape.

The pain came. It was unlike anything Falon could have imagined. Falon convulsed so violently from the agony that Gip kept the .45 locked, loaded and pointed at Falon's head at all times. Duct tape is strong, but so is torture.

"Okay, turn the burner off," Boots said.

Gip reached below the bed frame and switched off the heating element. The steam gradually lost its force and the awful whistling faded into silence.

Falon's writhing continued for several minutes, but eventually he lay still. He was covered in sweat. In addition to his burn wounds, his ankles and wrists were beginning to bleed from his exertion against his bonds. His face was lacerated from jerking his head back and forth against the wire mesh of the bed frame. What appeared to be the tip of Falon's nose was lying beneath him. He was exhausted and on the brink of shock.

Boots walked to the head of the bed frame. He would not let Falon see his face. This technique provided a psychological advantage to the interrogator. Let the victim wonder who his captors were. Let him imagine a face for the monster that controlled his fate. Although his breathing was still erratic, he was beginning to calm.

"So, my friend. I hope you have enjoyed your tea," Boots quipped. "I wonder if you'd like to have a chat. If I enjoy our conversation, I can promise you a swift ending to this messy ordeal. However, if you scream or refuse to answer any of my questions, the tape goes back on, and it will be some time before you get another chance. Nod if you understand."

Falon nodded weakly. Gip violently jerked the tape from Falon's mouth. Although he gasped for air and hissed at the pain, Falon did not scream.

"Let me explain the situation," Boots said, his voice shifting from convivial to metallic. "We have enough first aid supplies to keep you alive for at least a week. And, although there is plenty more fun we can have with the teapot, there are many other techniques I'd like to explore, just for practice. One must always hone one's skills, wouldn't you agree?"

After a few seconds, Falon responded, "Yes."

Boots continued, "If you don't tell me exactly what I want to know - if I don't believe every word - I promise you'll die like no other man ever has. Do you understand?"

"Yes, I understand," Falon replied in excellent English. He was in complete submission. The pain reset his brain, just like restarting a computer. When his mind came back online, it was stripped to the barest of instincts. Rational thought was impossible.

"Where are the girls?" Boots asked.

"What girls?" Falon said.

"Replace the tape, and turn the burner back on. This time, point it at his face. If he can't talk after that, he'll just have to write the answers on a pad," Boots said.

Falon's world had become amazingly simple. He knew only one thing – he must die. He acted accordingly.

"No! Please, I didn't understand. You mean Tartus' girls? I know where he has them! He lives in an old citadel east of town. It's called Kechla. The girls are in the catacombs below. They will be moved out over the next week or so. Is this what you want to know?" Falon knew uttering Tartus' name meant his death, but by then he was more afraid of living than dying - much more.

Mentally and physically broken, he began to resent Tartus, the man who had been his benefactor for almost twenty years. If it weren't for Tartus, he would not be undergoing such horrible torture. He had tortured and killed many in his career, but he was sure he had never inflicted such pain on another.

"Good," Boots said. "Now, I want to know exactly where every road to Kechla is, what it's defenses are and how many men Tartus has. Start talking if you want to meet your maker in one piece."

Falon talked, but not without occasional persuasion. His last conscious thought was sincere regret that he had let his kitchen knives become so dull.

Chapter Twenty-Four

Safi, Morocco

Drake and Gip paused in awe just inside the entrance to the Safi Museum of National History. The ceilings were practically a hundred feet high. From outside, they had assumed this was a five-story building, but it had just one expansive floor. The walls were granite, with every square inch covered with ornate carvings, sculpted directly into the walls. Most of the themes seemed to be religious or historical in nature. Centuries, even millennia of culture were depicted in painstaking detail in an architectural and artistic endeavor beyond the imagination of the western mind. The Sistine Chapel was a kindergarten finger painting in comparison. Near the rear wall, a curator sat quietly safeguarding a trove of historical documents Gip had hoped would help them.

"Okay, here we are. Now do you want to explain what we can learn in a place where all the books are in Arabic?" Drake asked.

"We don't have to read, we're looking for a picture. Look, Tartus lives in a historical monument. We ought to be able to find pictures or even a floor plan for this Kechla citadel. I mean, this is a stone structure we're talking about. I'm sure Tartus had done some remodeling, but I doubt he has moved any walls," Gip spoke in a hurried whisper.

"Gip, we might just live through this in spite of ourselves," Drake joked.

"I wouldn't make any long-term plans just yet."

The curator did not speak English. They were, however, able to communicate their interest by repeating the word 'Kechla'. After ten minutes, he returned with six dusty, leather bound books. They divided them and began to scan for pictures. After just over an hour, Drake found it – an artist's version of Kechla and the surrounding landscape. There were even detailed drawings of the interior. After studying them for a few minutes, he turned the book toward Gip and said, "Look, about fifty meters south of the main entrance, there is a plateau. It looks to be much wider than the building and faces the entrance. Now, look to the east. There's a hill. If you took position on the south ridge and laid down sniper fire, I could catch the reinforcements in a crossfire from the east." Drake was building enthusiasm. He'd already eliminated the probability of failure, an ability that distinguished between good soldiers and great warriors.

"Okay, that will take care of the outside guards, but you can bet your ass some will remain in the citadel to protect Tartus and the girls. How do we get in?"

"Look here," Drake said, tapping the picture, "See the aqueduct? According to this drawing, it runs right beneath the catacombs."

"How do we know it hasn't been sealed off?"

"We'll need more than a little luck. We'll also need sniper rifles with baffles to reduce sound and muzzle flash, plenty of ammo, small arms, grenades, claymores and a way to get the girls to the US Embassy in Rabat. That's approximately three hundred miles north of Kechla. How long will it take you to round this up?"

"If the two of us are planning to take a fortress guarded by twenty-five-plus heavily armed men, we're gonna need one helluva plan. Sounds like you've given it some thought."

"We've always known it was just the two of us. You and I are a Hail Mary pass being thrown by General Dalton. But, I'll tell you this, there were many points in the American Revolution where the course of the war changed due to Hail Mary passes thrown by the rebels. America specializes in long shots. I'm telling you, with these supplies, you and I can take this place. How long to round them up?"

"Well, I can have the firearms and silencers by nightfall today. This place is crawling with Soviet AK-47's. I tell you, the US could learn from those Ruskies. Their general-purpose rifles are among the best sniper weapons in the world. Grenades shouldn't be a problem, as long as we can make do with WWII surplus frags with ten second fuses. The truck will be a piece of cake. For indoor small arms, I'm pretty sure I can scrounge up a couple of M16's with M203 grenade launchers attached.

"As for the claymores, there are two options – we can raid a US or Royal Moroccan military base, or we can make them. I suggest we make our own. You'd be surprised how easy it is."

"You can make claymores?" Drake asked, raising one eyebrow.

"Sure! It's not much different from making pound cake. But, you don't want to be around if the cake falls, if you know what I mean." Gip smirked. "With the proper training, anyone can manufacture C-4 from commonly available items. It's a little tricky, but once it's finished, C-4 is surprisingly stable. We'll use a nine-volt current to ignite Potassium Chlorate - easily obtained from match heads. That primer explosion will ignite the picric acid blasting cap. It's the picric acid explosion that actually sets off the C-4." Gip became animated as he realized he would actually get to use his munitions training.

"Write this down," Gip continued, "Go to a hardware store and look at the camping stoves. They're powered by Hexamine tablets. Buy as many tablets as you can. While you're there, buy three gallons of battery acid refills. You'll find them in the automotive section.

"In the lawn and garden section, load up on saltpeter, at least ten pounds. Also, buy all their steel ball bearings smaller than a half-inch diameter. If you don't get at least fifty pounds, you'll have to shop around.

"We'll also need about two hundred yards of two-way insulated copper wire and fifty of the simplest switches they have. And we'll need fifty nine-volt batteries and all the matches they have.

"Stop by as many drug stores as it takes to get a half pound of aspirin and twenty-five pounds of Vaseline. I know liquor stores are hard to find in an Arabic country, but we'll need at least five gallons of grain alcohol.

"Finally, we'll need fifty one-liter soda bottles. You got all that?"

"Anything else?" Drake asked sarcastically.

"Yea, four of the largest glass bottles you can find – with corks- and six feet of plastic or rubber tubing, two shallow buckets and several bags of ice. I guess add a cooler to the list also."

"I think it would be easier to raid a military base."

"No way, man. Once you get the supplies, we'll have fifty commercial grade claymores with a combined weight of about a hundred fifty pounds within six hours. It'd take a hell of a lot longer than that to plan and carry out a raid on a military base, especially if we have to use non-lethal force. You would use non-lethal force on friendlies, wouldn't you?"

"No, I wouldn't," Drake replied.

"Yea, you're a real softie." Gip sneered, then added, "While you're shopping for all that stuff, I'll pay a visit to some rough looking mercenaries I saw hanging out downtown. These guys are always preparing for a rebellion, and they need cash. I'll pay them enough to replenish what they sell me with plenty to spare for other supplies. Weapons are necessary for a rebellion, but bullets don't sooth empty stomachs."

"Okay. You're the man. I'll meet you back at our room as soon as I can," Drake said, surreptitiously pulling several bunches of hundred dollar bills out of the satchel before handing the rest to Gip. They made hand copies of the pertinent drawings and returned the books to the curator.

* * *

Safi, Morocco

Gip enjoyed playing with his new chemistry set. Using two glass bottles, some tubing and an ice bucket, Gip had constructed what appeared to be a miniature still. Red fumes from the first bottle distilled into a pink liquid as they passed through a cooling coil. The second bottle was filling at a painstakingly slow rate.

"How much longer?" Drake asked, the frustration evident in his voice.

"Look, Man," Gip said, "You might as well relax. It's not like we're going in as soon as I finish. We're going in after dark, which doesn't hit around here until about ten o'clock," Gip answered.

"I know. I know. I just hate waiting."

"You don't say?" Gip's joke was wasted on Drake. "Earlier, I told you C-4 was a relatively stable compound, but the intermediate stages are not. If I let the temperature of the nitrator get above 55 Celsius, there's going to be a crater where this hotel previously stood. So, you think you can give me a little space?"

"I'm going for a walk," Drake said, taking his partner's advice. He closed the door gently behind him. As he walked the streets of Safi, he struggled with his actions during Falon's interrogation. It wasn't so much his actions that disturbed him, but his feelings about them. In Falon, he had seen all the injustices in the world concentrated into one container of flesh. For each nerve ending Drake activated, a wrong seemed to be righted. But, that damned dove would not leave him alone. Drake knew he was on the wrong path. He could be a professional soldier, even if it meant being a professional killer, but if he began to derive enjoyment and self-satisfaction from torturing, he would despise himself forever. Somehow, he had to come to peace with Tammy's rape, his murder of his friends and his hatred of his father. He knew the answer to that trinity of anguish was right in front of him, but he was blinded to it by the details. He needed a broader perspective.

When he quit trying so hard, he caught a glimpse of a solution in his mind, but it evaporated as quickly as it appeared. The answer was formless and hidden in shadows, but it did exist – Drake felt that.

He would find the answer, but first he had an impossible mission to execute. He turned his thoughts to the details of the Kechla Citadel. Every fortress ever built has weaknesses. Every castle had a back door. Drake's mind painstakingly walked through the attack again and again, each time adding a level of detail.

* * *

Two hours later, when he had finished the nitration process, Gip collected the pink crystals of Cyclonite and gently kneaded them into a bowl of Vaseline. His brow was prominent with sweat, stinging his eyes, but he didn't dare make any unnecessary movement at this stage. *If Drake walks through that door right now, I could flinch and kill us both*, he thought. But Drake did not interrupt him. The home recipe C-4 was a viscous, pinkish paste. He made an amalgam of the paste and ball bearings, a viscous mixture he then worked into the soda bottles. Once he was satisfied with the stability of the bottles, he began the dangerous and delicate process of manufacturing the blasting caps. Gip was just collecting the newly created yellowish-orange picric acid crystals when his partner returned.

"How's it going?" Drake's robes were drenched from exertion. He rubbed a bright pink cheek with his forearm.

"I'm just about to finish the blasting caps. At this point, if I screw up, it'll just mean a couple of fingers." Gip did not look away from his task as he spoke.

"I don't know why anyone would want to do that for a living."

"Hey, nobody ever said being a Ranger was easy. In fact, they were pretty emphatic that it wasn't. Besides, munitions are only dangerous if you make a mistake."

"That's one big if!" Drake laughed.

* * *

The Kechla Citadel

Drake's face was blacker than the night. Even Gip, whose skin was naturally black, wore face paint to prevent glare. The quarter moon was about thirty degrees above the horizon. The surrounding landscape was rocky, but barren of plants.

The Kechla Citadel was a massive stone structure, about sixty feet tall and roughly two hundred feet on a side. It had cross shaped windows, eight on each face, providing excellent cover while affording both vertical and horizontal freedom of aim. A four-foot wall encircled the roof. There were two entrances, both heavy steel doors – a large one on the north face and a smaller one to the south.

Drake took position among the rocks lining the ridge just beyond the southern entrance to Kechla. Gip took the north side. The rock formations were populous and large, providing ample cover and concealment. Drake was surprised that a solitary guard patrolled the outer perimeter. But then, when was the last time anyone had been foolish enough to attempt a direct assault on the most powerful man in Morocco, who by the way was housed in a stone citadel?

The outer guard meandered in a giant circle around the compound. Six guards walked a pattern that hugged the walls of the citadel. All carried AK-47s and hand held radios, but only the outer perimeter guard regularly spoke into his. Drake and Gip watched and waited, each taking copious notes. Dawn was scheduled for 6:13 the following morning. At 5:30, they each began the three kilometer trek back to their hidden vehicle.

* * *

Back in their room, Drake and Gip spent two hours comparing observations. "Okay, for the southern face, we've got a six minute window every hour. To the north, we've got the same gap, occurring three minutes after the southern window. Agreed?" Drake said.

"Yea. It's not much, but it's better than nothing."

"As long as we know what we're dealing with, we can plan around the gaps, no matter how small they are. How long will it take to plant the claymores?" Drake asked.

"At least a half hour total per side, maybe more."

"All right, that's five cycles total, maybe six. If we work independently, we should have plenty of time."

"Oh yea, plenty!" Gip said, rolling his eyes. "All we have to do is penetrate the guard cycle about a dozen times, completely undetected. All for the privilege of going up against as many as thirty heavily armed men holed up in a castle. What could go wrong?"

"We'll just have to avoid making mistakes."

"You know, your talent for fighting is exceeded only by your talent for understatement." Gip chuckled.

Drake and Gip devoted the rest of the day to sleep. To perform at their optimum, they needed their biological cycles to be nocturnal.

* * *

The Kechla Citadel

The following night, Gip parked in the blind spot three kilometers away from Kechla. A huge sand dune blocked the truck from the citadel's view. Both men were grateful for their training as they hoisted two seventy-five pound satchels of claymores across the desert night. That bivouac they had hated so much was actually paying off. So were the thousands of push ups and hundreds of miles humped in full gear. The loose sand made it difficult to walk and more difficult to maintain balance. It took forty-five minutes to reach Kechla. This time, they easily avoided the outer guard, knowing his cycle precisely.

"Okay, we both know the time table. Let's make the best of it," Drake said. "You take the south. I'll take the north."

"You got it boss," Gip replied.

"Let's move out."

As Drake circled to the east, Gip began his descent toward the citadel. According to Falon, there were six guards who patrolled the immediate perimeter, the one guard on outer perimeter, and an additional twenty or more inside. So far, Falon appeared to have told them the truth. Gip moved slowly, especially mindful of his footing. One loose rock could bring this mission to a catastrophic halt.

Properly positioned, claymore mines are extremely effective. Packed with steel ball bearings, each charge has a death zone in the shape of a hemisphere fifteen meters in radius. The most useful property of explosives is that in the first few milliseconds of the explosion, they are quite easy to direct. A well-placed couple of rocks or steel plate could focus the explosive blast extremely effectively.

The ground cover ended approximately ten meters from the citadel, making Gip's job tougher. Aside from his brilliant white eyes, starkly contrasting the blackness of night, he was invisible. He waited through the cycle of the guards, frequently checking his watch. Seconds after the inner guard rounded the southeast corner, he moved in. Even in the cool night air, sweat broke on his brow. No wind, that was good, but that also meant no air conditioning.

Gip crept down and planted the first claymore. The door was in the kill zone, but was at the edge of its range. He would have to do better. His objective was to cover the entire south side with overlapping kill zones. He crept. Each step brought the danger of slippery sand or an unexpected rock, either of which could trip him and bring six armed Arabs running.

As he was planting the third mine, a guard appeared right on schedule. Gip knew he was coming, but thought he could get one more planted before it was too late. He was wrong. He froze in a crouching position. The guard looked directly at him. Gip narrowed his eyes to a slit, hoping to be invisible. As dark as the night was, his eyes were completely adjusted and he saw clearly. He knew the situation was the same for the guard. The guard's weapon hung from his shoulder. By chance or purpose, the gun was pointed directly at Gip.

Gip ran through his options. They were pretty slim. He could wait, hoping not to be shot, or he could draw his weapon and shoot the guard, most likely blowing the entire mission, even though the shot would be silenced. He decided to wait. Ice water exuded from his pores, covering his bald head with beads Gip hoped would not reflect the dim moonlight. The guard reached into his breast pocket and removed an object. Gip could not tell what it was in the darkness, but he had a pretty good idea it was a radio. His finger tightened imperceptibly on the trigger of his Glock .45. He moved the barrel slowly toward the guard. Seconds later the knotted cords in his stomach loosened when the man lit a cigarette. The guard resumed his rounds. A chilly wave of relief washed over Gip's body. He allowed himself a silent sigh. He noticed his hands were shaking. *That was too close. No more cutting corners.* By the end of the sixth guard cycle, Gip had buried the final mine.

* * *

On the north side, Drake watched patiently as the guards carried out their cycle. There was a small and obviously little used door that would have to be dealt with. Drake carefully worked his way down to the edge of the rock line and planted the claymores, covering each with copious amounts of sand. Only once did a guard almost catch him unaware. The man rounded the corner thirty seconds ahead of schedule. Drake quietly and slowly lay on his stomach in front of a rock formation that he hoped would break his silhouette. It did.

Drake was particularly interested in the aqueduct. Seventy-five meters north of the citadel was a grating that, according to the drawings in the library, led into the main waterway. There was an underground stream that for five centuries had supplied water to Kechla. The drawings showed water wheels in the catacombs that worked a complicated series of gears, rendering it as self-sufficient today as it was during medieval times. Tartus had chosen his home wisely.

When the guard had passed, he moved north to examine the aqueduct grating. The grating was made of heavy, rusted iron. The metalwork was crude, with the look of medieval craftsmanship. If this grating were five hundred years old, it would be impossible for Drake to pry open. Nonetheless, he knew exactly what he would need for tomorrow night's mission. He began to feel that the two of them just might make it.

* * *

Gip lay in bed restless. Trying to sleep in the middle of the day had never been easy for him. Drake had dozed off in seconds. The deuce-and-a-quarter truck was parked outside their hotel room, complements of the local mercenaries. Gip suspected he had paid slightly more than sticker price for the truck, but that didn't matter to Uncle Sam. For night sniping, he wasn't able to get the AK-47's but got a great deal on two Heckler and Koch MSG-90's, each with special baffling to reduce noise and muzzle flash. For close quarter fighting, they had two American M-16s with M-203 attachments to augment their Glocks. Surprisingly, the most difficult item to find was the blowtorch Drake needed to cut through the grating to the aqueduct. Gip found it ironic that their entire plan could have been foiled because the local hardware store had run out of blowtorches. Luckily, a downtown construction site was quite happy to donate to the cause at a five-finger discount.

Chapter Twenty-Five

The Kechla Citadel

Drake and Gip arrived at Kechla at just past twenty three hundred hours that night. They had parked the truck in the pre-arranged spot and walked from there. The citadel looked just as it had the previous night. Apparently, their claymores had not been discovered. Gip waited until the first gap in the guard rotation, and then he scrambled down and cut the phone line. Gip took position off the southwest corner.

* * *

Drake chose a spot just east of the southeast corner, giving him a clear line of fire into the southern and eastern sides of the compound.

When the outer perimeter guard rounded the corner, Drake jumped from behind a rock and thrust a bayonet at an upward angle just below the guard's right shoulder blade. This technique punctured the diaphragm, rendering the victim instantly mute. The actual cause of death was internal hemorrhaging of the liver and spleen, taking five to seven minutes, so he was taught. Drake had no idea whether the death was painful or not, and didn't particularly care. The objective was instant silence. The guard was not human, just a mission parameter.

* * *

Gip established his position. When the first inner perimeter guard rounded the southwest corner, Gip placed one shot in the center of the man's forehead. He went down with a gentle thump. *So far, so good,* Gip thought, *One down, twenty some odd to go.* Six excruciating minutes passed before the second guard found the body. As he lifted his radio to sound the alarm, his head exploded into a fine mist with the impact of the 7.62 mm jacketed round. Gip had an uncomfortable feeling that this was too easy. He would get confirmation soon enough – one way or the other.

There were still four guards patrolling the inner perimeter. They all appeared at once. *Shit*, Gip thought, *it's begun.* He popped the one on the far right in the solar plexus. Rich organ blood spurted from the wound as he was thrown back against the stone wall. The remaining three took cover and began pelting the rock formations to the south with their AK-47's. Gip lay on his back, surprised at how accurate they were. As planned, he rolled ten meters east and waited for Drake to fire. The idea was to spread the enemy out, making them believe they were surrounded.

From the east ridge, Drake squeezed off a round, instantly killing one of the guards with a shot below the left armpit, the same area one targets for a deer. As another guard turned to return fire, Gip shot him in the temple, removing most of his forehead. The cross fire was working as planned so far, but that trick wouldn't last for long.

With bullets ricocheting all around him, Gip rolled another ten meters east. During that time, six more guards came scrambling out the southern entrance and took immediate cover. The man in charge, realizing they were being flanked, sent a contingent to the east side. By the time they got there, Drake had low crawled to the south. He flanked them again, this time hitting the leader between the shoulder blades as he shouted orders in Arabic. His body jerked as the three round burst of tumbling jacketed lead ripped effortlessly through bone and organs.

By this time, Gip was in position to the southwest and shot another guard in the back of the head. As Drake and Gip had hoped, these were not professionally trained soldiers. This became obvious when the stick and move diversion tactics repeatedly fooled them.

Tartus' men began firing wildly to the south and east, their AK-47's on full auto. Sand and rock fragments flew harmlessly into the air. The shots echoed off the citadel and rock formations with a staccato effect deafening to anyone near the structure. Drake and Gip remained face down in the sand as their enemies wasted ammunition. As far as they knew, neither of them had been spotted yet. After one more shuffle, Drake and Gip were within sight of each other.

Gip raised his left fist and made a pumping motion. This was the signal for the claymores. Drake jerked his hand across his throat, signaling *no*. They had to draw guards to the windows before setting off the claymores. Drake peeked above the ridge. Tartus' men were getting smarter. They realized they were being attacked from the southern and eastern flanks and were laying heavy cover fire in both directions. Drake hit the sand and low crawled toward the northern entrance.

Gip was no longer able to aim his shots, but that did not matter at this point. He held his weapon above the rocks and fired blindly for a few seconds, then immediately rolled to a new position. They had reduced Tartus' forces by about one third in the first few moments of the battle. Now, with the element of surprise gone, the focus was to draw men to the windows by creating the illusion that Kechla was surrounded.

* * *

"What is happening?" Tartus demanded, kicking the kitchen chair across the room. His silk pajamas were already showing sweat stains. He glared at his head of security, Shahid, who stood stiffly in the archway to the enormous kitchen.

"Tartus, we're under attack," Shahid said, "I estimate at least twenty men, heavily armed infantry. They've already killed at least six of my men. The phone lines are dead and we have no men in radio range. If we don't stop them soon, they will surely blow the doors."

Tartus could not bear the thought of NATO soldiers overrunning his home. If Shahid were right, if they blew the doors, Tartus would spend the rest of his life in a Western prison. "This is a military fortress! You're telling me you can't defend it?" Veins stood out on Tartus' neck and temples. His normally squinty look was replaced with a visage of wide-eyed fear and rage. Obviously, Shahid was incompetent and needed direction.

"Tartus," Shahid began.

"Just shut up and listen!" Tartus interrupted, "Post one man in each window along the southern and northern walls. Have them fire continuously. That will prevent them from storming the doors. Put four men on the roof, one for each corner, to act as snipers. Divide the remaining men between the entrances. If they blow the doors, we can pick them off as they come through."

"Yes, Tartus," Shahid said, knowing that whether he succeeded or failed, he would die for this. His best hope was to die with honor.

"And somebody get me a weapon!" Tartus barked.

"Right away, Tartus." Shahid barked orders to the twenty-four soldiers he had left. Sixteen deployed to the windows, four to the roof, and two inside each entrance.

Tartus paced nervously in the kitchen, drawing heavily on his Pall Mall. Normally, he enjoyed his little American luxuries, savoring each draw he took from the unfiltered cigarettes. Tartus had mastered the art of living in the moment. In a business where torture and death were realistic threats, he could not afford to concern himself with the past or future.

His mind swirled in a maelstrom of angry and frustrated thoughts. Who would have the effrontery to attack him? He had no serious competitors in the area, no dissatisfied customers. He was quite generous to the local law enforcement; so he didn't expect any trouble from them.

Who? Falon had warned him that he suspected American agents had taken an interest in his activities, but he had also assured Tartus that he had dispatched the men efficiently.

Where was Falon, anyway? He hadn't shown up for dinner last night and hadn't checked in today. What if that rat had betrayed him? For months, Tartus had suspected Falon wanted a larger share of the business. Falon had expressed dissatisfaction with some of his more menial duties, but Tartus didn't think he would act on it. Perhaps he had underestimated Falon. But still, something didn't make sense. If Falon wanted to stage a coup, a frontal assault didn't make sense. As Tartus' second in command, he had ample opportunity to kill Tartus and assume leadership. How would Falon benefit by killing all the men who were loyal to him?

No, the Americans were the more likely culprits. Why now? After decades of uninhibited trade, why did the Americans choose to shut him down now? Could it be those American girls? Surely not. But, what if it were? What if he were unwittingly in possession of someone important, someone for whom the US would send a platoon of troops? How did they even know where he was? *Stop it*, he told himself. He evicted the fear and uncertainty from his mind. His thoughts focused on the task at hand.

"Shahid, come with me!"

"Yes Tartus."

"And bring the keys to the catacombs."

* * *

Outside, Drake had moved to the north side. Men occupied all eight windows, their AK-47s at the ready. By his count, there were over twenty men remaining inside the citadel, if Falon had told him the truth. So far, he had found no evidence that Falon had lied about anything. It was time for the claymores.

When Drake hit the button, the result was devastating. The men in the windows on the north side were shredded as thousands of steel balls passed effortlessly through the heavy wooden shutters, then through the soft tissue and bones of their bodies. After the smoke and dust had settled, Drake saw that all the windows were vacant. He shouldered his weapon and sprinted toward the aqueduct grating.

* * *

Gip was back at his original position, flanking the south entrance. He continued to move to and fro, rattling off automatic fire to create the illusion that he was an entire squad. Abruptly, the earth shook with a massive explosion from the north side. He was caught by surprise. His ears rang terribly. He ceased fire and low crawled his way toward the claymore switch.

* * *

Tartus' men were bustling with panic on the south side. After the enormous explosion from the north side, the firing from the rocks had stopped. The northern entrance had obviously been compromised. After much shouting, the men outside stopped their wild firing, eventually realizing they were shooting at no targets.

* * *

Gip peeked out and saw heads or silhouettes occupying all eight windows, rifle barrels waving back and forth across the rock formations. Although he couldn't see them, he guessed there were at least six more men hiding outside among the rocks.

Bracing himself against the sound, he fired the claymores. Again concussion rocked the night. Body parts were strewn about the compound, falling to the ground with a sickening, wet sound. A preternatural silence followed the explosion. No gunshots, no birds, no insects, no voices; merely the ringing in his ears. Everything outside the citadel was dead. Gip estimated about a dozen bodies in the south compound. He didn't know how many Drake had gotten on the north side, but with luck he had gotten at least the men in the windows. That left the four snipers on the roof, between two and five inside, plus Tartus.

Gip checked his watch. Drake would be in the aqueduct soon. It was time for phase two.

* * *

Drake was right on schedule. The iron grating yielded easily to the torch. Once Drake cut the last bar, the grating screeched loudly and fell into the blackness. Seconds later, he heard the splash. *Must be a pretty decent drop*, he thought. Careful not to touch the red-hot edges, Drake jumped into a pitch black free fall, hoping the water would be deep enough to break his fall.

* * *

Tartus and Shahid jogged down the catacomb's main corridor. The girls were screaming in panic. Tartus had heard two enormous explosions outside, followed by silence. He knew his men were dead. Who but the Americans would come in with such powerful ordinance?

"Shahid, how many men do we have left?"

Shahid spoke rapidly into his radio for a full minute. "I can contact just the four on the roof and the four inside." Shahid was visibly rattled. Whether the Americans won or lost, Tartus would kill him before the Sun came up. Tartus did not respond, but simply resumed his trot. He had no intention of sharing his thoughts with Shahid.

When Tartus and Shahid arrived at Lupe's cell, they found she was the only quiet girl among the bunch. She stood calmly, just inside the barred window to her cell. This sent a chill up Tartus' spine.

"Who are you?" Tartus demanded. Spittle flew from his lips. His face was contorted with rage.

"What's the matter? You can dish it out but you can't take it? *There's* a major surprise." Her mocking tone suggested confidence - the raid was for her alone. *This situation is getting worse all the time*, Tartus thought.

"Damn you, answer me or I'll kill you right now!" As he spoke, Tartus drew his pistol and leveled it between her eyes. Lupe believed him.

"I'm the daughter of Juan Hernandez, US Congressman from California. And judging from the ruckus I hear upstairs, I'd say he's come to bring me home."

Shit, Tartus thought, "A congressman's daughter? What were you doing in Brazil?"

"Ever hear of a vacation, asshole?"

Tartus almost pulled the trigger. It would be so easy to end her life, just a twitch of his finger. But the power of life and death that normally drove his engine held no thrill for him. Something nagged at him on a visceral level. Some intangible force paralyzed his finger long enough for him to get control of his reflexes. Logic prevailed. If she was whom she claimed, she just might buy him his life. He turned to Shahid.

"Open the cell. She's coming with me."

Chapter Twenty-Six

The Kechla Citadel

The aqueduct was completely dark. Drake was in freefall for a fraction of a second before he struck the four-foot deep water coursing down the pipe. Drake struggled to hold his head afloat and keep his weapons. The water was surprisingly cold, and his hands were already beginning to numb. The sound of rushing water filled his ears, making him feel a slight vertigo. There was a definite sensation of speed, but he had no idea how fast he was moving. He managed to get his flashlight out and pointed it ahead.

The aqueduct was a stone cylinder, approximately three meters in diameter. The walls were green and slimy, covered with centuries of growth. Drake was amazed at how usable its condition was after five centuries of neglect. He strained to see ahead. Based on the speed the twelve-inch squares of stone passed by, he estimated he should reach the citadel within the next few seconds.

The drawings in the museum showed the aqueduct turning downward and feeding back into the underground stream shortly after passing through the citadel. This would be a one-act play. If he missed the citadel, he would be rushed deep into the earth where he would drown in complete darkness. He tried to keep that thought out of his head.

He heard it before he saw it. The giant wooden water wheel creaked with each revolution. He heard the paddles splashing loudly. The tunnel curved sharply to the right, forcing him and the water to bank left. The water was shallower and faster moving now. He saw the water wheel just thirty meters ahead, turning slowly in the current; thereby providing electricity to all of Kechla. The wheel was at least ten meters in diameter. Drake wondered if it would rip him to pieces before he could jump to safety.

Propelling toward the wheel feet first, he dropped his flashlight, relying on the lighting of the catacombs. When he struck the first paddle, there was an audible crack as two of his ribs snapped. He gripped with all his strength as he was pulled under. His back scraped the bottom of the aqueduct, freeing centuries of moss and algae, as well as freeing some clothing and flesh from his back. The turbulence forced water up his nose and the pressure forced him to exhale a stream of bubbles. He wondered if his body would wedge between the wheel and the bottom of the pipeline, bringing the wheel to a sudden stop, suffocating him. Without the slime, he probably would have been ripped in half; his fragile body no match for the gigantic forces surrounding him.

The wheel pushed harder into his sternum, forcing out air he didn't even know he had. He was no longer moving with the water. It rushed past him, creating a suction caused by the Bernoulli effect. Bernoulli had discovered that the faster a fluid moved, the lower its pressure. This was the principle that allowed airplanes to fly. It was also the principle that nearly collapsed Drake's lungs. The water was pulling a vacuum on him.

Just when Drake thought the current would suck him inside out, he broke free. Even in his delirium, he knew he had less than a second to react if he ever wanted to refill his lungs with oxygen. He gripped the paddle with all his strength. As the wheel lifted him, he swung toward the side and took a leap of faith at what he hoped was dry land.

The painful thump of the stone floor actually found a remaining pocket of air to expel from his lungs. He struggled to inhale, but couldn't manage more than an impotent wheeze. Purple spots danced erratically in front of his eyes. The world went black.

* * *

Tartus gripped Lupe's arm tightly, jerking her along the corridor. Shahid walked behind them with his AK-47 trained on the center of her back, providing a strong incentive for her to cooperate.

"Unit One, report status," Shahid spoke into his radio.

"Unit One here. No activity at the north entrance."

"Unit Two, report status."

"Unit Two here. We are receiving fire at the south entrance. Sounds like five, maybe ten shooters. The door remains secure."

"Get me out the north entrance," Tartus snarled. The three of them picked up the pace. As they rounded the next corner, Tartus stopped in his tracks. "Who the hell is that?"

* * *

Gip had to get those snipers before he could begin phase two. Having seen no men coming from the north side, he assumed the snipers were the only men remaining outside the citadel. He chambered a round in the M203. He would have to arc the shot to drop within fifteen meters of the roof corner. He knew the range to the citadel was twenty meters. Add to that twenty meters of height. He set the sight for 50 meters and drew a bead on the southeast corner of the roof. When he squeezed the trigger, there was a loud thunk as the explosive projectile was sent skyward. Seconds later there was an explosion on the roof. He looked at the ground just in time to see a bloody leg land in the dust. The other sniper threw his weapon over the side and disappeared from sight. Gip immediately grabbed his satchel and double-timed it toward the door.

* * *

When Drake awoke, the first thing he noticed was the absence of air. He tried to inhale, but excruciating pain in his ribcage caused him to grimace. By taking mini breaths, he was able to maintain consciousness. He looked around, trying to get his bearings. Luckily, he had disembarked the wheel on the correct side. The area of the catacombs that appeared to have cells lining the walls was about one hundred meters west of him. He pulled back the bolt on his M-16, chambering a round from the fresh banana clip. *Thirty rounds, plus nine in the pistol,* he thought, *Let's hope that's enough.* He had lost his extra clips to the aqueduct.

Drake had taken no more than ten painful steps when he saw three figures round the corner ahead. He hurriedly raised the rifle, but hesitated. He couldn't believe it. One of the three was Lupe Hernandez. The man at her side jerked her in front of him and raised a pistol.

Drake instantly sighted just left of the man and placed a round in the center of Shahid's chest. Dark blood tainted with bile spurted as Shahid's legs collapsed under him. Before Shahid hit the floor, Drake was already on the floor and rolling. With no cover or concealment, the best he could do was become a difficult target.

Tartus fired five shots wildly down the corridor, using Lupe as a shield. She instantly felt a sharp pain in her right ear, swiftly replaced by a loud ringing. The muzzle flash temporarily blinded her. In the confusion of the following seconds, she turned in a circle, pinching Tartus' thumb closed on itself. He howled in pain and yanked himself out of her grip. Before he could raise his pistol, she kicked him in the groin. If his testicles had been a football, Lupe would have easily made a sixty yard field goal.

Drake now had a clear shot at Tartus, but he was disoriented from rolling. He was afraid to chance a shot, so he shouted, "Hold it right there, asshole!"

Tartus disappeared around the corner with catlike quickness. Lupe was left standing in the corridor, her hands covering her face. Drake immediately jumped to his feet. He didn't know how long it would be before someone else appeared around the corner. His ribs felt like rusty swords being thrust into his thorax with each step.

"Ms. Hernandez, I'm John Drake with the US Government. I'm here to take you home," Drake shouted above the ringing in his ears. Lupe closed the gap between them and gave him a hug that turned his snapped ribs into a meat grinder in his chest.

"Oh, thank God! I was afraid he'd never be able to find me."

"Who?"

"My father."

"I'm here with another man. We're here to take you all home."

"Just two of you? That's all?" She asked, her tone petulant.

"Ma'am, there's no time for this. We've got to go. Where are the other girls?" Drake spoke and behaved like a machine.

"They sent just two men for me?"

"They sent two men for all of you, and if you want the opportunity to complain to your father personally, I suggest we get moving."

"This way," Lupe said, leading Drake west toward the row of cells. Drake stopped to grab Shahid's keys before they hurried along.

* * *

Gip carefully molded the C-4 putty around the perimeter of the south entrance. For good measure, he stuck the leftover C-4 in a large lump in the center of the door. He guessed he had about ten times more explosive than he needed. God help anyone on the other side of that door when it blew. Gip sprinted back up the hill and took position behind a large outcropping of rock. He attached the wires to the switch and, after bracing himself for the shock wave, pushed the button.

Nothing happened.

* * *

Tartus was furious. He was down to four men inside, and he still had no idea how many enemy soldiers were waiting for him outside. Since the southern entrance was obviously under attack, he moved north. He ran through the maze of stone corridors for a tedious five minutes. By the time he reached the north entrance, he was winded and sweaty.

"Halt!" One of the guards pointed his rifle at Tartus.

"It's me, you idiots! Is there any activity outside?"

"None that we can hear, Tartus."

"Then get that door open, now!"

The guards unlatched the two heavy bolts that ran the entire width of the door. One took several steps back and leveled his AK-47 at the doorway. Tartus took cover behind a stone wall. The other guard cautiously poked his head out, having no idea whether he would lose it for the effort. The northern compound was clear.

* * *

Lupe unlocked the last of the doors while Drake constantly panned east and west, alert for any activity. Most of the girls did not speak English, but they responded to sign language. Drake was concerned they would be panicky, but he was surprised by their silence.

After what they had been through in the last three weeks, they were shocked numb by the rescue. Most had given up hope long ago. Drake kept them single file along the southern wall of the corridor. If any gunplay should erupt, their chances of being hit were minimized. Of course, the walls and ceiling were stone, so ricochets would be an uncontrollable factor. Drake did not want to face the decision he would have to make if one of the girls were hit. He knew he didn't have the resources to get many wounded out of the citadel.

Where were Tartus' men? Surely Tartus had alerted them to his location. How many were left? Drake guessed about six. Once he had opened the last cell, he led the long line of girls toward the south entrance.

* * *

"Shit!" Gip screamed. He was running out of time, and something was wrong with either the wiring or the primer. He fired another burst at the citadel to perpetuate the illusion of a contingent of troops outside. He ran back towards the door.

* * *

Salam, one of the interior guards at the south entrance, heard it first – the sound of many footsteps approaching. *This is it*, he thought, *the troops must have taken the north entrance.* He signaled the other guard and they turned their attention away from the south entrance and toward the great hall.

* * *

When they arrived at the entrance to the great hall, Drake signaled the girls to stop. They responded well to his signals – almost like experienced soldiers. Drake figured we all become soldiers when we have to. With his back against the wall, he peeked over his left shoulder around the doorway.

Rock and mortar sprayed as steel encased lead ate into the doorway, inches from his face. The barrage of bullets chopped the doorway and the wall in front of Drake's face to pieces.

Drake didn't get a good look, but he saw at least two men. They had been ready for him, and he knew they would advance on him, one laying cover fire while the other moved. By taking turns in this fashion, they would be on top of Drake in less than thirty seconds. Gip obviously had not blown the door. Several of the girls screamed out in surprise when the shooting began.

* * *

Salam heard the screams of women. So, the troops already had the girls. He wondered how many of the footsteps he had heard belonged to soldiers. Regardless, with no appreciable cover, they had no choice but to storm the archway. He raised his arm to signal the charge. It was promptly taken off at the shoulder by the exterior door as it passed him at over two hundred miles per hour.

* * *

The explosion shook the foundation of the massive citadel. Drake was reminded of the scene in Butch Cassidy and the Sundance Kid. Butch, in an attempt to access the safe on a train, had blown the entire rail car to smithereens. Sundance had asked, 'Think you used enough dynamite there, Butch?'

The south door, now a massive projectile, traveled the entire width of the great hall, through the archway where Drake took cover, and struck the wall beside Drake with such force that for an instant Drake thought the wall would collapse. It held.

The corridor was filled with the sounds of screaming women. Projectiles of rock sprayed them, tearing delicate flesh. Drake's eyes were caked with dust. His clothes, still wet from his swim, were encrusted with a paste of wet dust and mortar. He clawed at his eyes, knowing that at any second, those guards could round the corner. When he had some semblance of vision, he ventured a glance around the doorway just in time to lose his head – almost.

While one guard lay on the ground screaming and bleeding, the other was advancing on Drake's position. Drake heard another barrage of shots. Even though his ears rang in pain from all the concussions, he recognized the familiar sound of an M-16, as opposed to the guard's AK-47. Silence ensued.

"All clear," Gip shouted.

Drake looked again and saw Gip standing there with a grin on his face. He let out a sigh of relief.

"Glad you could make it," Drake called out.

"Man, the last thing I expected to see was your white ass. 'Though you aren't exactly white anymore."

"It's camouflage. I'm disguised as a wall."

They both laughed, releasing nervous tension. Drake signaled for the girls to follow him. When they were all in the southern courtyard, Drake said, "Any survivors out here?"

"Possibly on the roof," Gip replied. He cocked the M203 and lobbed another grenade toward the center of the roof to make sure nobody got brave. "Man, we better get moving. We've got a long walk back to the truck and who knows who else might be roaming around out here."

"Good news," Drake said, "I saw two jeeps and a deuce-and-a-quarter around on the north side. It'll save us one hell of a hike."

"Well, what are we waiting for?" Gip asked.

"Nothing. Just be aware that door will be guarded, if only from the interior. Let's move out."

The girls were covered in dust and some of them were bleeding; but for the most part they seemed miraculously intact. They moved as swiftly as possible along the east wall. When they arrived at the corner, Gip peeked around. Two men stood just outside the open door. He thumbed his M-16 to fully auto and swept around the corner, all but cutting the two guards in half.

As they loaded the girls into the truck, Gip said, "Drake, I thought you said there were two jeeps."

"Ah shit," Drake spat. He told Gip about the man who had gotten away.

"Do you think it was Tartus?"

"He was as far away from the fighting as possible, and he used the Hernandez girl as cover. Sounds like a natural born leader to me. Besides, when he had the opportunity to shoot me, he chose to run and save his own hide. That's not a desirable quality in a security guard."

"Well, there's nothing we can do about it now."

"Yes there is. I'm going back inside. You drive the girls three klicks, switch trucks, and proceed to our rendezvous spot. If I'm not there by dawn, take the girls to the US Embassy in Rabat. It's about a three hundred mile drive, so you can be there by nightfall."

"You're the boss. If you want to commit suicide, that's your choice."

"Thanks for the vote of confidence," Drake said, starting northward, making his way through the rubble covering the great hall. He retraced the steps he had taken with the girls just a few minutes ago.

According to the drawings they had studied, the living quarters were just east of the great hall. If Drake could find Tartus' bedroom, there would certainly be photographs. It took him less than ten minutes to find the most lavish bedroom. There was a picture on the dresser of a man in military fatigues with his arm around two men. They had machine guns slung around their necks. Drake didn't recognize the man on the left. The one on the right was Falon. The man in the middle was the coward he had encountered in the catacombs – Tartus. In the nightstand, he found what appeared to be a day planner, but he could not make out the Arabic. He pocketed the picture and the book and ran to the northern compound.

* * *

At twenty minutes past dawn, Gip was facing a difficult decision – one he didn't want to make. His instincts told him to go back for Drake, but he had the lives of thirty-eight girls in his hands. *Damn him for leaving me in this position*, he thought. As he reached into his pocket for a coin to flip, he saw dust on the horizon. *Either that's Drake, or this is about to get interesting.*

Minutes later, Drake sped over the hill in a jeep. As the tires screeched to a halt against the packed sand, Drake jumped out.

"Find anything?"

"Yea, his picture. Tartus is the one who got away. I also have some sort of notebook, but we'll need help reading it."

"What about the girls?"

"We've got to get them to the US Embassy in Rabat before we deal with Tartus. Briggs made that crystal clear."

Gip had moved the girls to the other truck because of the special modifications he had installed. Gip put the pedal to the floor and they sped toward Rabat.

Chapter Twenty-Seven

Shaqra

Shaqra was crowded for five in the morning. The men were dreary eyed from a night of drinking. Tartus was well known and respected among Shaqra's clientele, so when he burst in they made no fuss. He was dressed in silk pajamas stained with sweat, dust and flecks of blood. His feet were bare. He walked to the center of the bar, stood on a chair and proclaimed, "I need men! I'm paying cash!"

* * *

Gip had been driving the truck full of girls for a little over two hours before he encountered the barricade.

"What the hell is that?" Gip said, rousting Drake from his catnap.

"Looks like a road block. It's probably just routine, but just in case, have your hand on that switch."

"You got it."

Gip braked gradually, taking as much time as possible so he could think. Even if this were a routine roadblock, wouldn't the men inspect their cargo? Plus, his special modifications were camouflaged only to pass a cursory glance, not an up-close inspection. Still, Tartus' men must have to contend with the same issues. Gip's experience in Morocco suggested that anything could be bought with hard cash.

He came to a stop twenty feet shy of the barricade. A man approached the driver's side window and spat something in Arabic.

"Do you speak English?" Gip asked.

"Yes. Your papers, please. I need your shipping manifest."

Gip pretended to look through his pockets. "I'm sure I have them in here somewhere." As he searched, men began to encircle the truck.

As they spoke, men moved to encircle the vehicle.

"Quit stalling. Your papers now, please."

"Here they are," Gip said, producing a wad of American hundred dollar bills. The guard was not receptive.

"Please step out of the truck."

* * *

While this conversation took place, Drake surveyed the situation. He counted nine armed men on either side of the truck and three in front. There were three trucks parked fifty meters ahead. Drake could not see whether they were occupied. He casually lowered his right hand, searching for the makeshift device Gip had prepared for just such an occasion. If Gip had made the slightest mistake in design or construction, everyone in the truck would be killed instantly. Well, it was a little late to worry about that.

Beyond the barricade stood a lone man. Unlike his compatriots, he did not have an AK-47. His only apparent weapon was a sidearm, and it was not drawn. Drake squinted into the glare, trying to discern the man's facial features. Since he had been napping, his eyes had not yet adjusted to the brightness. Although he couldn't distinguish the man's face, he did recognize the pajamas. It was Tartus!

Drake pushed the button activating the claymores planted along either side of the truck. The truck shook from the concussion. The back blast partially imploded the cab, but the small steel plates did their job of directing the blast outward. Both doors buckled inward. There was a sound like clumps of wet cement splattering onto the dirt. Their ears, still recovering from the torture of the blast, once again began ringing. *Shit*, Drake thought, *If I do survive this, I'll be deaf.*

As shredded body parts rained down outside, Drake was already retrieving his M-16 from beneath the seat. He flicked it over to fully auto and pulled the trigger in one smooth motion. The three men in front of the truck raised their Ak-47s, but Drake beat them by a split second. He dispatched all three, shattering the windshield in the process. Fragments of glass filled the front seat. Drake looked to either side and saw that all the men were dead or dying. He tried to open the door, but it was jammed. Tartus was nowhere in sight. *Damn, he's a slippery bastard.*

Men began to pour out of two of the trucks ahead. The girls were screaming frantically.

"Go! Go! Go!" Drake shouted.

Gip floored the pedal and broke through the barricade. He maneuvered off the road to bypass the trucks. He and Drake heard the crackling of the AK-47's as they passed. They kept their heads as low as possible. The girls lay as flat as they could, covering the bottom of the truck bed as Drake had instructed them to do should trouble arise.

Tartus' new recruits ran into the center of the road and fired behind the badly dented truck. Since the side view mirrors were shattered, Drake had to stick his head out the window to see behind them.

"They're coming! Two trucks. Hand me the M-203."

Gip instantly produced his M-16 with the M-203 attachment from beneath his seat. Drake chambered a round and leaned as far out the window as he could. He estimated the range to be one hundred meters and adjusted the sight accordingly. When he fired, the barrel was pointing up at a thirty-degree angle. His first shot hit the ground about ten meters ahead of the lead truck and exploded harmlessly.

"Another round!"

Gip slapped the cylindrical grenade into Drake's hand. Drake opened the chamber and dropped it in. The truck then appeared to be eighty meters back and they were firing. Drake's second shot hit the lead truck in the windshield. The resulting explosion billowed out of the cab of the truck. The truck took a sharp left and flipped on its side, sliding thirty meters before coming to a stop. Just as men began to scramble out the back of the truck, there was a secondary explosion as the gas tank ignited. Most were killed in the explosion, but the few who had escaped were doused in burning gasoline. Some ran. Some rolled. All screamed. The second truck broke off pursuit, screeching to a halt. Typical mercenaries. Men who worshipped the almighty dollar promptly lost their interest when they realized they were unlikely to be around to spend it.

Gip kept the pedal to the floor as they sped toward Rabat. Drake and Gip had no idea of the condition of the girls, and they couldn't afford to stop and find out. They were fairly certain that they had suffered casualties. Statistics dictated that.

* * *

Drake was surprised at how foreboding The US Embassy in Rabat appeared. A fourteen-foot brick wall surrounded it, with razor wire angled outward. The gates were wrought iron. Two guards were posted inside the gates, wearing Marine dress uniforms. Gip pulled the truck up to the gates, honking madly. The guards gave no indication that they possessed the sense of hearing. Their eyes were fixed ahead, their spines rigid.

Gip shouted out the window. "Open the gates! We are Americans being pursued by hostile enemy forces."

* * *

Although his head did not move, one guard's eyes shifted focus to their pitiful remnant of a truck. The men he saw were in civilian clothes. Their skin was so thickly pasted with dirt, he couldn't tell their race. He had to assume they were natives, possibly terrorists. He unshouldered his M-16 and pointed it at the truck from hip level. He partner did the same.

"Move away from the gate. Now!"

* * *

Drake climbed out the window and approached the guards. He was tired, hungry, thirsty, injured and generally pissed off. He winced in pain with each step he took. The guards responded by chambering a round in each of their weapons.

"Sir, get back in the truck and move away from the gate or we'll be forced to open fire!"

Drake recognized the rank of the Marines as E-5, the equivalent of a buck sergeant in the Army. "Sergeant, I am Sergeant First Class John Drake of the United States Army. My partner and I are on a mission for the US Government. I order you to open these gates right now."

"Sir, I'll need to see some identification," the guard replied. His weapon was trained on the center of Drake's chest. The other guard's weapon was trained on Gip, still in the truck.

"First of all, don't call me 'Sir'. I work for a living! Sergeant," Drake looked just above the man's heart, "Hudson, is it? Sergeant Hudson, we are covert ops, we don't carry ID's. And if you don't open this goddamned gate right now, I can guarantee that you will be scrubbing toilets with a toothbrush in Nepal for the next five years." Drake had spent enough time in the military to know what motivated grunts.

"I'm here on direct authority of Major General Jeremiah Dalton of Fort Benning, Georgia, and I have thirty-eight females that were kidnapped by Moroccan black marketeers. One of them is the daughter of Congressman Hernandez. If I have to ask you again, I swear to god I'll shoot you where you stand, you pompous ass!" Regardless of the threat he made, Drake was smart enough not to draw his pistol.

The Marine recognized the names of the General and the Congressman. This got his attention. He radioed the head of security, and within sixty seconds, he opened the gates and let the battered truck roll onto American soil.

Drake took charge, barking orders to everyone he saw, regardless of rank. Medics rushed to administer aid to the girls. Three had been killed during the escape from the roadblock. Six more were injured, but not seriously. Lupe and her two friends were unharmed. The embassy had rudimentary medical facilities capable of stabilizing the injured until they could be moved to a local hospital. The rest of the girls were escorted to the living quarters where they were allowed their first shower in weeks. Clean and dressed in cotton robes, they went immediately to the cafeteria, which was still serving breakfast. A lance corporal made a list of their sizes and arranged for the purchase of western clothes.

Drake and Gip refused food and medical care, demanding to see the Ambassador immediately. They met no resistance.

Muddied and bloodied, Drake and Gip walked into the Ambassador's office. The expansive room was ornate, with hardwood floors, original Monet's and a bust of Richard Nixon in the corner. There was a large circular throw rug in front of his desk displaying the seal of the US president. The Ambassador was a portly man, with a light peppering of sweat on his bald head. He had a blonde Van Dyke beard that gave him an approachable look. He wore a conservative gray business suit not quite large enough to accommodate his frame. If he noticed the disheveled appearance of his guests, he gave no indication. He didn't even flinch when they plopped their filthy bodies into his pristine wingback guest chairs.

"Mr. Ambassador, I'm Sergeant First Class Drake and this is Specialist-5 Gibson," Drake said in a formal tone.

"Gentlemen, welcome. May I offer you some form of refreshment?"

"Maybe later, Sir. Right now we need to talk."

"Of course. I understand you've had quite an adventure in Morocco."

"I wouldn't use that particular word to describe it, Mr. Ambassador. 'Romp through Hell' comes to mind," Drake said.

"I'm terribly sorry to hear of your hardship," he said in a tone one might use to calm a frightened animal. "May I offer you something to drink? I just received a bottle of twelve-year-old scotch from my stateside brother. Such extravagances are difficult to come by here, with the local religion prohibiting drinking and all."

"No thank you, Sir," Drake said flatly. He thought of Shaqra, with the stolid bartender who served up booze by the bottle. Apparently, the Muslims had at least one thing in common with the Christians – hypocrisy. "We're in a bit of a rush, and we need your help. Maybe after we talk, we could get a hot meal."

The Ambassador spoke into his intercom, ordering a food for four. His assistant promised to have it ready within fifteen minutes. He returned his attention to the two ragamuffins in front of him. "I'll do anything I can, of course. Please tell me what you need."

"Sir, we just wrested thirty-eight girls from the hands of heavily armed white slavers. Three were killed in the escape, but we do have Lupe Hernandez, the daughter of Congressman Hernandez, as well as two other American citizens. The other thirty-two are assumed to be Brazilian. We must contact Major General Dalton at Fort Benning immediately to inform him of the status of our mission. Once that is done, we must entrust these girls to your care. Six are wounded, but all require medical attention for shock and dehydration. At some point, they will require deportation. Sergeant Gibson and I have more business to conduct, and as I mentioned, we must leave as rapidly as possible."

"I wish you could stay longer. I'm anxious to hear the details of what must have been a heroic endeavor."

"Mr. Ambassador, we simply don't have time for diplomatic pleasantries," Drake said.

"Of course. I personally assure you these women will receive the best of care. You may use my private line to conduct your affairs. It is quite secure. When you are finished, we will provide you with whatever transportation you need."

"Thank you, Sir. Mr. Ambassador, do you have anyone on the premises who can read Arabic?" Drake asked.

"Certainly. I am fluent in both spoken and written Arabic."

"I have something I need to show you." Drake produced Tartus' notebook. "This notebook belongs to a man named Tartus. He's the leader of a global white slavery enterprise."

"Interesting," the Ambassador said, taking the notebook.

"Sir, we need to know anything that might help us locate this man, Tartus."

The Ambassador perused the notebook for a few minutes. "Well, much of it is personal in nature – a list of names and phone numbers, a ledger of debts. Oh, here's something. There is a reference to a lunch meeting on the 17th, that's tomorrow, at a restaurant called Kahlid's in Riyadh, Saudi Arabia, on the patio. It does not say whom he is meeting. Kahlid's is probably one of the ritziest restaurants in Riyadh. Does this have any significance?"

"If we know where Tartus will be and when, it has great significance. Sir, we must ask you a favor."

"Anything, my friends."

"We need identities, passports and papers that will get us into Saudi Arabia today."

The Ambassador's eyebrows raised in curiosity. "What you ask is unconventional, not to mention illegal."

"Sir," Drake began.

"However..." the Ambassador raised his hand, palm facing Drake. "I think we can accommodate your request."

Chapter Twenty-Eight

Riyadh, Saudi Arabia

Tartus arrived ten minutes early for lunch. Although he was unable to deliver the goods he had promised, he kept the appointment. Damage control of this magnitude must be done in person. He scanned the patio. King Fahr was nowhere in sight, but two men who appeared to be bodyguards were already casing the restaurant. Sweat glistened on his brow as the midday sun beat down on him. He was beginning to regret choosing a patio table, but Fahr enjoyed eating outside.

He was still in shock from the events of the past seventy-two hours. Apparently, an American task force had wiped out an operation that took him over twenty years to build in a matter of hours. Had someone told him that just two men had taken down the Kechla citadel, he wouldn't have believed it. Based on the reports from his security detail, there had been at least an entire platoon of ground forces with coordinated artillery strikes as well.

When he had returned to Kechla, the dead were strewn everywhere. Many were so shredded that the parts could not be matched with the bodies. His grounds looked like some malign butcher had passed his men through a meat grinder. It hadn't been easy to find men willing to clean up that mess. He had lost thirty-four men – his entire staff, not to mention twenty-two of the mercenaries he had hired to recapture the girls. Falon was still missing, and at this point, considered dead.

Tartus was not looking forward to this meeting. He had pre-sold the American girls to King Fahr and hated to renege on his promises. It was not good for business. He strained to conceal his agitation, taking in deep, calming breaths.

Fahr approached from the sidewalk. Due to the lunchtime crowds, Tartus did not see him until he was a few meters from the patio. He recognized Fahr's beard before he saw the details of his face. The jet-black mane came to a sharp point about ten inches below his chin. The portion of his face not covered by hair was ruddy. Beady eyes a little too close together peered through wire-rimmed glasses.

"Hello, my friend," Fahr said, "It has been too long since we last met."

"Indeed," Tartus replied in the calmest tone he could manage, "How have you been?"

"I am fortunate in that I am always in good health. And yourself?"

"Everything is fine. Business is strong."

"What an odd response," Fahr said. "I ask about your well-being, and you respond with an assurance about your business." King Fahr was known to be an extremely perceptive man. Tartus had also grossly miscalculated the power and speed of the grapevine from Morocco to Fahr. Fahr expressed concern, leaning toward Tartus. "Is something troubling you?"

"Not at all, Honorable One," Tartus responded. "It's just that sometimes I can't get my mind off of the daily details of my work. I guess it shows, huh?"

"You appear upset. Your breathing is deliberately slow and controlled. And why do you keep your hands in your lap? What is it about them that you do not wish me to see?"

"Honorable One, you see right through me. I admit that I am a bit preoccupied at present. But, it is nothing that will impact our relationship," Tartus said.

"Then, you have what you promised?"

"Promise is a strong word, Honorable One. I may have been premature in passing along second hand information. My Brazilian connection radioed me with news that he had three American girls in his most recent shipment. However, once I inspected the girls, I deemed them to be inferior merchandise. Certainly not befitting a king."

"Why am I just hearing of this now? Three days ago you said everything was on track. You told me you'd inspected the girls yourself and everything was a go. Such a miscommunication could have dire consequences for our business relationship. I believe you'd better clean these girls up and deliver them as promised. I will judge the quality of the merchandise." Fahr's voice had the calmness of a man who possessed absolute power. There was no need for a threatening tone. His words were sufficient, as they were always translated into action.

"Honorable One…" Tartus' hands were shaky. He strained to resist wiping the sweat from his brow. "I have already disposed of the girls. They were diseased. I practically had to give them away. Surely The King would rather wait for the next shipment. I'm already working on a deal involving Southern California." He referred to the scam the American agent had proposed.

"You plan to kidnap American citizens from their own soil? I find this implausible. Even a man with your connections cannot make it through American Customs with such cargo."

"I have a man there who is setting up a travel agency. He will lure the girls out of America under the guise of a free vacation giveaway. Once they are in a location with friendlier authorities, we can make our move. This will work." Tartus was lying at the speed of thought. He needed two things. First, he had to mollify King Fahr. Second, he needed to buy time. Within thirty days, he could rebuild his staff. But, with Falon gone it would be a challenge to reestablish his connections. And what about Fejo? In retrospect, he might have been a little harsh with him. He hoped he hadn't alienated the man.

"Interesting," Fahr said, stroking his beard. "What you propose may work. However, I can assure you that my disappointment will know no bounds if you let me down again."

Something struck Tartus as odd. He couldn't quite put his finger on it, but something about the crowd was not right. Had he seen a familiar face? He turned to look up the sidewalk, scanning the crowd.

* * *

"I think he made me," Drake whispered into the microphone under his robes.

"Man, with that fake beard I hardly recognize you," Gip responded.

"I've got a bad feeling about this. See those two guys at the corners of the patio? They're just a little too attentive. I think they're Tartus' men."

"Look, even if they are, the plan will work. Let's do this thing."

Drake's hands were surprisingly steady. He and Gip had seen Kahlid's for the first time just a few hours before. Their plan was quickly formed and required quick execution. He put himself in a semi-meditative state, filtering out everything except his target. This helped to calm his hands, which was critical to accuracy, even at close range. Beneath the sleeve of his robe, he held a silenced

.22 pistol, the preferred weapon for close range assassination. Higher caliber weapons were noisy, even when silenced, and passed effortlessly through the human head, sometimes leaving the target alive. A .22 was quieter and tended to bounce around inside the skull, ensuring death.

Drake looked around him. As far as he could tell, he blended into the crowd in the Arabic garments the Embassy had given him. Twenty meters now. He matched pace with the crowd. Ten meters. Tartus was scanning the crowd, but his attention kept returning to his lunch companion. The other man was of no concern to Drake. There wouldn't be time for a second shot, especially with the bodyguards. Five meters. If Tartus looked his way again, Drake was close enough to take the shot. It would be messier from a distance, but it could be done. One meter.

* * *

Tartus was still listening to Fahr's admonition when he spotted the gun. His razor sharp mind took just a split second to sort out the facts. The American from the catacombs! How could this be? Who was this devil? He was already ducking when he heard a staccato series of explosions from across the street.

As Drake raised his pistol to shoot, Gip lit a string of firecrackers across the street. In a country where terrorism was commonplace, the percussion of the firecrackers caused a panic. The crowd screamed and scattered in every direction. Gip joined them.

Drake squeezed off the shot from arm's distance. A red dot appeared just off center of Tartus' forehead. He slumped to the right, falling beside the table in an unnatural heap. With him, the last pillar of the Moroccan white slave market died.

Fahr had already flipped his chair over and was hiding beneath the table. His bodyguards moved into action immediately. One raced to his king's aid, prepared to use his body as a shield. The other went after the sound of gunshots across the street.

Drake kept pace with the crowd, breaking into a jog and taking a left at the next street. He hastily removed his fake beard and black robe, revealing a white robe underneath. As he ran, he wrapped the beard and gun into a tight ball inside the robe. In the general panic, no one noticed when he dropped the package into a trashcan. He reduced his pace to match the crowd.

* * *

Riyadh, Saudi Arabia

King & Prime Minister Fahr al-Azon Al Saud was disheveled. He sat at his kitchen table, surrounded by his security task force. "How could this happen? How could an assassin walk right up and nearly shoot me?"

"Sir," his head of security began.

"I don't want to hear your excuses! You were charged with protecting the life of the most powerful man in the Arab nations and you have failed." He turned to face his second in command. "You, arrest this man. Execute him at dawn." If the security chief was surprised to hear this, he didn't show it.

"We will discuss this in detail later. I have a press conference to prepare for." Fahr spoke directly to his new security chief. "Do you think you can get me through this press conference alive?"

"Yes, Honorable One. I will triple the contingent of guards."

"Then do it. I don't want to spend one second alone for the next forty-eight hours."

Fahr struggled to understand the reason behind the assassination attempt. Who would do such a thing? Why? The Israelis? No, that wasn't their style at all. He remembered what the Japanese Emperor had said after bombing Pearl Harbor. He feared Japan had awakened a sleeping giant. Had he done the same? Certainly the Americans fought the embargo, but they wouldn't assassinate a head of state, would they? Such an action would imperil their status in the UN.

Then again, there was no link to America in this incident. There was no link to anyone. The attack could be blamed on any number of extremist groups. He thought of the news stories he had watched where American soldiers had wiped out entire villages in Vietnam. Civilian men, women and children had been slaughtered over ideological differences. Would a country capable of such acts hesitate to take one man's life when billions of dollars of oil were on the table? No, they would not.

He knew what he must do. The Arab nations would not oppose him because they could not risk appearing divided to the UN. Such divisiveness would weaken them in the eyes of the world.

* * *

The Prometheus

Commander Rymes was tense. Today was his opportunity to restore his good name. He had checked every system on the Prometheus and all were in working order. He was somewhat concerned about using brand new equipment that hadn't been field tested, but everything seemed in top shape. Within the next three hours, he would receive the launch codes that would enable him to fulfill his mission. He still had no idea what the targets were. In fact, he wouldn't know when he received the codes. He would have to hear about it in the news. Rymes tried something he rarely did. He prayed, not for his glorification, but for the safety of his men.

Killian strolled onto the bridge and immediately stopped in his tracks. A combat veteran, he recognized prayer when he saw it. He tiptoed away, leaving the commander to make his peace.

* * *

Langley, Virginia

Special Agent Robert Fulton watched the press conference with relish. King Fahr was expected to announce a price increase as well as a production cut. He glanced at his watch for the fifth time in as many minutes. His man in the Suez Canal would begin the rerouting of ships within an hour. Two hours later, he would transmit the launch codes that would ensure American control of the world's power supply into the next century.

On the television, King Fahr stepped to the podium. "Ladies and gentlemen, I'm here today to talk about unity. As the Arab nations are one, so we wish the world to be as one. Tensions have been high in recent times due to production concerns among what you call the Gulf Six. I assure you that, regardless of appearances, we wish for nothing more than peace."

Fulton squinted in confusion. Where was he going with this? His grip tightened on his glass of water.

"I represent all the Arab nations when I say that we earnestly want to reach a mutually satisfactory détente with our neighbor Israel, along with the rest of the United Nations.

"As a gesture of good faith, I am pleased to announce the end of our oil embargo on Western nations. Production will return to full capacity effective today, March 18, 1974."

Fulton was in shock. What had he just heard? Before he could process the information, his red phone rang. Only one person in the world had that phone number.

"Fulton," he answered. His voice was high pitched from the stress.

"Fulton, abort Project Crossfire at once," the DCI said.

"But Sir…"

"No buts, Fulton. Our problem has been solved and this new gesture of friendship will be a direct contradiction to what we had hoped to accomplish."

"Sir, the time is right. We can still strike. We can spin Fahr's statement as cruel irony."

"No, goddamnit, we can't! The risk is too high. We can't imperil our country's standing in the UN to fight a problem that no longer exists. Fulton, I am ordering you to pull the plug right now."

"Yes, Sir."

Fulton slammed the receiver into the cradle repeatedly until it broke in half. He screamed and threw his glass through the television screen.

"You slick little bastards! How did you know?" he shouted at the dead TV, "I was one hour from the pinnacle of my career, and you screwed me!"

He threw the TV over and kicked it repeatedly until he broke the big toe on his right foot.

* * *

The Prometheus

Rymes was tense. The launch codes would arrive any minute. He just hoped all the doors functioned properly, if nothing else.

"Commander Rymes, we have received a transmission marked 'urgent'."

"Let's see it, Sparks." Rymes quickly grasped the document.

Rymes sat with the codebook and deciphered the message. All missiles were to be launched to a single set of coordinates. The actual coordinates were unknown to Rymes. The ones he was now looking at were dummy coordinates. Only the missiles would know exactly where they were going. This double blind code system seemed a bit excessive to Rymes, but he accepted his duty. *This must be big, for such elaborate security measures*, he thought.

"Lieutenant Commander Killian to the bridge," he spoke into the PA system. Killian appeared within thirty seconds. "Killian reporting for duty, Skipper."

"Joe, this is it. I'm entering the launch codes now. Regulations require that you witness and double check my numbers."

Killian translated the encoded message. His coordinates exactly matched Rymes'. Rymes entered the dummy coordinates with Killian looking over his shoulder.

"Agreed?"

"Aye, Sir."

Killian took his post across the bridge. For the launch to occur, they had to press the go buttons simultaneously.

"On zero. Three, two, one, zero."

At first nothing happened. Rymes wondered if they had not been properly synchronized. Seconds later, they heard the mechanical sounds they assumed were the outer doors opening.

"Sir, this is strange."

"What?"

"The outer doors are closed. What was that sound?"

"I don't know. Maybe..."

Rymes never got to finish his sentence. The full complement of missiles exploded in unison, killing all hands below deck instantly. The inner and outer hulls were perforated along the entire length of the Prometheus, just below the waterline.

"What the hell?" Rymes screamed. "What is happening? Are we under attack?"

"Sir, I can't hear you!" Killian had been deafened by the blast. The ship was taking on water at an alarming rate. Within minutes the deck would go under.

Rymes and Killian spent the last moments of their lives furiously trying to figure out what was happening to the Prometheus. They never even came close to guessing that Special Agent Robert Fulton had murdered them before they were sucked into the vortex created by the rapidly sinking ship. Rymes watched Killian go down, but he swam with all his might nonetheless. The vortex would only last a few minutes. He just hoped he could maintain this pace for that long.

* * *

Langley, Virginia

Fulton sat in the emergency room, waiting to have his toe X-rayed. The news was on the television mounted in the top corner of the room. When international affairs came on, his ears perked. He could barely make out the words.

"In a surprise move, OPEC announced yesterday the end of the oil embargo. In response to this, Israeli officials announced that they would honor the UN's recent call for a cease-fire. Egypt and Syria have also agreed, pending further negotiation about Israel's status as a nation."

Fulton broke his other big toe.

Chapter Twenty-Nine

Los Angeles, California

Congressman Hernandez wrung his hands in nervous anticipation. He was dressed in his favorite blue suit, although he knew Lupe didn't care what he wore. He hadn't slept more than a couple of hours in a row in weeks. At first, he was angry with Lupe for running off to Brazil without permission. But, when the school called Monday inquiring as to Lupe's whereabouts, he began to worry. By Wednesday, his house was filled with Federal Agents. The FBI had assured him that ransom demands would be made soon, and that their success rate for this particular scenario was respectably high. That's what they called it – a 'scenario'. He grew to hate that word. His daughter was not some goddamned scenario from the FBI playbook.

By the end of the second week, most of the agents had been pulled from his house. They left one behind to monitor the phone. They delicately told him they were shifting their resources to investigate the possibility of homicide. By that time, the solitary emotion he was capable of feeling was anger. Although he knew it was irrational, he hated the FBI for their incompetence. As the third week wore on, he began to accept that he would never see his daughter again. This sank him into a crippling depression, even though the FBI shrink told him it was a natural and healthy process.

When the General from Fort Benning called him on day twenty-two to tell him his daughter had been recovered by a special Army task force, he didn't know what to think. Hope, once lost, was a difficult thing to recover. At first, he was suspicious, thinking it was a mistake or a cruel prank. But a few phone calls later, he knew the impossible was true – Lupe was alive and well.

Now he stood in the foyer, and in just a few minutes he would see Lupe. He would be able to hold her and know she was home. When the front doorbell rang, he jerked involuntarily. Inside the door, he paused to say a prayer of thanks. When he opened the door, he was surprised to see a soldier in full dress uniform standing at parade rest on his front porch. For an instant, he feared something had gone wrong, but after his initial shock wore off, he saw his beautiful daughter Lupe just behind the soldier.

"Daddy!" she cried, throwing her hands around his neck, "I thought I'd never see you again!"

"I love you, sweetheart. I love you more than you'll ever know." Tears flowed freely as they embraced. After a few seconds, the soldier recognized that his presence was no longer needed. The Hernandez family was whole again.

* * *

Ft. Benning, Georgia

"John!" Tammy ran to meet her husband in the driveway. "I can't believe you're home so soon!" Tammy had been told John's mission in Vietnam would last the better part of six months. And now, here he was, home after less than three weeks. She leapt into his arms, wrapping her legs around his waist. He winced at the pain in his ribs, but returned her bear hug enthusiastically. He held her silently, treasuring the moment, before he responded.

"The mission went well. We finished ahead of schedule." He tightened his grip. "I love you, honey."

"Oh, I love you so much," Tammy said, returning his hug. She felt his rib brace under his shirt. "What's this?"

"Just a few cracked ribs. I'll be fine in a couple weeks. And, the best part is, I'm off duty with pay until the ribs heal up." Suddenly, a hairy blur emerged from the front door.

"Vonnegut!" he shouted at the sight of his old friend. Vonnegut jumped up on his master, fortunately missing the broken ribs. John put Tammy down and vigorously scratched Vonnegut behind the ears.

"I've got some good news." Tammy was brimming with excitement.

"Which is?"

"I'm pregnant!" She jumped into his arms again. John suppressed a grunt as she squeezed his ribs. "I just found out last week. The base gave me some APO box where I could reach you, but I didn't want you to find out in the mail."

John was stunned. They had been trying for months, but now that it had happened, he wasn't sure how to feel. Would he pass along his father's characteristics to his child? Would The John's defective genes infect his baby, giving him the last laugh in their eternal power struggle? But, he already knew the answer to that question.

In an instant, John relived every moment of his childhood - every need that had starved, every time he had turned tears into quiet rage - and it dawned on him that The John had actually taught him everything he needed to know about fatherhood. The John's words reverberated in his ears: *There is no right. There is no wrong. There's simply whose side you're on.* This statement had been a convenient rationalization for John, but it now took on a different level of meaning. For the first time in his life, John had a side to be on – his family's. Maybe that's all he ever needed. Maybe that's all anyone needs.

One thing was certain. John would give this child everything he had lain in bed and yearned for his entire life.

"Well?" Tammy asked.

"Well…Whoopee!" he shouted, "I'm going to be a father!" He squeezed her so tightly he nearly crushed her with his love. This time his ribs didn't hurt.

At that moment, John abruptly understood everything. He'd had the power all along, but never realized it. He knew what he had to do.

* * *

Beaumont, South Carolina

John parked his Challenger in front of his parents' house. When he rang the bell, Gloria answered. "Oh my goodness! What an unexpected surprise," she said, embracing his aching ribs.

"It's good to see you too, mom. Is dad home?"

"He's in the den."

"If you don't mind, I'd enjoy a few minutes alone with him." John had been anxiously awaiting this moment, and he wanted to act while he still had the courage. He strolled into The John's lair.

The John was watching an episode of All in the Family. John turned the TV off, walked toward his confused father, and knelt. The next seven words he spoke took more strength than he knew he possessed.

"I forgive you, Dad. I love you." Such a simple statement - but it evoked profound effects in both the speaker and the listener. The John's eyes swelled with tears. He had no idea how to respond, but it was clear to John that his father was overwhelmed with emotion. As John spoke the words, he felt the venom being sucked from his soul. It was the most liberating sensation he'd ever felt.

* * *

Saint Mary's Cathedral, Beaumont, South Carolina

John entered the massive stone edifice whose door he had last darkened the week he'd killed his friends. He dipped his hand in the holy water, made the sign of the cross and genuflected. He walked calmly behind the pulpit, toward the confessional booths. Once he sat, the priest joined him within a few moments. John began to speak. "Bless me Father, for I have sinned..."

* * *

John and Tammy sat at the breakfast table, both staring at the landscape through French windows.

"John," Tammy asked, "You sure you're up for changing diapers and doing midnight bottles?"

"That's exactly what I plan to do. You know, for nearly twenty years, I've been trying to figure out what I want to do with my life. Now I know. It's all so simple! I want to raise this child."

As John spoke the words, he felt an unfamiliar sensation – contentment. He had no malice toward anyone in the world. Just as Tammy's confession of her dark secret had freed her soul, John had wrestled his demons and decided to let them go. For the first time in his life, he felt complete.

Outside the window, a dove lit on a branch. John could swear it was looking directly at him. He winked at the bird before it took flight again.

The End

Lightning Source UK Ltd.
Milton Keynes UK
UKHW012235260221
379474UK00008B/429/J

9 781034 461531